PRETTY BROKEN THINGS

PRETTY BROKEN THINGS

MELISSA MARR

ALSO BY MELISSA MARR

Signed Copies:

To order signed copies of my books (with free ebook included in some cases), go to MelissaMarrBooks.com

Adult Thriller

Pretty Broken Things (2020; psychological thriller)

Adult Fantasy

Graveminder (HarperCollins, 2011)

The Arrivals (HarperCollins, 2012)

Cold Iron Heart (2020; *Wicked Lovely* adult)

The Wicked & The Dead (2020; Urban Fantasy)

The Kiss & The Killer (2021; Urban Fantasy)

Young Adult

Wicked Lovely series (HarperCollins, 2007-2012)

Made For You (HarperCollins,, 2013)

Seven Black Diamonds (HarperCollins, 2015)

One Blood Ruby (HarperCollins, 2016)

Middle Grade

The Hidden Knife (Penguin, 2021)

Loki's Wolves (with Kelley Armstrong, 2012)

Odin's Ravens (with Kelley Armstrong 2013)

Thor's Serpents (with Kelley Armstrong, 2014)

Collections:

Tales of Folk & Fey (2019)

Dark Court Faery Tales (2019)

This Fond Madness (2017)

Co-Edited with Kelley Armstrong (with HarperTeen)

Enthralled

Shards & Ashes

Co-Edited with Tim Pratt (with Little, Brown)

Rags & Bones

JULIANA

The dead girl is in a grave that's shallow enough that it wasn't hard to find her. That's the sum of what I know.

Dispatch doesn't add that it's awful, not directly. All she says is, "This is one for you, Juliana."

There's an unpleasant familiarity to this moment. I've only worked at my uncle's funeral home for a few years, but I apparently have the stomach for the sorts of cases that he can't handle. Even the bodies the Carolina Creeper has left behind. If I thought prayer would change it, I'd pray that this wasn't his work. No prayer so far has helped, though.

"Is it . . ."

The woman on the phone doesn't reply. "What's your ETA?"

I glance at my watch. "Twenty. Thirty if there's traffic."

"At this hour? There's always traffic."

"So, thirty then." I disconnect and take a moment to find a quiet place in my head.

I could send my uncle. He used to do this part on his own, but the last few years, Uncle Micky hits the bottle every time he ends up at the scene of an ugly death, so I take the hard ones these days.

After years of you,

SOME OF THE worst ones I see when I close my eyes at night. It's like having a photographic memory—but only for the things I'd rather never have seen. Unlike my uncle, I don't drink. Much. I find my solace in other things.

Such is the fate of those of us who work as ferrymen for the dead. Morticians have a very high rate of alcoholism, divorce, and suicide. I worry about it. I worry about Uncle Micky,

and I can't help but wonder if that's my future, too. Did he used to be more or less okay seeing horrible things? Is his reaction where I'll end up if I stay in this business?

Today, though, a dead woman needs me. Protecting Uncle Micky from more nightmares and retrieving the dead, those are my priorities *today*. I'll deal with the rest another day.

I poke my head into the preparation room. "Is there gas in the bus? I'm headed out to Umstead."

"Filled it this morning."

Mildly, I warn him: "I'll need to drop the client at the M.E.'s office."

In this part of North Carolina, the medical examiner's office is supported by a network of professionals. I often do transport. I do a number of preparations, and if I need to, I could do autopsy. It's not unusual. Plenty of states subcontract their work. It's cheaper for them than hiring full-time, and it's extra money for morticians who sign on. My uncle is grateful for the extra income, but he's well past the point of being ok with the ugly deaths.

AFTER A LONGER THAN USUAL PAUSE, Micky looks up from the body he's preparing for viewing. He hears the part I don't say, that this death is not a case of natural causes, that there will be an autopsy.

"Are you good?"

I nod, even though I'm not. I know that later, maybe not today, but sooner or later, I'll feel this one. Still, it's easier on me than him.

Death is hard. Seeing the dead who've been mistreated is never easy—and there's more likelihood of violence death than a heart attack today. Sometimes, more often than I've ever said aloud, I worry most about the dead who seem to show up in my jurisdiction more than anywhere else. *His* victims.

I whisper a prayer that today will not be anything woman *he* killed.

In my retreat to my own thoughts, Micky's attention returns to the woman on the table. This is the part of the job where my uncle excels. He can reconstruct expressions, apply make-up, and by the time he's done, the mourners will see their loved one. It's an art. No one ever suggests that the people he prepares look "wrong."

Unlike Uncle Micky, I don't have the patience for the make-up. Restoration and embalming, those are fine. Retrieval runs, paperwork and marketing—because, yes, this is still a business and marketing matters—those are all fine, too. Make-up perplexes me; it always has. I can manage it more or less, but not like him. Not on the bodies we prepare, and not on my own face.

Uncle Micky holds my gaze just long enough to make me want to tell him it's okay. We both know he realizes that there's a rough call. Uncle Micky might not offer to go in my place, but he *would* go if I asked. He's good people. That's a tried and true fact.

"Can you handle everything here while I'm out?" It's not *exactly* saying that I'm okay or that I can handle it, but we aren't direct like that.

He nods. "You're a good kid, Jules."

"I'm thirty-two," I remind him.

He smiles. "I swear you were twenty-five last time I checked."

I snort. "And this is why I do the books. You're lousy with math."

He's calmer as he returns to the dead woman he's making seem alive, and I feel a little less awful about going to Umstead State Park to retrieve a murder victim. We are both better at some things than others, so we're better off if we stick to our own areas.

I walk outside, and feel like a wet blanket just hit me. Normal Carolina weather. It's always humid, or at least it feels that way.

Murder smells worse in humidity. The scent of things best never smelled gets caught in the wet of the air, and I swear it clings. To my clothes. My hair. My skin. Some parts of my job are the things that tv shows don't mention, and blogs gloss over.

And I know that there is likely a murder. Those are the call-outs that evoke *that* tone, and based on the location, I can already guess that it's not pretty. A hiker with a heart attack wouldn't make dispatch sound so tense.

In this part of North Carolina, the medical examiner's office is supported by a network of professionals. I often do transport. I do a number of preparations, and if I need to, I could do autopsy. It's not unusual. Plenty of states subcontract their work. It's cheaper for them than hiring full-time, and it's extra money for morticians who sign on. My uncle is grateful for the extra income, but he's well past the point of being ok with the ugly deaths.

I drive out to the park. I've hiked here. It's almost six thousand acres of land with trails, campsites, and lakes. A part of me wants to believe this was a shooting or an accidental death. The logic part of my mind can't quite do that. The park is well traveled enough that there is little chance of death by exposure or animal. A shooting here is likely to have drawn attention, but it's not impossible to stealthily shoot or stab someone in the park.

The worst possibilities play in my mind: a child, sexual assault, murder suicide, group suicide, multiple graves. Sometimes, my mind wanders down paths I wish it wouldn't. It's a consequence of my job: I see the unvarnished truth, the details that are half-hidden or totally soft-focused before the family or friends hear about it. The truth is that people are cruel.

It's why Uncle Micky drinks. It's why I check my locks more than once at night. It's also on the long list of reasons I'm lousy at dating. Better to be single and haunted by my nightmares than to raise a child in this world.

I park at Umstead, in the lot closest to the crime, and get out.

I force my steps to be even, my expression neutral, as I walk over to the taped off area of the park. My part-time function with the medical examiner's office means that I have credentials to get past the police tape—not that I need them today. The officers here all know me.

"Jules." Henry nods to me. His eyes take me in like he can read things in my skin and stance. He probably can.

I nod back, and for just a moment, I let myself look at him.

HENRY'S YOUNG FOR A DETECTIVE, the sort of man who has the indeterminate age that could be anywhere from early thirties to late forties. Ex-Army. Descended from freed slaves. One tattoo. Proud nose. Military haircut. No glasses. I run the details in my mind, sorting through parts of the box in my mind labeled "Henry Revill." He's born Southern, raised Southern, and undoubtedly will die here, too.

He also kisses like a man who enjoys desserts and fine whiskey, slowly savoring each moment. That particular detail is one I shove back into the box where I prefer to keep it. Late night mistakes are best forgotten, even when they're rich with promise . . . perhaps especially when they are.

"Male or female?" I ask, facing the inevitable now that I'm somewhat bolstered by the comfort of seeing Henry. I hope it's a man. The Creeper doesn't kill men.

"Woman." Henry's expression is unreadable, even to me. That's not an accident. Even that single words feels heavier in his rich deep bass voice, though.

I'm not going to think about his voice or any other aspect of the mystery that is Henry Revill.

Henry and I are just colleagues these days. When we were younger, we were something else. A few times, I've slipped up and went backwards. Right now, though, that past means we know each other too well to be standing over a body together without stealthily checking in on the other one's well-being.

I SLIP ON MY GEAR. My gloves are purple. Uncle Micky thought I'd like them better, but they stand out too much, too bright at the edge of death. The only thing keeping me from ordering a box of the black ones is fiscal responsibility. I continue my mental catalog, focusing on the minutia of my coveralls, glasses, and gloves.

It's too damn hot to want to wear any of it longer than necessary, but I'm not stupid enough to think that getting fluids on me or contaminating the scene forensically is an option.

Henry looks away as I shimmy into my coveralls. There's nothing improper about it. My clothes stay on under them, but to a lot of Southern men, modesty matters. *Respect* matters, especially respect toward women. And as much as we are in a modern part of the South, there are still those who look at a Black man with a different level of scrutiny. Henry and I having a past doesn't erase that reality either.

From behind me, I hear,

"We aren't making any statements."

Officer McAllister glares at the reporter who's craning his neck as if seeing what's behind the black tarps would be wise.

I know better. Those hanging tarps aren't erected just for the deceased's privacy. The tarp hides the sight of what's sure to be awful. Tarps do nothing for the scent of death. I know without looking that the body is not one of those that's been in the ground for years.

It takes a certain sort of mindset to bury a body here. It means that he—and most killers *are* men—managed to take his victim into a well-trafficked area. She was either alive and killed on-site, or he carried a dead body into the woods. Both tell us something about him. The fact that I know that probably tells any detective something about me. I'm only contracted to *transport* bodies, but after a few years doing so, I couldn't help but learn more than a little about investigations.

People talk. Morticians listen better than most folks realize.

"You ought to send the old man out on these," Mac mutters just loud enough that I can't miss it, but low enough that he can pretend I wasn't suppose to.

Maybe he's trying to piss me off so I can better face the dead girl. Maybe he's just more of an asshole than I realized. Either way, I don't reply. I might be a woman, but I'm stronger than my uncle when it comes to this. Hell, according to my mother, it's *because* I'm a woman. A Southern woman. No wilting lilies here.

I glance at Henry. His expression has grown even sterner. "Detective?"

Henry nods, and we step behind the make-shift curtain.

The dead don't typically bother me, but these days, I've had far too much familiarity with violent death. I've been the caretaker for five of the Creeper's victims.

"It's *him*, isn't it?"

Henry doesn't reply. He's behind me, but he says nothing.

For a moment, I need to recount facts again to settle my nerves: My feet are already covered in booties, and my clothes are under coveralls.

The only excuse I have to pause is to straighten the clear glasses on my face. I'm decked out in the equivalent of hazmat gear.

Just because I can handle this, doesn't mean it's easy. Anyone who thinks dealing with the dead is easy has something wrong inside of them.

Nerves in control I look at her:

The dead woman is covered in blood-stained clothes, leaves, and dirt.

I catalog: Brown hair. Caucasian. Late twenties.

I squat so I'm crouched beside her. The smell makes me glad I hadn't eaten.

I catalogue her injuries. Broken radius and ulna. Six stab wounds. Bruising from restraints. I don't need to see the crude tattoo on her wrist to know it's there. The Creeper. She was killed by him.

Still, I brush away the dirt gently until I see it: Flower buds. It's not an old tattoo. The ink doesn't have that washed out tone that older tattoos have. He marks them.

"He sent a letter this time, Jules."

I look up at Henry.

"Chief says you ought to be kept away from this." He glances at the girl. "But . . . I convinced him that you'd be safer around us, so we ought to make use of you."

I laugh. Henry's not enough of an asshole to really think that, but he knows how to keep me from the panic that is already starting to fill me. There's an art to managing people, whether it's at the police station or a funeral home. It's one of too many things Henry and I share.

"What did the letter say?"

After a pause, Henry says, "'Thank Juliana for looking after all of my pretty things.'"

"They're not *things*, and they're not *his*."

"I know," Henry says quietly.

I look at her, the nameless dead girl in front of me. I can't erase the last days she's suffered, but I will give her the respect he hasn't. That's why I'm here. That's why I face my nightmares. It's the same thing that drives Henry: we are their last resort, the ones who protect the dead after they are no longer able to be saved.

"He sent a message to *you*, Jules."

"My name's in the paper," I bite out the words, the lie. I know it's personal. We both do. "My identity is not exactly a secret. I work for the county, so he knows my name. It's not a crisis."

"You know it's not that simple."

I've tried to deny it, but this body, this time, it's moved the number too far past coincidence. I refuse to look at Henry. We both know. My Uncle Micky will know it too. The newspapers will examine it to the point of absurdity if they find out—and they will find out about this lost woman. Someone will leak about the note, too. People will speculate again. There's nothing I can say or do to prevent any of that from happening.

None of it means I know what to *do* about the larger situation. What's the right thing to do when a killer knows your name? They don't cover that in any of the various classes I've taken, not mortuary science classes or my assorted college courses or even the floral arranging ones at the community college. I collect classes and facts the way most people collect shoes. It's never enough. Sorting out facts helps keep me from sinking into depression. It's a far sight better than some of the things morticians do to keep it together—things I do.

"I can't, Henry. Just . . . help me get the stretcher." I stand. "She doesn't need to stay here any longer than she already has."

"Fine." Henry follows me to what I privately call "the body bus." He's almost casual in tone, then, as he warns me, "You know we're going to have to talk."

"I'll have the paperwork—"

"Don't be difficult, Jules. If he really is leaving victims for you to care for . . . if he's fixated on you . . . "

"Sure." I try to match his tone, aiming to sound casual even though I feel anything but calm. "But I live at the funeral home, Henry. My home ? It's safe, and I'm not careless. There's nothing to discuss."

He shakes his head, but he lets it go for now. That's all I can hope for. Later, when I've done my job and I'm in the privacy of my home, I'll face the realization that a serial killer is paying attention to me. Later, Henry will force me to discuss the unpleasant realities of the police department knowing that one of their own—because whether I wear a badge or not, I am *theirs*

—is in danger. Later, Southern tradition will insist that I am in need of extra defense because I am a woman. Somewhere in there, Henry will pretend it's not personal for him. Even though we both know that it is.

But right now? I'm going to do my job.

TESS

It's a Wednesday when I meet John Michael Anderson. He doesn't use his first name in person, and both of his book covers list him as J. Michael Anderson. The extra initial may be pretension, but he's earned a few pretensions. His debut was the sort of book that's nearly impossible to follow. It's rare to have more than one such book in you. I think he knows that; the critics certainly pointed it out often enough the past few years.

He's old than I remember him being.

Reid would be too. I think it before I can stop myself. Even after six years, I still think about Reid. What he liked. What he wanted. Where I still fail. He made me who I am. Even without the scars, I can still see the proof of it. There's a kind of thin that comes from soul-deep hunger, a kind of lost look, a kind of desperation. Sometimes I still see it when I stare into a mirror. Six years, almost a thousand miles, and more than thirty hours of tattoos, and I still see the woman Reid made.

I hate her. I hate the parts of me that still sound like *his* Tess.

But that's who Michael wants, too. I know why he's in my city. I know what he's seeking here. The oh-so-successful author wants a story, and Tess? The me that used to be? The survivor? She's a hell of a story.

There was a time I'd have done just about anything to have him look at me with interest. I did *him* back then, although I doubt Michael remembers me. I was just another fan on the road, and I didn't have the maze of ink on my skin that I do now. I hadn't started to find myself or draw the map.

These days, the edge of a tattoo somewhere can be seen no matter what I wear, but when I took a tumble with Michael, I was unmarked aside from my scars. I've been adding tattoos since I moved to New Orleans, alternating between two different shops in the Marigny depending on my mood. When I have the cash and the stability to sit still, I write my history, etching it in my skin when I remember the forgotten bits and pieces of my past that might one day make me whole.

Someday, I'll either run out of skin or of memories. Either way, I'll be whole then.

Today, I'm at Mardi Gras Memories, the absurd little shop where I work right now.

Michael walks in like it's casual.

"Tess, right?"

I ignore him. I'm not going to make this easy for either of us. There are moments in life when we know we are at the edge of a mistake. J. Michael Anderson is a celebrity, a person whose death would draw attention. Attention is bad.

"You *are* Tess, aren't you?" He's wearing the same thing I've seen in plenty of photos, the same thing he once stripped off in front of me: jeans, faded enough to look like they're older than they truly are, a casual shirt, dark leather shoes.

"I hated your last book."

He stills at that, laughs awkwardly. "You've read my books?"

I debate kindness. I remember the peace I found in his touch when I needed it. Kindness won't make him leave though, and I need him to leave.

Michael steps closer to me. "Tess . . . You *are* Tess, aren't you? I thought you were. They said—"

"Obviously," I cut him off before he can lie. I try to be truthful when I can, even when it's ugly, even when it hurts.

"I am Tess." I clench my hand against the urge to scrape my nails across my palm. I want to stay in the *now* without tricks or pills. Truth helps. I meet his eyes and repeat, "I am Tess."

I am not *Tessie*. I am not the woman who did the things I can't always remember. I am not the one who made those choices. Now, I tell the truth, as much truth as I can. It doesn't undo the past, but it helps me be in the present.

"I thought so." Michael smiles. His attention is all the more focused now that I've confirmed what he already knew. There was no chance that I would be someone else. I used to be. I remember that. I don't remember all the things I used to know, the people I used to be, but I know that I'm Tess now.

"Are you buying something or leaving?" I keep my voice meaner than I feel, but he is a mistake. Talking to him, seeing him, everything about this is a bad idea.

Michael opens his mouth, but instead of speaking, he closes it again and picks up a few strands of beads. In February, they're tossed from floats or strung out like decorations. When they hang like tinsel in the trees or balconies or are passed out like rarities from floats, they seem valuable. They glimmer in street lights and headlights. Here, on the counter, they're worthless. Sometimes people are like that, too.

I RING UP THE BEADS.

"You know, I saw you in Jackson Square," he half-lies, giving enough details to make the lie feel almost true.

"Mmmm."

He keeps going: "I asked one of the fortune tellers down there, and she said you worked here."

"I do."

Michael hands me a credit card. It seems odd to charge such a small amount, or really, any amount. I am strictly cash and carry whenever possible. Credit cards leave a trail, and I don't want to be found.

Ever.

Michael looks at me expectantly, and I realize that he didn't think he'd have to have to work so hard for my attention.

"What do you want?"

He glances to the side, not meeting my gaze. It's an obvious tell. "I've only been here a couple weeks, and I could use an insider's perspective."

"Really?"

"I want to learn about the city." He offers me a full-out charming smile, as if I'm stupid.

He could find plenty of tours. The Crescent City is a tour mecca. Guides share accurate (or not) tales on everything from voodoo and prostitution to murder and plantations. The tour guides are so numerous that they must adhere to a minimum distance law to keep from interfering with other folks' tours— and thus their livelihood.

I shrug. "I can recommend some people."

"What I really want is the *insider* view."

"I'm not a native or insider."

He gives me puppy dog eyes. "Come to dinner, at least."

"No."

"Coffee?"

This is a mistake. I want it not to be, but I can't pretend I don't realize that I'm on the precipice of a disaster. People do that. They say they don't know how they ended up in the depths of self-destruction. That's a lie. We make a thousand small choices that lead to our demise.

"A drink then?" he tempts.

"It's a bad idea," I tell us both.

MICHAEL's not the sort of person who goes about unnoticed. Neither am I if the right people see me. I know I look different these days, but under all the changes, I suspect I still look like who I am. Someone could recognize me. I've seen my picture on television. I'm a missing woman. Everything I've done, every choice I've made for years, it's all been about being safe. Safe means hidden.

Reid can't kill me if he can't find me.

And despite all of the reasons not to, I nod. Maybe I just want to be found, for it to be over.

Michael talks. Making plans. I know I reply, but I can't be sure what I say.

Maybe it's not self-destruction. Maybe I'm lonely for someone who knows me. Michael met me when I was Tessie, and he still fucked me. That means I wasn't all bad, right?

Or maybe I'm overthinking it.

One date shouldn't change everything—but

I still take another pill when he walks away. Rules let me survive. Rules keep me safe.

Michael has already enticed me to break one of them.

A FEW HOURS LATER, Michael takes me to dinner at Antoine's, the oldest French-Creole restaurant in the city. It's far more upscale than I find comfortable these days. It makes me remember a life I won't ever live again, but this isn't about me. It's about Michael. He's trying his best to figure out how to charm me.

It's working *despite* his efforts, not because of them.

I shake my head at how silly it all is. We both pretend. He shoves his real motives aside and flirts with me. I hide my aware-ness of why he's sought me out and my memories of being naked with him. It's quite possibly the least honest date I've ever been on.

"What?" he asks, making me realize that I must've made a sound of some sort.

I stare at my dish, weighing words as I study my *pommes de terre soufflées*.

Part of me wants to tell him that he's trying to buy me by paying for a high priced meal instead of giving me the cash, but I settle on a softer truth than the raw words I would usually use: "Dinner and stories of your movie, your tours, your carefully dropped hints about your success . . . most women probably say yes before the main course, don't they?"

"Maybe I don't want sex."

HE'S NOT LYING, but like most good mistruths, there is a lie and a truth all twisted up together in his words. I knew when we met that someone told him about my episodes, and he is intrigued. If you ask him, press him hard enough, I suspect he'll claim that the curiosity is simply part of his avocation.

That, too, is not a lie.

It is, also, not the truth.

He wants to know, wants to collect stories and characters because it gives him power, but I'm not easy about parting with my truths. Some truths lead to blood. Reid taught me that, too.

I'm done bleeding for anyone.

I finish my wine, and then I lean closer. "It is a shame that you're not interested. I had every intention of fucking you."

He grabs my wrist, and I see a hint of darkness, telling me that he's not as polished and civilized as he tries to be. That does more for me than any meal or story of his travels ever could. Maybe it just because it's familiar, but I like that threat the way a junkie likes a fix.

This is why we break the rules, this rush, this easing up on the precipice. I can see disasters looming if I stay on the path I'm approaching.

Outside, Michael shoves me against a wall and kisses me. Crudely, carelessly, like I mean nothing and everything in that moment.

It is exactly what I need.

JULIANA

I never wanted to be in a house that smells like death—and there is a smell. I know it. I'm proud of the work I do, but I can't ever escape the feeling that I smell like grief. For me, it's always been the mix of bitter coffee and too sweet flowers. Not every mourning is that. Sometimes, there's cologne. Sometimes, there's the bite of cigarettes from the grieving who quit years ago, but couldn't resist the calm of nicotine during the pre-funeral days. No matter what else, though, the ceremony around death smells like flowers and coffee to me.

When I was a kid, my uncle was actually the *fun* one in the family. He told the silliest jokes, and he was the first to go play in the rain with me and my sister—and the last one to add new rules to our lives. Uncle Micky was happy to have a tea party with us, but when he did so, we had proper tea and scones. My sister and I loved him, but as an adult I realize that his need to play was a result of the things he saw in his job.

My job, too, these days.

I guess I realized that Uncle Micky was lonely. It was just him in his big house in Durham, and sometimes when we visited, plans changed last minute because someone died.

When something bad happened, he was the only one who ever knew what to say. Maybe that's the truth of why I do what I do. I want to be like Uncle Micky because he was the only one who could help me when I thought I'd rather crawl in a hole and give up on living. I wanted to be someone else's Uncle Micky.

When my sister died, Uncle Mickey was one of the only two people who wanted to talk. No one else seemed to get beyond "I'm sorry to hear about Sophie" or "Sophie and Tommy are with God now." And maybe they are. I want to believe that.

"He's going to go too far one of these days," Sophie says.

"Should I ask?" I don't like Darren, but I'm cautious. Everyone who says anything negative about Darren gets kicked out of Sophie's life when she takes him back. My hand tightens on the phone. I want her here where I can see her and protect her.

"I love him."

"Uh huh."

"We just fight so much . . ."

"Sophie? Did something happen?"

My sister pauses long enough that I open my mouth, but then she says, "No. It's okay. He's just . . . upset a lot."

Afterward I realized that I couldn't save her. I know that. Sometimes people are beyond our reach. I think about the things I could've done, the things I could've said. Maybe there was nothing. Logic says nothing I do today will bring her back, but every so often, I can't stop thinking about her voice. I hear her voice, and I think about the women the Creeper kills. Did they have sisters they'd call? Do they have kids at home?

Tommy is harder to think about than my sister. My nephew was the only person Darren treated like he was fragile. For all my issues with my brother-in-law, I never doubted that he loved his son. He claims he still does. Hell, he claims he still loves my sister. He writes to me sometimes, long rambling letters that remind me that the human capacity for self-delusion is incredible.

And every once in a while, I am terrified that he's not completely wrong. Some of them I've read and re-read:

Sophie would forgive me. I know she would. Someday I'll be with her again, and she'll tell me. With God's grace, we'll live together in his kingdom with our son. I can't be angry with you, Juliana. Sophie would disapprove. I wish you could understand what happened.

The rest of the letters I've asked not to receive. I'm not sure if they reach the house, but one way or another they are turned over the police, to Henry. I can't read them. It makes me feel weak to admit that—so I don't. It's my secret. Only Henry and Uncle Micky know. I can't handle my own grief sometimes when I think of my nephew.

I'm not sure why I can handle the grief of mourners or the heartbreak over the women the Creeper has killed, but my own grief is too much to unpack even now. I haven't seen or spoken to my sister's killer since the trial. Sophie's husband. Tommy's dad. How do men kill their children? Their partners? How do they do the things that I see written on bodies?

"Jules?"

Uncle Micky is in the room. The little girl in me still looks at him and sees home. My parents are good people, but my uncle's the one who kept me safe.

"Rumors are already starting." Uncle Micky stands far enough away that I don't feel crowded.

"About?"

"The body you and the Revill boy—"

"He's thirty-eight." I shake my head.

Uncle Micky ignores my attempt to redirect. "Are there things you aren't telling me, Jules?"

If I listed all the things I hid, we'd be in this stand-off a while. I can't. Not today. I walk over and wrap my arms around my uncle. It's not exactly an answer, but for a moment, I want to be a small child, safe from the monsters in the world. I used to think that the bad things were the stuff of stories, and I believed that things that go bump in the night skittered away when the lights cut on.

Then my brother-in-law murdered my sister and my nephew.

Then a killer started leaving bodies at my doorstep.

The world is full of monsters, not make-believe ones, but flesh and blood men who target women. The two men are not connected. They aren't connected to other men like them either. I'm well aware that there is no great conspiracy. It's not that complicated.

Some men simply like the power they can have over others.

At the end of the day, that's why Darren writes to me from his cell. It's why the Creeper sent a letter. And it's why I'm not going to allow fear to reign over me. My fear—any woman or child's fear—gives men like that power. I won't do it.

MICHAEL

Despite my inquiries about Tess, I hadn't been prepared for the woman herself. Nothing had prepared me for her brashness. Above all, the stories I'd collected hadn't prepared me for the way she seemed to study me.

Tess *judged* me. Not just that, she saw me in a way I wasn't sure I liked. I've never felt as replaceable as I felt when she disrobed and looked back at me like I'd missed a cue along the way. Not just that. Sex with Tess felt vaguely like a doctor's exam. I'm not sure it was an exam I passed.

She was *satisfied*. I know her orgasms weren't faked. Despite that, I was dismissed like hired help. There were no invitations for future dinners or desserts, not even a vague suggestion that we ought to "get together some time." She simply sent me on my way with a little wave and a kiss on the cheek.

I don't know if she plans to see me again, but I will see her. She's about to be my salvation. Whether she wants to or not, Tess will save my career.

"Think of it as a storyteller's journey." That was the excuse my agent, Elizabeth, offered when she told me to "take some time" before writing my next contracted book.

I've never failed at anything, not until the release of *The Ruins of a Carriage House*. To say failure was unexpected is such a mild explanation. To say I'm desperate to restore my reputation is even less accurate. The pressure to deliver the next promised manuscript has become a nonstop murmur in the back of my mind as I wander cities. It's become the proverbial devil on my shoulder.

I could buy out my contract, pay out the signing advance and end the whole thing. Sometimes I think about it. I don't *need* the money, but quitting is a level of failure I'm unwilling to accept. It means the end of a writing career the *New York Times* once heralded. I won't quit.

I just need to find the right story, the right character, and then everything will be golden again.

A SOLITARY GRAVE was the start of what critics agreed would be a remarkable career. The prose was nuanced. The story was both heart-breaking and terrifying. The protagonist was the sort of broken man who overcame his own foibles and the world's weight. It was, in sum, well-received and exceptionally lucrative —even more so after the film.

My sophomore effort, on the other hand, was soundly dismissed. "Maudlin and disjointed," pronounced one the industry reviews. The critical reception from every outlet was either scathing or, at best, vaguely kind. The consensus, however, was that perhaps my *first* book was the anomaly.

The next book will be the deciding factor. It will tip the scales in one direction or the other.

I'm on a "post-modern experiment in storytelling." I need a compelling character. I've considered a few:

a red-nosed man who talked about working in a steel town, an angry vagrant in the Pacific Northwest, a bankrupt tobacco farmer in the American South. They were all interesting in that way of strangers in transit, but theirs weren't stories that I wanted to continue to spin out. That was my goal—find the germ of a story as I had with Jorge, and then run with it until it became more. With Jorge, I took far more of his tale than anyone knew, but Jorge died not long before *A Solitary Grave* came out, and his daughter was content to sign a non-disclosure agreement with a generous check attached.

New Orleans is the first city where I think I might have found the start of a story. I'm not sure I'll even need to offer a check for this one. In a city of broken souls, artists, and madmen, it takes a truly spectacular person to stand out.

Tess stands out.

"Back again?" Molly, the bartender, asks when I walk into May Bailey's. The bar, on Dauphine Street in a little boutique hotel, is tucked away. It feels like so many things in this city: hidden in plain sight.

"Nowhere else is quite as irresistible."

It's not a lie. There's a lot of loud bars in the city. Bourbon Street is a mass of tourists, cheap drinks, and nearly naked women. There are other bars, catering to a different sort of tourist. New Orleans is a city founded on sin and illusions. The very land was stolen from the swamp—there is nothing substantial supporting it.

I like that, the idea that this is a city resting on something far from solid. It feels right that this city is where I'll find what I need. The city stretches along a tempestuous river, giving life and taking it in equal measure over the years. It is, in sum, everything a writer could want. If I were capable of love, I'd fall in love with this city.

And even within such a place, there are pockets that are odder than what passes for normal here. May Bailey's Place is unlike every other bar I've tried in the city. From the faded elegance of the bar to the jaded history of the location, it is remarkable.

Molly, however, smiles in the way hundreds of other bartenders across the country as she pours me a drink. The bar is mostly deserted, and I wonder—not for the first time—how it stays in business. Maybe it's only because of the tours or the hotel that the doors remain open.

It has a very intentional charm, calling back to its history as a brothel. Photographs and assorted memorabilia hang on the wall, and every so often a tour group or a lone tourist clutching a book will wander in and stare at the vestiges of the past on display here. A few take pictures; others buy a drink or two. The bar seems to lack regulars, which is part of its appeal. A changing clientele means an endless buffet of stories.

However, Molly's mention of a former bartender, of *Tess*, was ultimately that caught me. I spent days asking questions before finally approaching Tess. I did ask the fortune teller about Tess. I did see her in Jackson Square.

I wasn't *stalking* her; I was researching.

It's different.

Molly had described Tess as a fragile creature, prone to flights and fights in equal measure. I knew I'd found my new Jorge when Molly had added that Tess was running from something so awful that she rarely spoke of it even when she was so far gone on pills and liquor that she would wander into cemeteries, parks, and alcoves to sleep.

"I met Tess."

Molly scans the room as she answers, "Everyone does if they stay around long enough."

"She seemed pretty together. I expected her to be a little more disorganized." I swirl the cubes in my glass, not looking at Molly in case she can see the hope in my eyes. Sometimes I think bartenders, the good ones at least, have a preternatural gift at reading people. I don't want to be read.

"Tess has good spells and bad spells." Molly shrugs. "When she's having a good one, I always hope it'll stick, but sooner or later, it ends. Poor thing never gets too far away from what's been chasing her all this time."

"Did she ever hint at what it was?"

Molly stares at me longer than polite before saying, "Don't go thinking I'm unaware of who you are, Mr. Anderson."

I put my hands up in surrender. "I'm curious. That's all."

"Uh huh." Molly's stare feels unending, and I know that I'm being weighed and measured. Whatever she sees is enough for her to add, "And don't you go asking her questions about the past. Sometimes sleeping dogs bite when you disturb them."

"I didn't ask anything."

It's true, too. I was very careful not to ask about Tess' past, her secrets, her tattoos, or anything that would make her run. Even when I saw the scars hidden under her clothes, I didn't ask questions.

I want her to tell me her story of her own volition. I'm letting her direct our contact. I held out my hand to Tess like I would with a feral thing. Now, I'll wait.

"I'm not cruel," I tell Molly.

I'm not sure the same can be said of Tess. There's something about her that's not as sweet as Molly had led me to believe. I don't know if I should hide it or accent that trait in the book.

"Leave the girl alone," Molly says before she walks away.

I settle into the odd little bar and muse over the possibilities. Maybe it's where I am; maybe it's Tess' comments about prostitution. Is that why tonight was so peculiar? Is that why Tess has such scars? I imagine stories: Tess as an entrapped prostitute, sold by an alcoholic mother or abusive father; Tess as a runaway, mentally compromised by the horrors of a human trafficking ring. In my book, *The Story of A Sparrow*, Tess will be younger, of course, but I think she'll still have some of the tattoos that spiral across her skin. Perhaps, I'll make her a single mother who had a schizophrenic break when her whole family died. The possibilities roll out as they haven't since the days when I met with Jorge. Unlike him, Tess is reticent to share her past, but I can be patient. I know in my bones that she's worth it.

"I like her, you know," I tell Molly when she comes to bring me a new drink. "She's a sweet girl. Maybe she just needs a friend, someone to accept her as she is, a girl with no past."

Molly shakes her head and takes my empty glass.

A Girl With No Past might be a better title. I send myself an email with the two title possibilities and a note that my heroine needs a supportive friend who helps her open up about her tragic past. I think I'll keep her first name though. Naming her Tess will be a nice allusion to Thomas Hardy's novel. It'll evoke sympathy for her, remind readers that she's a victim. I like that. My protagonist, the victim of a violent teen life, taken in by a seemingly kindly woman who forces her into a life of prostitution so deviant that Tess changes her name to that of Hardy's character when she flees to safety. I think I'll make her an English major, too. That feels right for a girl who reads Hardy for pleasure.

She needs a nemesis, though. The person who gave her the scars. I think I'll call him Edward. It brings to mind all sorts of allusions—Rochester.

Once I hit send on the emailed notes, I tuck my phone in my jacket pocket and enjoy my drink. I've got a good feeling about *A Girl With No Past.*

UNTITLED

A Girl with No Past

When I met Edward, I was twenty-four, waiting tables at a restaurant and picking up shifts at a bookstore, going to college part-time and feeling a million years older than the sorority girls in my classes. Even with working every shift I could, I lived in a lousy area and could barely afford it. Durham wasn't exactly affluent—which was part of why I was here instead of up in New York or Boston.

He wasn't always a monster, or maybe he was, but I needed a monster. He loved me. He rescued me. That's the part people don't understand. It's easy for people to look at him and think they understand why I didn't run. It wasn't that, at least not only that. Being loved like you're the air is addictive. Being taken from a place where you have no direction and given purpose, meaning, it's everything. Sometimes people talk about what they'd do differently, but my secret—the thing I don't whisper even now—is that I'm not sure if I would.

Being loved by Edward made me.

It started so blandly. A favor for a roommate. Money troubles. It wasn't a big deal, except it changed everything in my life.

"Tessa?" My sometimes roommate, sometimes friend Elle had a wheedling note in her voice. "You know I wouldn't usually ask for a favor."

"But?"

"But I have this great opportunity." Elle had the game down to a science, and I had to respect her despite the way her choices impacted me.

"Of course, you do."

She cozied up beside me on our thrift store sofa, ignoring the personal space norms. Whatever her favor was, she was pulling out the extra tricks to get me to agree. "You should let me do your hair."

I made a keep-talking gesture with my hand and turned so she could get her hands more easily into my hair. I knew she was trying to con me, but that wasn't going to stop me from enjoying it. I'd been single longer than I wanted to admit. I didn't have the time or energy to juggle two jobs, school, and a man.

"It's not like you'll even need to go every night," she continued.

"Go where, Elle?"

Her fingers worked through the messy braid I had, loosening the strands so they fell around my shoulders. I was overdue for a cut, but spending any money on something so frivolous seemed fool-

ish. I wasn't going to prove I could make it on my own if I dipped into the accounts my mother's attorney managed for me. So far, I'd managed one way or the other.

"The Red Light."

"No." *I started to stand.*

Elle's fingers tightened in my hair, holding me in place. "Tessa . . ."

"Let go, Elle."

"Just hear me out." *She released the tendrils she had coiled around her fingers.*

"I can't—"

"Just waitress. You don't need to go on stage." *Elle did that thing where she widened her eyes and pouted. It earned her plenty of bills in her G-string. Something about looking like an innocent girl worked for her.*

It also made me want to laugh. "Stop that. You look ridiculous."

"I do not." *She pouted more, exaggerating it until it looked truly absurd.*

"Why do I let you talk me into things?"

Elle launched herself at me, dropping a smacking kiss on my mouth.

"Because you get bored being so smart all the time?" *Elle teased as she flopped back with the most honest expression she had.*

She spent so much time playacting that it was easy to forget that she was genuinely beautiful underneath the games. I trusted her the way you trust anyone who juggled addictions and bad habits like it was an art—which is to say that I didn't trust her to do anything other than what was best for her.

"Waitress," I repeated. "Fully dressed."

She giggled. "You've been to the bar. The uniform isn't bad. The shoes . . ."

"But your boss knows I'm not going on stage," I stressed. The first time I'd picked Elle up, the manager tried to convince me to do a twirl around the pole. The topic had become one that was perpetually revisited. It wasn't uncomfortable enough to make me refuse to pick Elle up at work, but I wanted to be clear from go: I was a waitress, not a dancer.

"Kari knows that I'm getting a waitress to sub, and one of the regular waitresses is taking a turn on stage. Charity, the one with the pretty tattoo of the Bible verse on her thigh."

I nodded. Charity was one of the many anomalies at The Red Light. Anyone who thought that the girls in adult entertainment jobs were one-note or predictable clearly hadn't met them. The Red Light wasn't the most upscale of the clubs in town, but it was only a tier lower than them. The girls—from bartender to dancer—were a strange mix of lost lambs and driven businesswomen.

"So . . . what do I need to know?"

Elle hopped to her feet. "There are two waitress moves you need to learn. The first is the bend. You make sure your feet are exactly the right distance apart to make your ass look its absolute best. Then you extend to reach across the table. This is for getting tips from other tables mostly. If you have the boobs for it, you can use it for tips at the table you're serving too. Make sure, though, that you bend deep enough to have gravity cleavage."

I laughed at the Elle-isms she used, but stored the knowledge away all the same. I could use a little help from gravity and underwire.

"The other is the semi-squat. You bend at the knees. This is a little less comfortable, but you'll get used to it. It lets you get closer, and it lowers you so you're putting the assets at the customer's eye level." Elle demonstrated.

If I didn't know how much the wait-staff made, I'd have refused, but my one remaining job wasn't going to pay the rent, and tuition for next term would be due soon. I could either look for another job now or I could sub for Elle and save up a fair bit while I looked. There really was no contest.

"The only other thing is Edward," Elle said in a quiet voice. "If he picks you as his waitress, you do it. If he doesn't, you don't bother him."

"Got it."

"He seems to like you," she added. "I've seen him talk to you."

I shrugged. When we talked, we ended up discussing books or my classes. He was kind, and he never seemed to so much as notice the nearly-naked girls on stage or the waitresses hovering nearby. When Edward gave me his attention, it felt like there was no one else in the room. I liked it more than I cared to admit.

The fact that he was handsome didn't hurt either. Unlike a lot of the men who came into The Red Light, Edward carried himself with the sort of careless confidence that made me think he could've walked into one of my mother's parties and blend in with the bankers and lawyers that hung on her every word. He had one tattoo that I'd glimpsed, but his entire look was one that spoke of money.

If he was there, he sat like he ruled the bar, his back always to the wall in the far corner. The light there was lowered, and the table was reserved for him permanently.

"No one tells him no." Her voice softened as she repeated that particular rule yet again. "Whatever Edward says goes. If you can't say yes to him, you need to quit."

I laughed. Elle didn't.

"I got it," I assured Elle. "Wait tables. Wear criminally high heels. Don't piss off Edward."

Elle nodded. "Exactly."

It sounded so easy.

TESS

Michael found me hoping for my story, but he discovered more when I took him to bed—not that I'm an acrobat. It's the potential for danger that he sees when he tries to read the scars and tattoos that I've collected. It's not the actual sex act. That is functional, no different than eating or shitting.

It was different with Reid.

My hands shake at the thought. Sometimes I admit that I'm running from myself as much as I'm running from him. He made me see a mirror that told me truths best not admitted. He remade me, and I'm not sure that being Dr. Frankenstein's monster would be any worse than the thing he created in my place.

I open one of the pill bottles Tomas brings me. Klonapin. I already took a few earlier, but some days are shakier than others. Michael trying to burrow his fingers in old wounds makes me feel like my tethers are coming loose. Worse still, more and more I want him to untie me.

I want to be finally done. Whether I'm found or not, exposed or protected, I want to have a life again. Maybe Reid has forgotten me. Maybe I'm running from a fear that I don't need to hold on to. It's been years.

Maybe a life lived in hiding isn't enough.

Maybe I'll be freer if I share my story. I'll be absolved for the things I didn't do right. Maybe it's no different than the tattoos I compulsively get.

Or maybe this is that self-destructive streak my old therapists said I have.

WHEN MICHAEL COMES BACK after my shift, I'm outside the shop smoking. I'm closer to the door than the city ban allows, but if that's the worst crime I commit in the next few months, we'll all be lucky.

The acrid taste of my hand-rolled cigarette is strong enough to be unpleasant without a few fingers of whisky to chase it, but liquor isn't usually the right choice with all of my medicine, and I like the act of smoking too much to surrender it. I like rolling my cigarettes, too, but it's the smoking that's the most calming.

It's a focus.

Pull in the smoke, let it linger until just this side of pain, visualize the sins of my past escaping between my lips.

"Well, Tessie can butt the fuck out or buy me a beer."

"*Tess*," I repeat, but I'm not feeling so much like Tess right now.

Tessie is caged.

The Klonapin helps, but I don't remember how many I've had today. I try to do better at that, at keeping track of my pills now, but Michael's attempts to stare into the parts of me underneath the now unravel me more than I like. Tessie is in there, under the layers that I've added to become Tess.

I reach into my bag for the bottle.

Lucas reaches into his pockets too, pulling out a few crumpled bills and coins. "I'll buy him one. It's okay." He sounds more nervous by the moment. "You don't have to do anything. It's okay. It's okay." He starts crooning the words. "It's all okay here, Tessie."

And I realize that he knows more than either of us want him to. He didn't think I was reaching for pills; he thought I was going for a weapon. He knows what I am, knows things that aren't okay to speak, but no one believes people like Lucas.

Would he tell? Is he a threat? It's one thing for me to tell Michael bits and pieces of what I am, who I once was, but I control my story. I define myself. No one, no *man*, will ever define me again.

"I'm *Tess*."

Strangers, drunk tourists who've found there way down here and locals who know me, are taking notice. Attention isn't good. I can't risk it.

"Don't mean no thing, girl." Lucas straightens up, sounding clearer for a moment.

Strangers, drunk tourists who've found there way down here and locals who know me, are taking notice. Attention isn't good. I can't risk it.

"LUCAS DON'T SHARE NO GHOSTS." He pats his chest, over his heart, twice.

I nod. I want to believe him. I want to apologize.

And I want to slit his throat. I don't want the Klonapin right now. I want to feel safe, but the answer isn't pills tonight.

There are things that a woman does to keep safe, things that maybe aren't right, but they still need to be done. I want to be safe. No choice I've made has been more important than that one.

I let go of the pill bottle and pull a twenty out of my wallet. I hand it to Lucas. "Go. Get of here."

It's enough money for both of them to get drunk--or it's enough to take a bus. I'm guessing that Lucas will use it to buy beer, but he could run if he wanted.

I don't want the Klonapin right now. I want to feel safe, but the answer isn't pills tonight.

"It's not your fault, Tessie," Lucas says. "And no one knows. *No one.*"

They walk away, and I have to tell myself that no one listens to the mad and drunk. No one would listen to Lucas. Plus, he shared his stoop. I shouldn't hurt a man who shared his stoop.

He knows things from my *underneath* though. Knowing means talking, and talking means he's choosing whether or not I'm not safe. It gives him power. That won't do.

I hope he takes the money and buys a bus ticket. I want to be okay. I want to be Tess who is *now*.

I'm still standing in the street when Michael joins me.

"What was that?"

I shake my head.

"Tess?"

"He spilled his beer," I manage to say. It's all I can say. There are too many other words twisting in my throat. I feel like I'm choking on them.

"Okay . . ."

"Sometimes I need to do things," I offer. It's truth. It's been a truth for a long time. It is now and always true. "I want to be safe, Michael. Sometimes that's everything."

And I see the flicker of something far from monstrous in his expression. He might want my words. He might even want my body. Right now, though, in this instant, Michael cares. I'm not sure why, but he does. If he knew the things that Lucas knew, would he still look at me like I was a lost girl in need of a hero? If he knew that I wanted to find Lucas' stoop tonight to make sure he didn't spill my secrets, would he still pull me into his arms as he just did?

The questions are unanswered, and I'm not sure that's a bad thing.

"Come on." He leads me to music, puts a drink in my hand, and wraps his arms around me.

For this moment, there's a man with shadows who wants to keep me safe. It makes me want to keep Michael, to be whatever it takes to make this feeling last. I miss mattering to someone. I want to have that again.

I suspect everyone wants it. This difference is that I have *had* it. I know exactly what I lost—both the good and the awful. When I was with Reid, I learned how far I was willing to go to be safe.

I dance in the frame of Michael's arms. The most he does is the occasional sway of the perpetually awkward upper-class man. He can't let go of his boundaries, even here, even in a city with sin in her very bones and beams.

"Are you okay?" he asks between sets. "Earlier in the street . . ."

"Lucas let me share his stoop."

"The bum?"

"I was having a bad time. He watched me so I could sleep."

"At your house?"

"No, on his porch, Michael. I don't let people into my house."

Letting strangers into the space where you bed down is asking for trouble. Letting people carry your secrets is asking for exposure.

My gaze darts to the door. I can't help thinking of Lucas. He knows enough of my secrets that he is a risk. I remind myself that no one listens to the ravings of the drunk or mad.

I know that.

Except the others who are just as drunk or mad *do* listen. Lucas listened to me more than I realized he had. I saw that tonight.

Now I need to fix it.

I need to leave, and I need to get Michael out of here and handle Lucas.

MICHAEL

After we drink, after Tess dances, after we return to my rented flat and fuck, I watch her dress by the light that slips through the drapes. The windows here are as tall as doors, with exterior shutters that span the height of them. The shutters, drapes, and windows are all flung open now. It seems peculiar to me, but Tess likes them open. Even when she's naked, she prefers that the shutters and curtains are open.

My agent would have fits if she knew.

My family would threaten me.

It's *my* livelihood though, my reputation, my money. My grandmother could go to her lawyers and deny me my trust fund, but I think she's also the only one who would be amused by my indiscretions. She knows more than my mother realizes, and she takes pleasure in my inappropriate choices. I think she may have been far less modest in her youth than my family pretends.

"I can't stay." Tess announces it abruptly, as if I couldn't figure that out without her words. She's dressed almost as soon as she stands.

Unlike most women who seem to believe that a cuddle is more important than the sex itself, Tess has no patience with affectionate touches.

It's one of the things I appreciate about her, but it sets me off kilter all the same. There aren't many times in my life where I've felt like the one with no power, but watching her refuse to look at me prickles the vestiges of childhood's tattered baggage. It's not the sort of thing that even my overpriced therapist would've bothered with when I used to drag myself across Manhattan to her office. I wouldn't say I have abandonment issues, but I'm human. No one likes feeling discarded, and I'm simply not used to it.

"You don't have any pets," I point out.

She pauses, pulling her hair over her shoulder and braiding it silently. There's an expression she gets, as if she's trying to figure out a puzzle. Whatever all is wrong with Tess—and there is far more broken than even she might realize—there is an awareness that she must mimic functional. That's what it is though: mimicry.

"I like animals." She smiles, and I wonder how she exists in the world. There's something helpless about her when she's like this. It's the side of her that the bartender sees, the part that makes people warn me to be kind to her. I must resist getting drawn in by it.

"Me too," I lie. I couldn't care less about animals, unless they're seasoned and on my plate. "But neither of us have any, so there's no reason you couldn't stay here."

Tess laughs like so many women at too many parties in my life. It's disingenuous enough to set my teeth on edge. For all of the vulnerability in her, Tess also has a condescension that is familiar—and in that moment I know one of her secrets.

"You came from money." I realize it's true even before I see the worry that flashes on her face when I say it. Tess doesn't admit I've gleaned a detail she'd rather I hadn't. Nothing more than a tightening around her eyes and lips tells me that she's upset by my epiphany. Instead, Tess saunters toward me with a sway in her hips that I will describe as rolling in the book.

THE REAL TESS isn't the character I need. She's too brittle, too close to fractures. The fictional version will need to have softer edges to sell the sparrow image I have of her character. The real Tess has the sort of talons that call to mind something more dangerous. Right now, they are glinting.

She leans in and trails those talons over my stomach in a way that shouldn't frighten me, but does.

"Goodbye, Michael."

I've noticed that it's always a vaguely hopeful phrase when she says it, as if she's trying to make every exit a permanent one.

"Good*night.*"

She presses her lips tighter together, straining the smile she's offered, but she flutters her fingers at me.

Definitely from money.

The door falls shut with a click.

I wait.

Three. Two. One.

The press of her palm on the door as she makes sure it's closed is the last of her presence. In this, and in so much more, Tess is a creature of habits. I collect them to piece together the story she thinks I won't get out of her silences and evasions. She has a comfort with being seen even while mid-sex-act, but she also has a pathological need to check security of doors and windows. She needs to inspect the corners of rooms, light the spaces where unwanted surprises could lurk. She may not speak it, but at some point, she's felt unsafe in her home.

Tess looks for faces in the shadows. Not in restaurants. Not in the street. The places where most women I've known would seek out threats are not where Tess expects danger to wait. In both my rented flat and her own, she keeps a light on in the bathroom. Earlier I turned it off to watch her reaction. It's back on now. It took all of six minutes before she had to find an excuse to do so.

I stare at the light as I wonder at the possibilities for a plot.

Sometimes I don't think any secrets she reveals will be as complicated as the scenarios I imagine when my fictional Tess blends into the details of the real Tess. Was there an attacker? Is she running from a rapist that targeted college girls in her small liberal arts school? Did she walk into the darkened room and find him there? I laugh at the camp of that idea. It's been done too often, too many ways. There's nothing new. It's horrible in reality, but every writer knows that some territory is harder to make exciting and fresh on the page. No. That history wouldn't create the broken sparrow of my novel.

I grab my trousers and get dressed. The second drawer of the bureau holds the notebook where I've been jotting down my notes and passages that will become the novel that solidifies my reputation. It's a strange truth that sometimes writers just *know* when we're holding something special in our hands. It doesn't mean we'll be able to pull it off, but it does mean that we know there's gold in the dirt where we're burrowing our fingers.

Tess is gold.

I don't skim the parts already written in my notebook. Not tonight. I want to capture the unvarnished truths from the cracks in Tess' defenses. I want to contain her in the clean, white pages so later I can dress her up like those paper dolls my sister had when we were children. As time passes, I'll add the costumes, the cut-out dresses that can be added and removed to the paper doll of a woman who will carry my name back up to the top.

The scratch of nib on paper is a comforting sound in the quiet of my temporary home. I can hear the voices of tourists in the streets of the French Quarter, the too sharp laugh of drunk women. They look in through the still-open windows, but it bothers me as it didn't when Tess was astride me. Writing is more intimate than fucking. It might not be *my* soul I'm trying to ascribe to paper, but it is still the bones and breath of a real person contained by the ink in these pages.

I close the notebook before I get up to close the drapes. Once prying eyes are unable to see, I shove the book back into the drawer. It nestles between carefully folded undershirts. The city is too hot for so many layers of clothing, at least for me. I see Southern gentleman—or those playing at being old South aristocracy—with their pressed shirts over undershirts, with vests and ties and hats. Some wear a suit coat too. A few add the eccentricities of cane or antique jewelry. They add a strange false elegance to the city, much like the dripping vines and ornate ironwork. The surface of the place, the pieces caught in old photographs and tourist brochures, zero in on the timeless grace of the Crescent City.

They don't include the drunken women in their sharp heeled shoes or the pervasive stench of vomit and piss that steams and rises in the morning sun every day. That's the heart of this city, though: filth and the consequences of bad decisions. I don't know why I bothered with any other city. New Orleans is the epitome of the stories. She's beautiful and dark, simmering with jewels that look enticing in the flickering gas lights that are still used in the French Quarter, but her feet are mired in things we try to wash away every morning.

They come back. All the dark things come back.

Tess' secrets will come back, too.

TESS

There is nothing wrong with sex. There is nothing wrong with Michael. He's a perfectly serviceable lover. If I thought sex would ease my stress though, I'd still be selling my ass on Bourbon Street. Every buttoned-up-too-tight man wants a woman they wouldn't ever bring home. They fuck us, and then they return to their tedious lives, safe and oblivious, and for years, I have benefitted from their need to take a stroll in a world they can't even truly imagine.

Sex is a thin bandage on a seeping wound, for me. It doesn't make me forget my problems. Talking doesn't fix them. Drinking doesn't. Sex doesn't.

Running hasn't really fixed my problems, either.

But I'm alive. That is *something*.

And it's something I won't let anyone take away from me—which means I must deal with the reality that that Lucas knows things he ought not.

I should die for my mistakes.

That doesn't make it okay that *Lucas* knows any of my secrets. I remember red, remember gurgling sounds.

Tessie is the person I try not to be. She's a woman who made choices to stay alive. She's a woman who loved a man who turned out to be a monster.

I fist my hand, and discover a knife there.

Sometime between fucking Michael and now, I must have stopped at my home. The minutes get blurry when Tessie starts stretching inside my skin. She's me, or I'm her. We were once both Teresa.

It feels far too familiar to hunt. It's almost like Reid is with me. I can hear him whispering, memories of the things he said or maybe just a part of him that he left behind in my skin. He left his mark so deeply inside me that I can still hear him. I look at the people I pass, see the traits that mark them as lambs waiting to be culled.

"Tessie?" Lucas is on his stoop. He pats the floor beside him when he sees me.

I close my eyes. I want there to be another way, but this city is my home. "Don't shit where you eat" is what my mother used to say. Admittedly, she said it with a clipped accent and in reference to fucking the help, but the point is the same.

"Walk with me?" I ask softly, letting Tessie's voice free. Tessie is softer, weaker, unwell. Tessie seems vulnerable—but she is the one who survived Reid.

"You okay?" Lucas is stumbling, drunk on the money I gave him.

"I need company."

He ambles into the dark with me.

We walk toward Crescent Park, and we talk about . . . things as we walk. To be honest, I'm not entirely sure what all I say. I tell him things. I ramble, no more or less incoherently than drunks and madmen. It's late, and the city is ours at this hour. Over in the quarter, in between neon lights and harsh music, there are tourists. In the Marigny, floating on sultry jazz and friendly locals, there are my people. Further into the city, there are families in their homes.

And here at the edge of the Mississippi, there are no faces either familiar or strange. Crescent Park is deserted.

Lucas is not the first man I've walked to the park. There are things we all do to survive.

I don't want to be found unless I choose it. I don't want anyone to tell my story.

I don't want to die.

There are things we all do to survive.

"I don't tell no tales, Tessie. What you did, you did."

He's right. There are truths that a person can't understand until they've lived them. Lucas had a family once. I think he might have even had a job. Things change. *People* change.

· · ·

"IF I HADN'T, he'd have killed me," I explain. I slip off my coat and toss it on the ground. Then I walk toward the bank of the river and stop.

Lucas follows, too. The river is spilled out in front of us. There's something about that rolling water that seems to purify me.

Reid kept the girls in water sometimes.

"Sometimes, he'd fill the tub," I explain.

I don't look over at Lucas. If he understood, maybe he would live. That was what Reid told the women. If they could only understand . . .

The knife is at my side now. My right arm is steady, and the shadows are thick.

Lucas stands on my left. He's tall.

"He just wanted them to be good, to be clean. I always tried to be good, too. After the first year, I tried so hard. I'd tell them what he liked so he wouldn't hurt them as much."

"I AIN'T NEVER TOLD no one, Tessie. No one knows you're the missing woman what was on that news all the time."

"But *you* know," I point out. "You know, and you drink, and one of these days you'll slip. I slipped. I told you. I'm sorry for that."

He steps away then. If he were sober, maybe he'd run. He's not.

"I'm so sorry." I truly am, but sorry doesn't change anything.

Then the knife slides into his belly. He stumbles. Falls. I'm on top of him. He struggles. It's not easy to die.

We resist it. Sometimes we resist enough to buy a little time.

I bought time.

In the end, though, when it's time to die, we die. Lucas knows things, and knowing is power.

It's why Reid wouldn't let me leave. I knew things.

I know things.

"I GAVE YOU MONEY TO LEAVE," I remind him, but he's already dead. "I tried not to do this."

Afterwards, I strip down, pile up my clothes, and light them.

Then, I purify myself in the river. I get the soap from my coat pocket and wash myself. The water takes away the blood. It takes Lucas away. The blood, the dirt, the body, the water fixes it.

Then I put my coat on to hide my wet body and walk home, as pure as if I'd been baptized. This city is good for me. I won't lose it. Not the river, not the music, not the peace I have here.

Lucas should have taken the money and ran. It's what I did. It's why I'm still alive.

JULIANA

I'm out of my home alone, knowing full well that I need to be cautious, far too aware that a killer knows my name and face. I realize I need to think about safety. If Henry knew I was walking around, I'm guessing the lecture I'd get would be loud. He'd be angrier than he's ever been with me.

He's a good friend, and I know he means well. He's also the only man whose come close to being a lot more than a friend, and I know that he can see the fears I'm trying to outrun right now.

I just . . . feel like I'm losing something if I let anyone control me. I've seen the bruises and wounds on the women the Creeper has killed. He wants control. They are restrained. They are injured over a period of weeks or days. I don't know if it's breaking them that makes him kill them finally or what. I am not an investigator. The *dead* are my priority, not the pursuit of the living.

The Creeper is determined to pull me into his perversion, but I'm not willing to be controlled. Cowering would give him power. It doesn't spare a life. My sister cowered. Sophie still died. Her husband, the one person who swore to stand at her side and protect her, took her life.

Cowering isn't a path I'm willing to take.

Despite that, I'm not so foolish as to spend my evening aimlessly walking around in public. I let myself into my more-or-less boyfriend's building, walk to the third floor, and use the key Andrew gave me last year. I sent him a text a half hour ago. He didn't reply, but the worst that can happen is that he's not home. He never travels more than an hour or two from home, so if he's not here right now, he will be soon.

He's not the sort of man who would ask me to cower—or to submit to anything. He doesn't try to take control of my life or freedom. It's why he's in my life.

And he won't call me out on the way I test myself.

I needed to get out of the house. I needed to know that I wasn't crippled by the fears that I couldn't quite put to rest. I don't know how to sort through what it means that a killer has decided to notice me.

The Creeper is the one person I've never met but whom I know. I know he's right-handed. I know he's of average build. Both were theories I shared with the Durham police because of the bruising on Christine Megroz's body.

I see things that let me know him better than I would ever want to know anyone capable of such violence. I chose to protect the dead, to shepherd them to their rests, to ease their families' pain.

I didn't choose to be a detective, but a serial killer has forced me to think about motives, about his identity.

AND I ALREADY THINK ABOUT death too much. I see all of the ways we can end, and I see the things that we don't share with the public. It keeps me awake sometimes—but I don't drink.

Instead, Andrew is my version of too much to drink. It's a sad truth about those in my profession that we need ways to reaffirm *living*—drink, affairs, and driving like we're invulnerable. Uncle Micky suggests that we're not so different from teenagers.

"JULES?" I hear him before I see him.

ANDREW IS WEARING A TOWEL, clarifying why he didn't reply. I swear the man showers three times a day. I won't say he's overly body-conscious, but he's definitely aware of his body in a way that's unusual to me. I like his attention to his cleanliness and fitness most of the time, but I sometimes worry that his obsessive showering is a hint that the scent of my work lingers on my skin.

I drop my things on his sofa and close the distance. He's a smart man, sweet in ways I appreciate. If I were a different person, I'd tell him I need to talk, but I'm here to feel alive. Andrew is handsome in the way typical of the sort of man who spends more hours exercising than in the library, but I know for a fact that those muscles actually come from riding a bike or walking everywhere. He's an environmentalist and a part-time researcher.

He doesn't resist when I remove his towel. He doesn't need words from me, not to tell him what I need, and not to tell him how I feel.

Andrew understands me.

He knows me well enough to understand all the words I'm not saying, and in short order my shirt and skirt are on the floor. Andrew is the sort of lover who borders on perfect. We fit. He knows that sometimes the only thing that matter is feeling the world go silent. It's not a show. It's not about racing to orgasm. Those are perfect other days, but the desperation that drives me when the job gets too much is different.

Skin on skin is all that matters when I feel like this, which means that being bent over the back of the sofa is exactly right. His hands roam from holding my hips to stroking up my sides.

Touch is everything.

My mind falls into that glorious place where there are no thoughts, no fears, no worries or self-consciousness. All I know is that I am safe here. I don't need words or voice; I have no need to see him. In these moments, I am alive as I can possibly be.

Andrew gives me a space where I can fall apart. Tears come with my orgasm, and I can't say which I needed more.

He leans down so he's holding me and kisses my neck. "Do you want to talk about it?"

I shake my head.

"Are we going to anyhow?"

I snort. "Probably."

He stands up, letting me have space to come to my feet. He treats me with a level of kindness I'd fond uncomfortable initially. With Andrew, everything—no matter how simple—requires consent in some fashion.

"Tea?" he asks.

"What's with the tea thing? Uncle Micky has corrupted you, hasn't he?"

"So, coffee?"

I bend to pick up my clothes. I'm not going to bother getting dressed, but if I don't pick my things up, they'll end up in his wash—as if too long on the floor makes things instantly dirty--or perhaps it's just his theory that washing our things together is an encouragement of a primal bonding. Andrew's current research area is biology, and it's led to a few peculiar theories.

"I can stuff my bag in the closet."

He grins and holds out a hand. "Or . . ."

I give it over. His quirks are more than made up for by his kindness and tolerance of my own eccentricities.

He says nothing as he takes my clothes out of my bag to fold and sees the stack of manila folders under them. Instead, he pulls the folders out and puts them on his table before he folds my clothes. It's as close as we get to him offering to help me. A lot of our conversations are ones with no words in them.

"Coffee?" he asks again.

"Please."

He glances at the folders again and makes enough coffee for both of us. Tea is more of a social drink for him. He doesn't drink alcohol, and it's only on rare occasions that he drinks anything other than coffee, fruit juice, or water. People often assume he's a recovering alcoholic, but in truth, it's a lot like his fastidiousness with cleanliness and order. Andrew likes things the way he likes them.

I'm not interested in poking at his reasons why, and he gives me that same consideration. Maybe that's all love truly is: two people who accept each other as they are without needing to change or control the other. If so, I love Andrew, but it's not a word I've ever used. It's not the fairy tale sort of thing the movies sell, but it reminds me of what my parents had when I was a kid. There's a stability to it that makes me wish we could use that word sometimes, but using it would mean things change. I don't want that. What we have is enough for me.

"You're a good man," I tell him as I get out a couple of cups.

He looks over his shoulder at me. "Really bad day, eh?"

"Body dump."

He nods, waiting for the rest.

"Carolina Creeper," I add.

"Those are always hard." He motions to the fridge. "Do you need food?"

"No."

For several moments, the only sound is the steady flow of coffee. It's comforting. Like everything with Andrew, there's a familiar warmth to the simplicity of it. There's nothing confusing or complicated between us. It's peaceful.

And I am about to ruin it.

"He sent a note."

"Who?" He meets my gaze. "*Who* sent a note?"

I hear it, the unspoken urging to tell him he's misunderstanding me. I want to. I want to lie. To him. To myself. Saying it aloud, telling Andrew, makes it real in a way I have been trying to avoid.

"The Creeper."

"Jesus, Jules!" He's across the few yards separating us in a heartbeat. His arms are around me, and his hand cradles my head as he holds me like I'm precious and vulnerable. If I hadn't cried when my orgasm hit earlier, I'm fairly sure that the tears I prefer to never shed would be impossible to ignore now. Sex is a much better way to release emotions.

"I'm fine," I lie.

"You're not." He only leans back far enough to look into my face. "What's the plan? What are they doing to keep you safe? Do you want to move in here?"

I shake my head.

"No what? No there's not a plan or no to moving in?" An edge creeps into his voice, and I know it's fear.

"No to all of it. I sort of haven't talked to Henry or any of them since I found out. I had to take care of the woman and—"

"Bullshit." He steps back then, arms releasing me, putting distance between us. Anger. Worry. Frustration. He's feeling all the things I can't, and I wish briefly that he was a bit less in touch with his feelings. "You're avoiding dealing with it."

I walk around him and pour the coffee. Once I'm done, I add the creamer and sugar he likes and hold out his cup. For a moment, I think he's angry enough that he's not going to take it.

"I came to you. That's what I'm doing so far."

He sighs. "You need to talk to Revill about your safety."

Any other time, I would've called Andrew out on the tinge of hostility he has toward Henry, but tonight, I ignore it. There are reasons for his jealousy and possessiveness, but I came to *him*, not Henry.

I like the lack of pressure. I can accept being loved by Andrew. I can let myself love him because he's so safe. Henry isn't safe. He loves the way a mortician typically drinks—and it terrifies me.

Darren loved Sophie that way. My sister is dead.

I know that Henry isn't like that. He's a good man. There *are* good men. Sometimes, though, when I see the women who die at the hands of men, I remember that in most cases, they thought their killers were good once. How can anyone trust? How do we know which love is safe?

Darren killed my sister. My nephew.

The Creeper is out there, blending into society.

Men like him are out there, and I cannot trust my own judgment to be sure that any man is truly safe.

I shake my head.

"I need to find him."

Andrew and I both know I don't mean Henry. Finding *him* is never hard. He's right downtown in the new police building or out on a call or a lead, but even if he were out, anyone there would tell me where and page him if I showed up at the office.

Finding the other one . . . finding the Creeper . . . well, no one's managed that. It's sheer arrogance to think *I* can find him.

But then again, he isn't sending anyone else letters as far as I know. He's paying attention to me. Maybe he *wants* me to find him. The thought of that, of him wanting anything from me, makes me fill with so much fear that I feel like I might vomit.

"That's Revill's job. Not yours."

"The Creeper didn't send a letter addressed to Henry. He said he wanted me to take care of his 'pretty things.'"

"Jesus." Andrew pulls me in for a hug. "Move in here. Let me take care of you. Stay with me so he can't get to you."

It's not the worst idea ever, but I can't, especially now. I will not let some sociopath control my life, rush me into decisions I'm not sure are wise, change how I live, force me into commitments. I watched Darren dominate my sister, make her smaller and smaller until one day he just killed her.

No one will ever control me. Ever. Not the Creeper. Not Andrew. Not Henry.

"You know I . . . care about you."

"I figured that out the first time you shoved me onto a bed."

I roll my eyes. "I *care*. It's not just sex. I care . . .I . . . "

"I know, Jules." Andrew looks like he's not sure whether to laugh at my discomfort. "So why not move in?"

"No. I'm staying at my home with Uncle Mickey. Right now, that's where I belong." I don't want to discuss it, but Andrew deserves some answer. I push past my tendency to keep my fears to myself. "He's obviously trying to manipulate me. I can't let him."

I see the sympathy. Andrew lost a sister and his parents when he was a kid. He understands loss. It's not pity in his face, but he's looking at me in the way that reminds me that he knows better than anyone why I find the mere thought of marriage or kids terrifying. My sister's death just about broke me. My nephew's death . . . there are no words for how I felt when I heard that Darren killed Tommy, too.

I walk out of the kitchen, trying to move away from memories best left forgotten. I need to stop thinking about Darren. He's in jail. There's nothing more to say there.

I walk away and stare at the files I brought with me.

Silently, Andrew follows me to the coffee-table. He doesn't offer to help, and I don't ask. We both sit and take a file. It's not the first night we've done this.

"What if they never find him?" Andrew asks several minutes later. He doesn't lift his eyes from the stack of articles he's pouring over.

"They will." It's not an argument, not really. I can't think that.

Even if I wasn't on the Creeper's radar, I owe the dead women. Someone has to remember the lost. That's my job.

The Carolina Creeper case has bothered me since the first body was on my table, but this time, it's worse.

His latest victim is in my basement. Again. He's obviously trying to draw me in, but I don't know why or what he wants. Is it a warning that I'm in danger? Or does he want to be stopped? Some of the articles in the past speculated on my physical similarities to the victim that was never found. I look like her, and I handle the dead.

"I have to find him. Or maybe the department will because of a clue when he wrote to me. I don't know. I can't . . . I just . . . I can't ignore it."

I look at Andrew as I realize that he was aware of the latest body before I came to his place. He *had* to be; everyone in Durham is. I suspect people in the whole of the state and other states, too, are. There was already another write-up that got picked up by the AP. So, all of the Associated Press affiliates had summaries of the killer. What was omitted so far was his presumed fascination with me.

I stare at Andrew, but I don't ask why he didn't seek me out or prompt me when he undoubtedly knew what sent me to his arms. I don't blur the lines of the safely constructed box where we exist. He chose not to come to me, but he didn't reject me. I'm not sure what to do with that.

"I couldn't prepare her body because of his fucking letter." I try to keep my voice level, keep both my anger at the killer and my frustration with my lover out of the words I need to say. "He killed another woman, and I couldn't do my job."

"You *are* human."

I wave his words away. "I don't know how to find him, but maybe I can find Teresa Morris. That's the best bet we have. She's the most likely clue . . ."

It's not exactly a new plan. A lot of people would like to find Teresa. She's the only person I can think of who might help me find the killer, find the missing bodies of the girls who disappeared . . . unless she's dead, too.

I hear myself getting louder, my voice too sharp. "I need to do *something*. I have to."

He drops his voice to that soothing tone and reaches out to touch my hand cautiously. "Jules . . . you could just leave it alone. Take care of yourself, but stay out of the investigation. Let them do their job, and you just . . . stay safe. Maybe tell them you won't be able to deal with any more of his victims."

Andrew moves closer to me and tries to hug me.

I pull away. I know he means well. I know he cares about me, but his words make me feel weak. I am not weak. I will *never* be weak. "Fuck that."

Andrew doesn't flinch. The man has the patience of a saint. He has to in order to be with me.

"No one would think less of you. A *killer* sent a letter to you, and you're letting your emotions—"

"I'm not." I glare at him. This bubble of rising rage isn't what I'm to feel, not when I'm with Andrew. He's meant to be calm and steady. He's in my life because he can level me when I become emotional. Right now, it's not working. I am livid. "I am not being emotional. I'm not letting this asshole manipulate me either."

"Be smart, Jules. Talk to Revill, but don't get involved." Andrew doesn't reach out again. He looks like he wants to, but he holds back. "Think about it, Jules. Please? He's dangerous, but maybe if you let it go—"

"No." I take several steadying breaths until I know my voice will be level. When I'm sure I sound calm, I say, "He wants my attention. It can't be just because of my job. There are other morticians, others who work for the coroner's office, but he wants my attention. There's a reason. I'm going to figure it out."

Andrew shakes his head. "And if the reason is simply that he wants you?"

"Don't."

"Listen—"

"No, *you* listen, Andrew. I'm not stupid, or being stupid. I know he's out there. I knew better than most women. I *see* the bodies. I . . ." I swallow hard before I can continue. "But that doesn't I'm going to tuck tail. I need him to stop."

I wonder if any man can understand the fear that women know intuitively. The victims of the Creeper have had those fears all realized. My sister was overpowered by a man who claimed to love her. I can't decide if that's worse than a stranger. Either way, it's the stuff of every woman's nightmares at some point. Andrew has rarely sounded so insensitive.

"He can't stop killing. If he could, don't you think he would've?"

I shudder. In some ways, killers like the Creeper are not so different from any other addict. The difference, of course, is that this sort of addiction destroys a lot more lives.

It's not going to destroy mine.

"He'll stop because we'll catch him." I open the next folder. "Read or don't. I'm going to find something."

UNTITLED

A Girl with No Past

"Did your roommate quit?" Edward asked after only an hour at my temporary job.

"No." I filled him in on Elle's temporary absence and my job woes.

"You'll take care of me. Won't you, Tessa?" He nodded, pronouncing this in that way of his that made it apparent that this wasn't truly a question.

I nodded—not that it mattered. The manager wouldn't allow me to tell him no. That was the rule at the Red Light: Edward was never wrong.

"So you're only here until Elle gets back?"

"That's the plan." I felt odd just standing and talking to him, but Kari had been explicit that I should do so as long as he wanted.

"Just to wait tables," he clarified.

"Definitely! Can you picture me up there?" I gestured toward the stage. I was a little in awe of how girls like Elle and the others could dance so confidently. I wasn't unfit or unattractive. If I had been, I couldn't even wait tables at the Red Light. That didn't mean I felt bold enough to spin around a pool or gyrate on the ground wearing only a G-string and garter.

I'd taken the job in a sort of desperation, and maybe a secret fantasy of my mother discovering that I'd rather let men ogle me than take her money. Maybe it was petty. Maybe I wasn't being a survivor as much as a fool.

"I can picture a lot of things," he said.

I forced a smile. He wasn't unattractive, but he made me nervous.

In truth, he was handsome. Muscular without being bulky, no visible tattoos or scars. Blue eyes. Luscious mouth. Everything else about him was so carefully cultivated. His suits were off the rack, but tailored. His haircuts were salon quality, but not attention drawing. The look of his mouth, though, when he smiled was the stuff of fantasies. It was like he had a decadent side that explained away the cold in his eyes.

He worked at one of the myriad companies over in RTP. If I had to guess, I'd think he was in charge. I didn't ask. A lot of suits came into the strip club. Men like them liked to pretend they were civilized, but they still visited the place where they could treat women like objects.

"I need a whiskey." Edward slid two bills across the table, drawing my attention away from my thoughts. *"I need a whiskey."*

"You don't pay. Kari said—"

"It's not for the drink, Tessa. It's yours."

I blinked stupidly at him for a minute. He'd just tipped me more than I made in an entire shift at the bookstore.

I brought his drink back and smiled as I accepted the tip waiting on the table.

"Tell me about you," Edward ordered.

"What do you want to know?"

"No secrets, Tessa. Tell me about you. What state? What's your family like?" His breath curled over my skin.

"Massachusetts. Awful but . . . wealthy." I swallowed.

"But you're here," he said. "Letting men look at you."

I nodded.

"Do you like it?"

There were a lot of things I could say. I could tell him that I liked the money. I could say that I liked knowing that the men who looked at me wouldn't ever be ones I would let touch me. I could even tell him that I thought about how shocked-horrified-jealous my old friends would be. Something about Edward's words scared me, though, so I said nothing.

"Little rich girl playing at being bad . . ."

I shrugged. "I'll inherit enough not to need to work, but . . . I hate my mother. I hate her husbands. I hate the stupid lies and—"

"But you want to be taken care of, don't you?"

I shook my head instinctively. "I can take care of myself."

It wasn't a challenge, but I know now that he heard it as one.

JULIANA

Since I learned about the letter from the Creeper, I can't stop thinking about them, the flower bud girls. Courtney Hennessey. Maria Adams. Christine Megroz. Yolanda Waters. It bothers me that he thinks of them as *his* because no woman belongs to anyone but herself. I suppose the same is true of men. We are our own keepers. We define ourselves, possess ourselves, and what he did to these women cannot change that.

Murder is not ownership.

His possessiveness is part of what the police need to understand to find him, though, and I'm sure Henry is thinking about it. The Carolina Creeper not only holds them captive, but he also marks them. He tattoos them. So many killers—and I have researched far more of them than I ever planned as I try to understand this one—keep tokens, like talismans from their crimes. In some perverse way, it's akin to the holiday mementos regular people tote home from every excursion. The police don't know if he keeps anything, but they—*we*—know that the

Creeper sends his victims out with a memento. A tattoo, a specific one: Flower buds.

Of course, journalists have speculated. Why that one? Is he a florist? Is it symbolic? Is it about the language of flowers? There are a lot of questions, and not very many answers.

The only truth I know for sure is that he's out there. Right now, he has another victim with him or has another victim he's still watching. He has a pattern, a type, a timeline, and he's good at it.

He kills in the South. That's the best we can tell: He's regional. No DNA. No forensic evidence that leads to him. White and in his thirties is the likelihood, based on profiling. I have read every snippet I could get—not that I am technically *allowed* to do so, but when a killer seems interested in you, friends sometimes bend rules. Henry has bent more than a few rules so I can sleep at night.

We don't know how to find him, though. I don't know if we'd even find the victims if he wasn't so eager to share.

The Carolina Creeper is good at what he does, and I am afraid. I admit it to myself. I've admitted it to Andrew, by word and silence. I don't need to admit it to Henry. He knows me. I suspect he knew I was afraid before I did.

I'm not good at being afraid, so I'm going to find him. I have to. It's the only option—and it's all I can do to avoid total obsession with it.

A few days later, Andrew and I are spending another date reading horrible things. I'm fairly sure he's using vacation time to do so.

I look up at him and smile. He is oblivious, reading glasses slipping down and forehead furrowed as he studies case files. I wish I could push past my fears. He deserves it.

"Thank you," I say, as he looks up questioningly.

"If you're going to do this, I'm here to help, too. Well, as much as I can." He gestures at the pages in front of me. "Read. I have an hour left today to do this."

Someday, maybe I'll be able to be better at this relationship thing. For now, I lean over, kiss his cheek, and then get back to reading.

The biggest anomaly in the cases is the missing heiress: Teresa Morris.

There are only two realistic choices: The Carolina Creeper has either killed her or he still has her. I can't decide which would be a worse fate. She was one of the last girls to go missing in North Carolina, but she gets a lot of attention because of her family—especially in the last year: Her mother died about fourteen months ago, and her entire estate was left to her missing daughter.

I find Sterling Morris' final act of faith unsettling. She died believing her daughter was alive. I never want to have another woman with a flower bud tattoo under my gloved hands, but I cannot imagine wishing for anyone to survive what he does to the women.

Years of being trapped there would be more than I'd wish on an enemy. What sort of woman would wish that fate on her daughter? Or did she just foolishly think that her daughter was elsewhere? Safe and not his victim?

I've made use of my connections through the police department to get files from around the state, and I've looked for the missing girls. Andrew has used his ties to the paper to help me as often as I've wanted. Henry has left files out where he knew I'd see them. It still isn't enough. I have no answers. Amateur sleuthing doesn't work like it does on TV. I haven't found some magical clue that would lead to the killer's apprehension.

Instead, the Creeper is watching me. I know it. His letter proves the fears I've tried to ignore the last year.

The man whose victims I've prepared for their graves, the man whose actions make me unable to sleep far too often, knows my name. He knows where I am. He knows *who* I am. The sheer weight of that realization makes me shudder. Too often we imagine that killers are people we'd notice, but in reality, they often aren't. Richard Ramirez, Paul John Knowles, Charles Schmid, Paul Bernardo . . . a lot of serial killers are charming and attractive.

"Jules?" Andrew slides a paper from one of my files toward me. A missing person's file. A thin, dark-haired woman. "What about this one?"

The woman in the picture is a light skinned Latina girl of the right age.

"She's a likely candidate." I read her name: "Ana Mendoza."

"A lot of women are likely candidates," Andrew points out. This is what he does. He switches to devil's advocate. I think I need that as much as I need the rest of the things that he gives me.

"She's not as pale as he usually picks," I admit.

"As far as we know. There could've been others, ones we didn't realize were his . . ."

That's the part that's maddening sometimes—or at least *one* of the parts. For all we know there are dozens more who weren't included in the list because they weren't perfect matches. Until I can examine their bodies, or the police catch the Carolina Creeper, we can't say for sure. Even then, we might not be able to find them all. That's more common for killers than the myriad crime shows or thrillers admit: There are bodies that will never be found.

"Ana vanished from Wilmington," Andrew reads.

I stare at her face. Heart-shaped, pretty, wide-eyed. I want her to speak to me, to let me know if she's one of the women I'm looking for. The dead don't truly talk, but their bones do. Their paper trails do. A lot of forensic information gives voice to the women who no longer can ask for help.

"She's a strong maybe." I take Ana Mendoza's picture and add it to the maybe file. There are so many dead girls, so many men preying on lost women. I'd tried to tell myself it was a coincidence that he left their bodies where I'd be their caretaker, but I'd worried. It hadn't only been the journalists drawing the unpleasant conclusion that it wasn't an accident. They were fascinated because of my brother-in-law's crimes, as if some people draw murderers to them. It doesn't work that way, although most articles about Darren mentioned that I introduced him to my sister and I work with the dead. A part of me wonders if the Creeper's interest in me is the fault of those journalists. It doesn't matter why, though. What matters is that a killer is watching me—and not from behind bars like my brother-in-law.

"NEXT FILE." I drop my gaze to the stack of photocopies of pictures of missing women. Some are no longer missing. Their files include autopsies. Most don't. So many of the women in these files will never be found. So many *not* in these files won't even be reported as missing.

Andrew reaches out and squeezes my hand. "It'll be okay."

All I can think about are the rest of the girls whose bodies we haven't found. I think about Ana, and Maria, and Courtney, and Christine, and Yolanda, and the others whose names I don't know yet. I want someone to stop the Creeper because of them. I want the list to stop where it is, no names added, no new bodies with ink etched on their wrists.

I want to not see them on my table.

I SLIDE a stack of missing person and Jane Doe coroners' files out of the folders. "No, it isn't, but it *will* be fine once he's stopped."

There is no other option. He has to be stopped. He wanted my attention, and now that he has it, I'm going to find a way to help the police stop him. I have to because I have his attention . . . and I don't want it.

TESS

"Why don't you stay at my place?" Michael's hands stroke my skin, tracing tattoos as if he can read the stories by touch. If we reach a point where I need to share all of my words, we'll start here: in bed, naked, where I'm not the only vulnerable one. I don't want to discuss my skeletons, though; I want to be a blank slate. I want to be someone other than the woman with these memories.

I want to not expect pain to accompany caresses.

"I only sleep at my own house," I explain for what might be the sixth time so far. If he were anyone else, I'd be well past done speaking. I'm enjoying Michael even though I know it's a series of mistakes to do so, but I'm on the verge of trying to be someone Michael wants to keep in his life.

Maybe I miss a life with comforts, or maybe I want to be loved. I can't say for sure. What I know is that I want to stay in

Michael's arms, and it's been a very long time since I wanted that.

It doesn't mean I lack limits. Having lines that you won't cross— or at least won't cross easily is essential. I still have limits. I *have* to have them, my rules, my pills, my forgetting. If not, I'm not sure what I'll become.

"I don't see why you can't come to my place for the night. Did something happen in your past, Tess?"

"Yes." I don't admit more, but I see his eagerness. He looked for the woman I used to be, and I want him to see *me*. So, I roll over and set to distracting him. It's not unpleasurable. He has a good body, trim and firm, and he has the sort of penis that justifies some of his arrogance. Nice girls tell you that size doesn't matter. It's a polite lie that we use when necessary, but it is a lie.

Afterwards, I leave. It's what I do. This, too, is a rule. I don't stay. I don't feign affection. The sex is as satisfying as anything is these days. I'll return, not because of the sex, but because I like the way he craves me. I enjoy being wanted, but i

t certainly doesn't make me want to spill most of my secrets.

Two weeks later, Michael starts pressuring me to travel with him. Like everything, he's expecting me to capitulate. He wants compliance, even though he tries to pretend he isn't bored when he gets it.

I refuse until my temper is frayed.

"I don't leave the city," I point out bluntly and firmly once my laughter and distractions fail to get him to drop the subject.

Travel has never been an issue, not that any of my other lovers mattered enough that I would've cared. The problem with Michael is that as much as I dedicate myself to finding ways to keep him happy, the truth is that I do it all for my *own* happiness. More and more, Michael pleases me. His presence in my days, at my table and in my bed, sometimes makes me feel almost as if I could forego my myriad pills—not that he knows about my reliance on the pills. Like the stories that explain my tattoos, the pills are as much of a secret as I can manage.

"We could turn it into a holiday," Michael argues the next day.

He's done so well at not trying my boundaries that I am unprepared for the onslaught of arguments. On this, he's not bending. I don't know how to refuse both his request to travel and his pleas for my history. There is no way to give him an explanation *and* maintain my silence.

One of my rules the last three years is that I don't leave New Orleans overnight. I haven't left the area even once since I arrived. Sometimes, I might go over to Slidell or maybe as far as Baton Rouge for a day if I'm having a good spell, but New Orleans is where I feel safe. It's where I sleep.

My doctors are both here. My jobs . . . the dozen or so that I've had . . . have all been in the city, mostly in the Quarter. There's so much turnover that one more fucked up chick with a lot of short-term jobs isn't shocking. I'm a hard worker when I keep my meds all straight.

But as the days pass, Michael keeps pressuring me. He offers me every temptation I would've wanted in my life before Reid.

"We could go to a show. Wouldn't you like to see Broadway, Tess? Or the Met. The only work is a few meetings I need to go to, and then you can come to dinner. Meet my agent."

He reminds me of the life I knew before I defied my family and left. Shows and shopping, lovely meals and banal conversations, these were the pillars of life before I met Reid. Michael's offers invite me into worlds I've avoided since I escaped. I figured *he* would look for me there.

Maybe he no longer searches for me. Maybe he never did.

I debate agreeing to the trip. It's been years since I've been to Manhattan, but I didn't know if I could pretend to be well that far from my city. Could I pretend to live that life for a few days in order to make Michael forget about the years I don't want to remember?

"We'll have a great time," he tempts.

The question isn't going away, no matter how much I wish it would.

"It's really not a good idea," I stress again.

Still, he doesn't let go, and I can't tell him why I don't sleep away from my house, not without telling him things I'm hoping never to share.

"I don't travel with women, Tess. You realize that, don't you? I need to go, and I want *you* with me."

And I capitulate. Being made to feel special is my weakness, as it was with Reid, as it was with mother and her many lovers. I am not so different from her, from the woman I once was.

"I'll come with you, Michael."

Even as I agree, I fear that this is the biggest mistake I've made in years, but I want this. I want to be normal again, to have a life, to be well and whole. Michael makes me want things I haven't dared to dream of. He holds the illusions I crave in front of my eyes, and in my secret heart, I am still Teresa wanting to be loved the way Reid once loved me--before things went so incredibly wrong.

Maybe the pills will be enough. I can double up for a few days, either enough to stay asleep or enough to stay awake. Hesitantly, I nod my head. I can't make my tongue say the words, but I agree.

I'm leaving my city. . . for a man. I'm going to go to New York for a week. It's not what he *most* wants, but I have another plan, one he set into motion by hiding from himself. I see hints of who he is, and I think that this is my solution. If I give him what he doesn't realize he needs, he might stop trying to get the thing I am loathe to surrender.

Michael is like a lot of men: he's terrified of growing up. Commitments, marriage, kids, a house, they are the stuff of nightmares for him. I envy him a little that he knows so little of true nightmares, but if I envy him for that, I'll have to envy a lot of other people too.

Sometimes, I do. I watch them as they stumble down Bourbon Street, women tottering on high heels that they were foolish enough to wear for a night of heavy drinking and men so obscenely drunk that not even the strippers who take on extra jobs would be able to feign interest. They are such easy marks. Once upon a time, Reid would've been whispering in my ear, telling me how weak and stupid they were.

Tell a man he's brilliant, fuck him like he's the best there ever was, *listen* to him, and he'll tell you how to own him.

I'm listening to Michael. I'll be exactly the woman he needs. I can do that.

"Take me to New York."

UNTITLED

A Girl with No Past

At the time, I didn't realize it. Edward was training me the way he'd train a dog. I was rewarded and punished. The methods might have been unusual, but the core of it was the same. Every decision I made was influenced by Edward. I missed classes when he wanted. I kneeled down in front of him in the shadows of a parking lot. I hadn't slept in my apartment for at least a week.

Maybe I had a bit more of my mother in me than I thought. I shouldn't need a man to make me feel value. I didn't want that, had left her world where marriage was about status and connections. I had no urge to preserve family connections or forge new ones.

"Do you trust me, Tessa?"

There wasn't a true answer to that, not really, but I knew the right one to give. "I do."

"*Good girl.*" *He put his hand on the small of my back and steered me to one of the private rooms.*

Inside the room, he tapped out a bit of cocaine, and I watched as he turned the small pile into a line. "*You need you to relax.*"

"*I'm relaxed,*" *I lied.*

"*You can trust me,*" *he swore.* "*I'll take care of you. That's what we both want, isn't it?*"

He stood and kissed me. His kisses were unlike anything else; they were the kisses of a man who needed me. Edward, a man with money and power and danger, chose me.

"*Do you want to make me happy?*"

"*I do.*"

"*Such a good woman.*"

He demonstrated how to inhale the line of powder, and then he drew another one for me. He held my hair back over my shoulder as I bent down and inhaled. I felt it flood my system almost immediately.

Edward's hands slid to my hips. "*Keep me happy..*"

"*Yes, Edward.*"

"*You'll never belong to anyone else the way you belong to me.*"

From that day forward, I was his.

JULIANA

My day starts with a cup of coffee in the privacy of my room as I read over more newspaper references, alerts for my name, and my stack of mail. In it is a letter from Darren that escaped the monitoring.

He'd obviously sent it to someone else, who then sent it to me. If I'd know it was from him, I wouldn't have opened it. Too late, I realized it.

My Dear Sister,

I'm sorry that you have become caught in such danger. If Sophie was alive, she'd be worried. I pray for your safety. Some of the people inside these walls are evil. This killer is surely the same. Take comfort in the Lord, sister. I will continue to pray for you each day.

yours in faith,

Darren

My hands shake as I read his words. On the surface, they are innocuous. A man praying for my safety, that's not terrible. And yet, it was his twisted version of religion that he used to justify Sophie's death. Some men hide behind Christianity—or other religions—as if a good and kind god would find their violence righteous.

I force myself to calmness, or a facsimile of it, and I refold the letter. I tuck it into its envelope. Later, I will give it to Henry. The police can follow up on who helped Darren. *This* letter, at least, we can trace.

I doubt that they had much luck with the Creeper's letter.

Most of my mail is sorted, but this had the return address of an association I am a member of. It took care to get it out and to me. Most of the letters I receive from awful people are stopped. Being the subject of speculation in the media because of the Creeper—and because of Darren—means that I have a strange, sick fan-club out there. I have never responded to any of them, including my brother-in-law.

Truth be told, I am most comfortable with distance from the world. In my job, I meet people but because we meet over grief and loss, they do not seek me out later. You don't befriend the woman who sells you coffins or dresses your late relative's body.

In some cases, there is no one to meet. It's been almost a week since I helped lift the unnamed woman out of the grave. We do not know her name. There is no relative to comfort. I know now that she'd been dead less than two weeks. Last month, she was walking around. I wonder what her laughter sounded like. I wonder what her life was like. Unless we catch the Creeper, I'll never know.

With the deceased who die natural deaths, or who die in accidents, I hear the words of their family. People talk. They hold onto the lost a little longer by sharing memories.

In my job, I've hugged more strangers than I can count. I've listened to the stories of innumerable people, many of whom I dressed for their final public appearance. I've sat with them in silence. That's my mission, the responsibility I took on when I became a mortician. I know some people find it macabre. It's uncomfortable work—and I've made my share of off-color jokes at funeral industry conventions. Sometimes we laugh to avoid crying or crawling into a bottle of gin.

That doesn't change the core belief that drives me: I am as much a caretaker as a priest or teacher or nurse. My charges are unable to tell me what they want, but often they've left instructions or told loved ones. Even if I don't have the specifics, I know that everyone wants to be treated with love and respect as they leave this world. Whether it's a standard embalming, a natural burial, or a cremation, every last person should be given respect.

The Creeper disrespects them and me by dropping the dead in shallow graves, unwrapped, dirty, and with no more care than trash. He insults them in their last journey . . . and he's intentionally done so where I am the one to care for them. It's disturbed my peace to the point that I've slept like shit. Nothing like dreams of a killer to make rest elusive.

I need more coffee the way an addict needs a fix on a very bad day.

Walking into the kitchen to find Uncle Micky at the table with Henry does nothing to improve my mood. It's a tiny breakfast nook, and seeing them sitting there over tea and coffee seems funny. . . well, aside from the surly look on my uncle's face.

"Fuck," I mutter. There's nothing else to say, not without another vat of coffee.

As I meet Henry's eyes, he gives me a look I've seen far too often, somehow vaguely amused and disappointed all at once. He doesn't say anything. He will. I don't know when, but he will talk to me alone. For all of the slack we cut each other, he is still an officer of the law, and I am still a stubborn bitch. Those two things mean we reach conflict regularly—at least that's how I explain it to myself or anyone who asks. I don't mention that we were the same way as kids, or that the way we spark led to the kind of kisses and touches that defy words.

"Were you going to tell me?" My uncle lifts his gaze from

his floral tea pot. "Were you going to tell me?"

Both men are holding their delicate white china cups. Uncle Micky looks natural. He has an entire routine to his tea. It's soothing to him, and at this point in my life, I find it comforting more often than not, too. Henry is drinking coffee out of one of the matching cups, and it's not that he looks unnatural because of the cup or the coffee. It is simply wrong for him to be at my table with my uncle at all.

"Coffee first," I mutter.

I skip the pretty cups in favor of an enormous mug with "I'll sleep when I'm dead" written on it. It's not one I'd ever use in the business part of the house, not where mourners might see it, but it's the right size for mornings.

"Juliana . . ." Henry starts.

Mutely, I shoot him the sort of look I wouldn't dare in the field or in public. He's a detective. He's entitled to respect—or he is usually. He's come into my home telling tales. That changes things. Sure, I told Andrew I was going to talk to Henry. I meant it too. I just wasn't ready to do it just yet.

"Coffee first," I repeat more sternly.

"She's still like this in the morning?" Henry smiles at me. "Here, I thought she'd get sweeter with age."

I flip my middle finger up without looking. My right hand is busy holding the carafe of happiness that pours into my mug. Uncle Micky prefers to start with tea. By mid-morning, he'll switch to coffee. I don't bother with tea. Or cream. Or sugar. I just need coffee.

"Henry brought scones," Uncle Micky says.

"Bribery? Isn't that illegal?"

Henry grins. "Pretty sure scones aren't considered bribes, Jules. They were a friendly gesture to a colleague who's had a rough week."

I snort, lifting both middle fingers from my cup.

"Micky deserved to know." Henry slides a cranberry orange scone my way.

I pull out a chair and sit. "These are homemade."

He shrugs.

"Definitely a bribe." I can't resist though. Henry may be pissing me off, but the man is an exemplary baker. "This is your grandmama's recipe, isn't it?"

Henry shrugs again, but once I take a bite, he doesn't need to confirm anything.

"Are we going to talk about this?" Uncle Micky asks. It's not truly a question. They were waiting for me. Henry gave me a couple days to settle myself and admit that I needed to deal with being in the gaze of a killer.

I just don't know what it means to deal with it. There isn't a thing I can think of that is a good solution. Tell the killer I took out a restraining order? Somehow, I don't think he's the law following sort. Hide away until he's caught? He's been killing for years, and I can't stay hidden or under protection for years.

"I'm sure he already told you everything," I tell my uncle, not coldly but honestly.

Henry leans back in his chair and studies me. He does that far too often for me to be unnerved by it. He can't turn off his job the way I can. In public, I am a consummate professional. I am polite, reserved, approachable. I am the woman you can come to in your loss and pain, and I will remember your name when we are in line at the grocer. I don't intrude, leaving the choice to speak up to the bereaved—because even years later, that's what they are to me. They are the bereaved, and I am not going to remind them of their grief by approaching them. Here at home, though? I am Juliana. I am a woman with a temper. And right now, Henry Revill has sparked it. Again.

"Someone had to tell him," Henry says unapologetically. "You not dealing with it stopped being an option once the Creeper sent a letter to you."

"You weren't surprised by the letter."

Henry shrugs. "Too many bodies when you're around. Too many bodies that end up being yours. That meant either you were connected or guilty of something."

"She's not guilty of a damn thing!" Uncle Micky might be the sweetest man I know, but he's still the closest thing I have to both a guardian angel and a father.

"*We* know that." Henry looks at Micky. "You aren't either. We follow every lead, no matter how improbable when it comes to a case like this."

"There wasn't ever a shred of chance that Uncle Micky was a killer." I take the scone sitting untouched on Henry's plate. If he wanted the damn thing, he should've eaten it before I walked into the room. "You checked out everyone who works here then."

"And Andrew." This time Henry doesn't sound at all sympathetic. Andrew's dislike of Henry is matched by Henry's increasingly obvious disdain. In truth, no one in the police department seems to get on with Andrew. I have to wonder now if it was because of this.

"When?"

"Two bodies ago. The papers weren't the first to wonder at the connection. The department saw it. You had to have considered it."

He pauses, and I nod. I considered it. I chose to reject it. Thinking that the Carolina Creeper was watching me felt solipsistic . . . and paranoid. I'd prefer to be neither.

"So, we paid attention. Checked out your associates." Henry's speaking to me the way I speak to the bereaved. "We want to keep you safe, Jules. He's obviously interested in you."

Uncle Micky makes a sound that might be a gasp or a cry. I can't tell, and I can't look at him right now. I reach out and rest my hand on his arm. His other hand covers mine, holding it there.

My gaze is fixed on Henry, though. "I'm not going to stop doing my job, Revill."

His brows raise at my reversion to his surname. "No one thinks you will, Miss Campbell. That doesn't mean you can stop us from doing ours either. I gave you a few days without pointing out that we've started keeping an eye on you, but—"

"You're following me?"

"Protecting you."

I snort, and despite myself, I look away. I don't feel comforted by the idea of my colleagues trailing me, studying where I go and what I do. I especially don't feel comfortable that Henry is doing so. It makes me feel weak. Admittedly, a part of me also cringes when I realize that they'll all know that I deal with bad days by running to Andrew's bed. I don't want anyone to know that—or maybe I'd just rather *Henry* not know that detail. I feel a flash of guilt, like I'm betraying Henry. After all these years, I still can't get past the thing between us.

"Jules?"

I look back at Henry and shake my head. I can't do this, none if it. Henry saying my name like that . . . it's too much. I am not a girl in need of a rescue. I am not a woman in search of a man. I am a professional who just happened to catch a killer's attention. "Back off, Revill."

"I need to do my job. If it were Micky in danger, if it were anyone else, what would you say?" Henry says, more kindly than I might deserve. "Don't make this about—" He stops himself, takes a breath, and tries again, "Don't make thing difficult."

There's no way for it to be anything but difficult. I don't want to be a victim, but I don't relish the thought of years under surveillance either. It doesn't matter, though. Nothing I say right now will matter. Henry will do what he believes is right, regardless of what I say. He would no matter who the Creeper targeted. The fact that the letter was sent to *me* complicates matters further. I know it. I suspect a lot of people know it. Henry and I might not address the thing between us, but it's still there.

"Uncle Micky?"

"Yes?"

"Sort out whatever details the detective wants to put into place. I need to look after . . . *her*. I need to do my job." I stand and toss

Darren's letter to Henry. "Deal with this while you're meddling. It came here to the house."

Then I walk away.

I can't fight them on the protection, but I can't agree either. I can't stop the killer. I can't make him stop watching me. There's ultimately nothing I can control in this moment, but I can do my work. I can take care of the dead. It's not enough. I still feel helpless, but obviously, I'm good enough at what I do that a killer has noticed me.

If he left one message for me, maybe there are others.

So, I descend the stairs to read Uncle Micky's files on the Creeper's last victim again, hoping that there will be something there to share with Henry, something that will speed the process of finding and stopping the Carolina Creeper. I don't know what else to do.

A Girl with No Past

My mother had been sending messages. She twisted guilt and demands together into what her string of husbands have always heard as "things I must do to appease Sterling." Unlike all of her men, I know that nothing appeases my mother. It never will. If she's ever satisfied, it's only a state she'll linger in long enough to weigh and reject it.

I haven't been to my apartment in weeks. Today, Edward had his oldest brother, William, drive me here to get a few more of my things. I was packing them when she called again. I shouldn't have answered, but I did.

"Tessa, how are things?"

"Why?"

"Darling . . . I'm your mother. Shouldn't a mother ask?"

"What do you want, Sterling?" I close my eyes. I'm not hurt. I remind myself every time I hear her tinkling laugh or crisp accent that I'm not hurt. She can't hurt me now. Edward keeps me safe. Edward protects me.

"Does a mother have to want something to call her own daughter?"

I wait in silence. It is the only answer that works. Engaging her in arguments serves no purpose, but acquiescing is beyond me now. Silence is my defense.

"I want you to come home the month after next," she says after a small sigh that is the Sterling Morris equivalent of giving in.

"I live in North Carolina now, mother." I look around the dive of an apartment. The carpet is the vaguely brown color darkened by dirt and stains. The furniture is thrift store bargain, made tolerable by a lot of Febreze and cheap but new blankets as furniture covers to hide the age and stains.

My mother's skin would crawl at the mere thought of standing here.

I have money. A fund that comes with oh-so-many strings. But using it would give her hope that my defection was temporary. All I'd need to do is tell her I wanted an allowance from my fund, and I could live alone and in a far nicer place.

I'd rather try to prove that I can survive on my own than concede anything.

"Please come for a visit."

"What's in it for me, mother?"

She sighs again. "I'll pay you to come."

I laugh. It's the closest she's come to admitting that she's willing to use her money to control me.

"You're asking to hire me, Sterling?" *I tease, crueler than I am with anyone else. She makes me that way. She made me that way.* "Shall we draw up a contract?"

Another sigh.

"Fine. Tell me when. I'll come if I can get off work." *I resist telling her where I work. That detail may be too much for her to overlook. I know she still thinks my independent streak is temporary. Hearing that I'm working at a strip club, that I'm dating a man who frequents the club, would provoke fights I'd rather skip.*

The Red Light is temporary, too. I'll get a degree. A career. Freedom. That will be enough, and then I'll be old enough to access my account, too.

"And you'll dress appropriately," *Sterling adds.* "Use my account. Indulge yourself—"

"*Indulge* you, I believe is what you mean to say."

"Dress like my daughter," she continues blithely. "Speak like my daughter. Give me three days of—"

"How much?"

"Don't be vulgar, dear." Sterling sighs yet again. "Don't be vulgar, dear."

And I wonder if that sigh used to work on me. Admittedly, she wasn't going to win any parenting awards, but most people's parents fail in something. Sterling Morris wasn't particularly awful, but when she accused me of trying to seduce her latest windbag of a boyfriend, I realized that she was everything I never wanted to be.

A mother doesn't turn on her daughter.

A mother doesn't choose money over her child.

Her needs weren't ever particularly deep. She wanted to be dressed in the designer du jour, seen at the right restaurants, and fawned upon by men who could afford her—or who were embarrassingly young. The latter were the ones who met her at the beach house rather than in public.

"Shall we discuss vulgarity then?"

"Two thousand, Tessa. That's what I will pay my child to pretend to be an adult."

"Five."

Sterling said nothing in response. If I didn't know my mother, I might feel sympathy for her. She'd failed us both though, and I *was enough like her that I couldn't forgive her.*

"Five or hang up," I told her. I could use the money, and somehow it didn't seem the same as accepting the fund that was in my name. This was a one-time business transaction.

"And you'll pretend to be the loving, polite daughter." Sterling's voice was no longer cajoling or falsely kind. Here was the woman who had raised me. "Dress appropriately, speak politely. Talk to your old friends. Be everything I would expect in a daughter."

"As long as there are witnesses, I will. If it's just us, no."

"What would that cost me?"

"You can't afford it."

"The money and ticket will arrive this week," Sterling said, and then she hung up.

JULIANA

After the burial of the Creeper's last victim, after the upheaval of admitting that my life is under scrutiny by both a killer and the police, life somehow resumes a normalcy that seems unnerving in its calmness. It feels more like the quiet before disaster, and I half wonder if I *want* the disaster. I am better suited for a crisis than a lull.

Henry has already followed up on the letter from Darren, who has subsequently had his mail privileges further limited. I know a letter ought not to upset me as it did. He's behind bars. Words cannot hurt me in any real way—but I think that we allow so many little attacks by those who can claim power. He is still trying to do so, power over my sister after her death and power of me. Would Sophie want him to worry and pray over me? I don't know, honestly. My sister was broken by the million little ways he shaped her. By her death, she seemed like a stranger to me.

And I guess I started to look at her life and the lives of the dead women on my table. How many times had some person taken away their control? Their voices? Their freedoms? Sophie and the women whose lives I study as I think about the Creeper have made me look at the places where I am asked to surrender my power.

Today, I'm at the coffee shop a few blocks from the police station when Andrew walks in the door. He has a black eye. My first thought is that it looks oddly attractive with the vaguely-confused librarian look he's always rocking.

"Ouch." I motion to his eye.

He drags a chair out and drops into it. "I'm clumsy sometimes."

The tenderness that had come over me when I saw him vanishes at his lie. "Seriously? Clumsy?"

Andrew looks down awkwardly.

"I'm not trying to . . . I don't want to fight, but don't *lie* to me."

"It's a family thing." He offers me a smile that is anything but happy. "I know you try to let me in, Jules. I do, too. We both have limits."

I'm not sure what to do with that, but he has the knack for making me feel guilty if I get angry, as if he waits for my temper so he can air a grievance he's held in silence. Last time he accused me of only seeing him for sex. That isn't true. We go on normal dates. I just want to share a home with him.

"I've been patient, haven't I? When you shut me out, I wait."

"You have," I allow. It's a long-standing issue. I was far from receptive to his initial attempts at inviting me to his place or meeting him at mine. I'm cautious. There are things worse than a black eye, and after Sophie, I am verging on paranoid. It probably doesn't help that I see them on photo after photo, M.E. report after report, body after body, and I don't ever want to be one of the women in such photos.

"So can't you be patient with me too?" Andrew reaches out and takes my hand.

I meet his gaze. "Not if you lie to me. I don't need every answer, Andrew, but I don't *lie* to you. You don't get to lie to me either."

"Fair enough . . . I was punched."

"By?"

"A relative. That's all I'm saying."

He shakes his head. "We both have our secrets, Jules. I can agree not to lie to you, but that doesn't mean I'll tell you everything. There are good reasons I don't introduce you to any of my family members."

Talking about his family is absolutely forbidden. I know that, but I guess I thought he didn't see them, that they were far away or something. "Do they live here? I thought--"

"Don't."

"You saw a family member, and now you have a black eye. I care about you, you know?"

He nods. "And I love you. That's why I'm not answering questions about this."

As usual, I ignore how easily he says he loves me. I can't say it, not unless I'm sure. "I won't judge you. A lot of folks have relatives who are embarrassing. A drunk? Argumentative? What? A junkie?"

"Let it go." An unfamiliar tone creeps into his voice, more aggressive than I have ever heard him when he spoke to me. "Trust me, Juliana. Just let this go."

For the first time since I fell into his bed, I wonder if I was wrong about him. I wonder what Henry turned up when he investigated Andrew. A brief guilty thought flickers in my mind: I could ask.

My nerves are on edge, and I know that. Logic says I'm being foolish to doubt Andrew. Reliable, patient Andrew.

Being under observation destroys people. I see horrors in every shadow, in the eyes of people I meet and people I know. Everything becomes suspect. Everyone is a potential villain.

Seeing threats in every face, wondering if each person who stares too long is a danger . . . I can't be that person. I won't. Secrets are not a thing I can handle right now. I need *answers*, not more secrets.

"If you want to touch me again, you'll tell me the truth." I feel a twinge for drawing a line, but whatever he's hiding was enough to make him try to lie to me.

Andrew gives me a sad smile. "I suspect you'll need to use me before that happens . . . and Jules?" He waits until I meet his eyes before he continues, "I won't tell you no when the time comes. I don't have conditions the way you do. I love you, and I accept you for who you are. I know you can't say the same, though. I've known from the beginning."

WE STAY LIKE THAT, me ignoring the complications he's just thrown between us and him watching me with a tender expression and a black eye.

I don't know what I'm supposed to say or do. With the dead, I know. With mourners, I know. With the police, I know. Andrew, however, has pushed me off kilter.

"You know we're not the only ones desperate to find her," Andrew says after the quiet grows too heavy to ignore.

I look at him. "Her?"

"Teresa."

This is what we do when we fight. He says his piece; I say mine. Then we put it aside for whatever distraction we can accept. Andrew doesn't need to get into an elaborate explanation of how and why he's bringing up the missing heiress. All he does is offer me the topic so we can move on. I let out the breath I'm holding and accept the distraction.

"I was thinking about him sending you that letter. Maybe he thinks you know more than you do. About her. Or maybe he just knows you're paying attention—which means he's watching you."

I shudder. Usually the way Andrew sounds so sure makes me feel comforted, but this . . . isn't. "I don't know how I could know anything the police don't."

"You talked to Sterling."

"A lot of people talked to her," I point out. Meeting Teresa's mother was painful. She wasn't cold, but she had reached the point of self-delusion. It was embarrassing to watch. She'd claimed that her daughter was dating a "criminal element," and he was obviously convincing her daughter to stay hidden. On some level, Sterling Morris was certain that her daughter wasn't the victim of a serial killer—and her parting shot that I looked like his type, too, made me hate her more than pity her.

A folder with photos of another body is under my hand. I tap it. Opening it without warning is not something kind to do to people who are not in the business of dead bodies. "Ana Mendoza died at least three months ago."

Andrew gestures to the file. "What do you know?"

I open it. The photos aren't the best, but they still show more details than I'd like. Ana suffered. It wasn't only the tattoo that made clear that she was one of the Carolina Creeper's victims. She had bruises in varying states of healing and internal scarring where no woman should ever have scars.

"She was definitely one of his." I don't share all of the pictures, but I point at the tattoo and the bruises on her arms. I point out a stab wound that is visible without showing her private areas. I do my best to respect the dead's right to modesty.

"He hurt her," Andrew says. It's a question as much as it's not. He might not care about the dead women in the same way I do, but he's squeamish about how they've been hurt.

I think of the autopsy notes. "Hurt" isn't enough of a word for what had been done to Ana. The M.E. could tell that she had sustained injuries for weeks. Not all of the women had revealed as many details, but Ana was found before all of the evidence was gone.

THE DOOR to the coffee shop opens, and Henry walks in. It's no coincidence, I'm sure, and it's not just because the shop is near the police building. The reality of having a protective detail is that someone always knows where I am.

It's not like vanishing in the age of technology is easy. Most people are a text or call away twenty-four hours a day. There's still the illusion that we can ignore those calls, that we can escape the world for even a few moments. It is an illusion all the same. I always check my messages. In my job, I have to.

I have accepted that reality, but looking at messages isn't the same as having my location be traceable at all times. Everything in me tenses at the admission to myself that until the killer is caught or I am dead, I will be a person who can be found in an instant.

My hate for the Creeper grows.

But he is not here to face my temper, and Henry is.

Andrew tenses as Henry approaches. "Revill."

Henry nods, but he doesn't speak to Andrew. Whatever politeness they sometimes manage is absent today.

There are only two reasons that Henry would approach me when I'm with Andrew. Whenever he's seen Andrew with me in public in the past, he's simply nodded and kept moving. Today he approached, and that means this is either about a case —or my safety. "Is there a call?"

"No." Henry meets my gaze in that way that says he realized most of what I was thinking. "No calls."

I take a breath, let it out, and try to force a smile to my lips.

I want Henry, the whole department really, to let me have the illusion of privacy. "Do we need to do this?"

"You know that answer." Henry's voice, a deep weighty thing at the best of times, makes him words feel ominous.

Arguing with Henry in front of Andrew—or with Andrew in front of Henry—is on my list of things not to do. Ever. I can pretend their discord is simply that they don't like one another, and undoubtedly, that's part of it. So is jealousy. I'm not sure whose jealousy, and I'm not fool enough to ask. All I know for sure is that they both care for me. Beyond that, I'm not opening the discussion with either man.

"Jacobs has to go over to court, so I'm around this afternoon." Henry shrugs like it's not a big deal, but he should be off duty today.

I doubt Andrew knows that, though, so I don't mention it. "So . . .?"

"So, I thought if you wanted to go over those files of yours this afternoon, we can put in a few hours." Henry glances at the folder that Andrew had closed at his approach before he adds, "Maybe I'll see something you missed."

"Andrew?" I reach out for the file. "I need to head home anyhow, and there's no sense in you driving *and* Henry following us."

Andrew gives me the same false smile he had earlier when I asked about his black eye. "You know I don't mind."

"I'll see you . . . tomorrow . . . though?"

With a wry twist to his lips that feels like an invitation to argue, Andrew stares at me, and then at Henry, and then stands. "Sure."

Despite Henry watching us with undisguised curiosity, I grab Andrew's hand. "Henry? I'll meet you at your car."

Both men pause. Andrew's smile evolves into something closer to genuine, and Henry gives me the same implacable look he reserves for any time he disapproves but doesn't want to say that. I ignore all of it and gather my things.

"I'll be out front," Henry says as he leaves.

Once the shop door closes behind him, I step closer to Andrew. "I hate this."

"Move in with me. Let me guard over you. Shelter you."

I close my eyes and lean my head against his chest. "I don't want to fight with you. Not about this or whatever you're hiding or any of it."

He tilts my face upward and kisses me, gently not possessively, and then says, "He'll keep you safe. Revill's good at his job . . . but be careful. Okay?"

I nod.

Neither of us mention his mutual dislike with Henry. It's there, unspoken like far too many other things. These days, Henry is my colleague, my sometimes friend, and that's all he can ever be. The past is over, and there is no future with a man who needs and wants things that I am not, no matter how much I'd wished I could be her. I'm not able to let go of my fears, and unless I can, Henry will only ever be my friend. I'm not sure Andrew believes that, and I'm fairly sure Henry doesn't.

And if Henry could settle for less . . . I don't know. I used to think I'd be his, and after we got passed the flinching at folks' issues with a white woman and a black man—and in the South, it is still a point of tension—I thought we were done with our obstacles. I am the obstacle now, though. My fears. My refusal to let myself be consumed.

Andrew is the safer choice. Andrew, steadfast and kind. Andrew who is staring at me in love, but not rage as I go off to spend a few hours alone with Henry.

"Maybe Henry will find something I didn't," I say. "My job isn't investigating. I just . . ."

Andrew nods. I read case files, M.E. reports, newspapers, anything I can about the Carolina Creeper. I did that before there was the possibility that he was interested in me. Now that he is . . . I can't stop. I need to do everything possible to get my life back.

"I could take care of you." Andrew stares at me from behind his black, swollen eye and urges, "Move in with me, Jules. I can keep you safe."

"No. Not now at least." I shake my head. A woman doesn't get very far in this world if she looks to men to keep her safe. Not that men don't try. Not that they're all bad. But I'm not a delicate blossom to be protected. No one who succeeds in this world is—and I will succeed.

Andrew switches gears. "I can call my cousin over at the N & O."

The News and Observer is the paper in Raleigh, one third of the so-called Triangle.

"I don't think—"

"We need to find her, Jules," he quickly clarifies. "I'll just see if they'll circulate Teresa's picture again, maybe get one of those digital progression things to show ways she could look now too. That's how we'll find Tess if she's alive. Someone will see her. They'll recognize her, and then . . . we'll have a lead."

"Tess?"

"Teresa," he corrects. "We'll find *Teresa*. The newspapers and—"

"It wouldn't hurt." I don't add that we are more likely to find a clue forensically.

Maybe a progression would lead to someone recognizing their Jane Doe as our missing heiress. I'm not so foolish as to think I'll be the one to find her, but maybe someone will. Then her body will be in my hands.

Like all of the victims' bodies, Teresa's body will lead to new information. Sooner or later, the Creeper will leave some trail that will let us find him.

The fact that he's sent a message to me makes me need that timeline to be shorter.

UNTITLED

A Girl with No Past

Edward didn't want me to see Sterling. The sheer idea of it made him unhappy. Edward unhappy was never a good thing. I wouldn't say that I was truly afraid of him, not yet. I was just desperate for his approval.

I'd moved in with him the week after Sterling's invitation. I'd given up my jobs, my apartment, my classes. He was my world. I left the house sometimes, but only with him.

"You could come with me."

"To your mother's house?"

"It's a job. She's paying me. I'll dress up and say the right things, and she'll give me a check." I felt stupid telling Edward that I sold myself to my mother so she could parade me around as if we were a family.

We were at his house. It was a four thousand square foot house with a three-car garage and shed. Behind it was a river that he would go out on with a canoe. The buildings were set back on a twenty-acre lot, and a privacy fence with a coded gate lined the front boundary. It wasn't the sort of old money estate that my family called home, but it was moneyed enough that I asked more questions about Edward's job. He worked at a tech company at RT, one he'd founded.

He looked around the kitchen as we spoke. I had cleaned it while I cooked. It was perfect. He liked things to be perfect. "You've done a good job."

He pulled a box out of his pocket and slid it toward me. He liked to bring me presents.

"May I eat?" I smoothed my hands over the skirt of my dress.

"You may." He nodded toward the plate he'd prepared for me.

"Open your present first."

I lifted the box, unwrapped it carefully so as not to rip the paper or the bow. Inside, a thin chain for my ankle nestled in a box. "May I wear it?"

"Not yet."

"Yes, Edward." I stayed where I was.

The last time I made him unhappy, he took away my clothes and locked me in the shed for a day. There was no toilet. No furniture. No water. No food. No furniture. No water. No food.

But when I did a good job, he treated me like I was made of spun glass. Really, what did it matter that he picked out my clothes? Was it actually important to earn money when he provided everything we could need? I hadn't ever had a burning career passion. I simply hadn't wanted to be trapped by Sterling's whims.

Edward smiled at me. "We could get married. That way you'd never need to worry about anything. I'll take care of you."

It wasn't a proposal in the way that I'd expected as a girl, but Edward made me happy. He took care of me.

"I love you."

"You don't want to marry me, Tessa?" *The edge was there, the one that I knew could lead to things I didn't like.*

"I do, but—"

"What? You want to whore around? You want other men to look at you? To fuck you?" *He threw his plate.*

"I'm sorry." *I was frozen in my chair.*

"I offer to take care of you." *He stood.* "And this is what you do? You aren't working any more, not at some menial job, not at a job where you act like a whore."

"I'm sorry," *I repeated.*

"Sorry that you don't get to act the whore? Is that what this is about? Are you not satisfied?" *He grabbed my hair and jerked my head back.*

"I want to marry you."

He stared at me. "You need something to do? Fix it."

He knocked the rest of the dishes onto the floor, shattering them. "There. You have a job."

He watched me clean. I picked everything up, washed the floor, and eventually, I stood in front of him. I was bleeding from several small cuts, and somewhere in the back of my mind, I thought that the ways he watched those cuts was scarier than being locked in the shed had been.

"Shower, and put on the blue dress with the little flowers," he said. "We'll go out to dinner."

I nodded and walked away.

"You need to do a better job, Tess," he called after me. "I'm patient, and I know you don't mean to make mistakes . . . but if you want this to work, you need to trust me completely."

I turned back to look at him. "I do."

"We can pick out a ring tonight. My brothers are coming over tomorrow," he explained. "You'll be a good wife, won't you?"

"I will."

Edward stared at me, looking for something in my expression. If I knew what he wanted, I'd have given it to him. When he was like this, I didn't know what to do or say. There was always something, though, some word or act that would make him forgive me. When he did, he was amazing.

"I love you," I said.

I did. I really did. I just didn't know if I loved him enough. I screwed up, and he got mad. Mostly, being mad meant embarrassing me or sex that was a little rougher than I enjoyed. Other than the shed incident, it wasn't so bad.

"You're not going to see your mother," he announced. "We'll get married that day instead. Isn't that a better plan?"

"Yes, Edward."

"No one will ever tell you what to do again, Tess. No one will ever touch you again without my permission. I'll take care of you." He stood and walked toward me. "Come on. Let's shower before we go out."

And just like that, he was sweet again. He took my hand, led me to the oversized shower in the master bath, and knelt before me. He kissed me, licked me, nuzzled me. After the first orgasm, he slowed, but he didn't stop. After the next, he smiled at me. I stroked his hair while he lavished so much attention on me that I couldn't imagine being anywhere else.

Edward treated me like I was everything he could want until I could barely stand. He stared up at me while I was still trembling with aftershocks. I saw awe and love in his expression, and in that instant, he looked like every fantasy a woman could ever have.

"I love you, Tess. No one will ever love you the way I do." Even then, even feeling as sated as I did, his words sounded like a threat and a promise, but they were true either way. "You're mine."

"Always."

MICHAEL

I call Elizabeth as soon as it's a decent time in New York. Maybe things with Tess won't continue to develop like I hope, but already I have more of an idea for a book than I've had in years. The draft is going well, and every tidbit I learn, I revise into the pages I've already written. I see it glimmer more and more each time.

"She's the one," I tell Elizabeth.

"The one?"

"Look at your email," I explain. I'd sent her a picture of Tess. "She's the one. Tess. The woman in New Orleans is the one."

There's a brief pause before my agent lightly prompts, "To marry or write about?"

"She's the character, a young woman with a dark secret. She's running from something awful. I don't know exactly what yet, but she's a mess of scars and tattoos. Mostly, she's lucid, but the word in the square—"

"The what?" Elizabeth sounds vaguely charmed.

I slow down, explain that I've been mingling with the locals in New Orleans to set the world of the story and to gather information on Tess. It's a heady thing, this early stage of writing when the world and characters are so close but still elusive. I know the pieces will coalesce. I'll make them.

"The story will be tragic, redemptive, and Tess is the lynchpin." I try to sound calm, but not bored. With most people, I need to hide the excitement of the process, but agents are like bloodhounds. They want to have the scent to chase. There's an excitement that they seek as much as writers do. The difference, I think, is that they do it for the money, for the acclaim of having the project—or author—their contemporaries covet.

That's not what drives me. The money is nice, but I have plenty of that. The acclaim is nicer, but I could have quit after the first book, preserved my reputation, and spent years riding on that success. That would've been safer. I needed more.

"The critics who dismissed me will eat their words when they read this," I promise.

"As they should."

I can't help but cringe at her tone. Elizabeth is precisely the sort of woman that I will marry some day: cold, cultured, and conveying most emotions with only the slightest hint of actual expression. She's every woman I'm supposed to want.

I shudder at the thought.

When I disconnect a few minutes later, I admit to myself that I'm loathe to leave not just Tess, but New Orleans itself. There's something gorgeous about New York, and I'm not trying to abandon the literary world or the polish of that far more familiar city. There's also something alluring about New Orleans, her secrets and her characters.

And, increasingly, Tess has become a character to me, perhaps she already was before I met her. I know all books have that foolish disclaimer that announces that everything under the cover is a lie.

That's pure legalese.

Surely, I'm not the only writer teasing stories out of shop girls or drunks in bars. Truth be told, they're getting something out of it too. What use does Tess have for her secrets? She pays her rent several months in advance when she can because she knows that she's as likely as not to go off on one of her "episodes" and forget.

When I'm not with Tess, I'm studying her, collecting the bits of stories about her, and trying to understand her world. It's no different than the research in the depths of archives or museums. Writers study and sort. We gather the pieces to assemble a tale. I am assembling the pieces of Tess—and adding my own to make the story better.

I make my way down Royal Street, high on my impending victory, on the joy of the story and the acclaim ahead of me.

I'm stopped by a man who lowers his horn at my approach.

"You're Tess' writer," the trumpet player, a man whose name I can't recall, says.

It's amusing to be Tess' anything. *My* name opens doors in a lot of places. My reputation does, too. Here, though, with the people who exist on cash-under-the-table or change-in-a-bucket, I am no one.

"How is she this week?" he asks.

"Fine."

"Don't be too sure." He shakes his head. "Clovis says the girl's done paid up her rent for the next four months."

I don't know what to say. There's the Tess I see, and there's the Tess the locals know, and the Tess I write, and I'm not sure how much they have in common sometimes. One or all of them is an illusion.

He lifts his horn and plays, knowing in some seemingly innate way that the tourists coming toward us are likely to drop money in his open case. There's an art or science to busking that I can't figure out.

Like a lot of the people I meet because of Tess, he'd be a fine character himself. He's a modern town crier, a newsman with a horn, a person who distracts and distances himself by putting others in my path. In a way, I trust him more because of it.

Too many people want to talk to me when they hear what I do. Most of them tell me about their cousin in Baton Rouge or their auntie clear up North—and you can hear the capital letter when they pronounce North just as you hear it when they say South—

who wrote a storybook for kids or their dentist who wrote a romance using a woman's name to do it. Everyone's an author or wants to write a book. Nevermind that they'd scoff if I decided to wield a dental pick or a trumpet with no experience whatsoever and call myself a professional after a few moments of well-intentioned practice. I learned when *A Solitary Grave* released that pointing out some truths resulted in surly looks, so I nod and hold my tongue as I gather the pieces they will share with me.

"Poor Tess," the trumpet player laments when he is no longer distracted by the sweet couple from somewhere in the Midwest who lingered to hear maybe a half a song. "Sometimes I swear the devil hisself is chasing after that girl."

I wait. That's the trick with people this far in the South: they'll tell tales as long as you stand still, buy a whiskey or a joint to share, drop a few bills in the hat. They do it well. I've been listening to stories in a lot of cities, a lot of bars, and quite a few planes and trains. There's nowhere quite like the South for tales. Maybe it's the humidity. Everything feels more languid when the very air insists that you slow down.

"The devil?" I prompt after a moment.

He laughs, a husky sound that seems to rattle and scratch in his lungs before finding its way into the air. "I don' have the answer you're trying to con outta me, boy."

I don't bother trying to deny that I want answers. These aren't people who are easy to lie to. They live in a way I don't understand, and in some way, they only tolerate me because of Tess. I simply nod.

He lifts his horn to his lips again, but before he starts to play, he adds, "All I'm gonna say is if you poke a hornet's nest long 'nough, you don't got no room to bitch when you get stung. Tess might be crazier than a box of magpies when she's off in one of her spells, but those spells always end . . . and what you don't see is that Tess . . . she simply ain't *right*. Whatever trouble sent her here cracked something in that girl, and broken girls are dangerous."

I don't laugh even though I disagree. Tess is unpredictable. She's embarrassing at times, but that's the worst of her. She's a victim. I don't know of what yet, but I'm sure of that much.

I toss another twenty into his hat. "Thanks."

He nods his head at me and starts to play. It's not a song I know, but my jazz repertoire is fairly lacking. The best I can do is recognize the song as one I've heard in the streets. Maybe that's progress enough. I know it's not one of the handful that are played constantly for tourists with as little jazz or blues knowledge as I have. My familiarity with the city, the music, and the streets is all coming together a little at a time. People say hello, nod at me, but all of it is the result of being here with Tess for several weeks.

She's becoming the face of the city to me, the body of the lush woman that is New Orleans, and I'm figuring her out. I'll walk these streets and trace the planes of her body, and turn it all into a bestseller.

Then everything will fall into place.

JULIANA

Andrew has been absentee for several days now. I'd say he's avoiding me, but it feels like more than that. I do my job, handling the preparation of an eighty-three-year-old man whose family reminds me a bit of the vultures that swoop down on road kill. Some people make me wish for the ability to go back in time and show a stranger the love that we all deserve.

The truth is that I think most of us could stand a little more love, a bit more hope, and a lot more peace in our lives. These are, also, the sorts of thoughts that come from too long alone with the dead.

Between the location of my work and Andrew's absence, I am forced to admit that my complete lack of a social life is exceedingly apparent. There is, literally, no need to leave the house. So, I've been using it as an excuse to lose myself in my research.

. I'm haunted by the Creeper's victims. Every flat surface of my room is growing littered by stacks of files—unsorted and sorted cases, my years of notes, and newspaper clipping. Coffee cups are scattered throughout the organized chaos. The worst are the photographs slipping out of their manila folders. I absently tuck them back in every time I notice one. Seeing them without warning, even though I've seen them before, hurts in a visceral way.

When my research is interrupted by a call from

MY COLLEGE ROOMMATE, Sharon, I'm exited in ways that might be atypical of a woman my age. A distraction! It's a welcome thing right now.

"Hey! How are--"

"IT's HER, Jules. The missing woman. I know where she is . . . or at least where she was."

"Who?" I can't assume. Just because my mind is on this case, I can't expect it to be at the forefront of anyone else's mind.

"The one you were looking for last year. Teresa." She pauses. "I saw the articles, too. Another body. Not her. *She's* alive, Jules. Your missing woman. Alive."

"Are you sure?" My voice cracks. I'm only awake thanks to the mixed blessings of caffeine and willpower. The letter from the Creeper and absence of Andrew have my stress levels high enough that I float between insomnia and nightmares.

"It's her, Jules. I looked up old pictures of her before I called."

I close my eyes in something akin to relief

So many dead women.

So many lives I can't save.

It's not like I'm a savior or even a vigilante. I just want to make a difference in this world. I want to do something *good,* an act of strength against the tide of monsters out there. I know my family worries.

Uncle Micky doesn't comment beyond offers to cover my dark circles and none-too-subtle remarks on the absence of clean coffee mugs. We don't discuss the fact that both of my parents have called. My mother suggested that therapy might be wise. My father asked if I'm still going to the range.

We all cope in our own ways. I need to research. I need to try to stop the Carolina Creeper. I need to help these women.

I need to save myself.

Despite all of that, I can't decide if the call from Sharon is a good thing or not.

"Jules? If it's not her, it's her twin," she says, calling me away from my worries and weary thoughts. As if I'm confused, Sharon adds, "The heiress."

"She was an only child. No twin."

Sharon's voice softens as she adds, "I've seen her pictures often enough, Jules. You're not exactly subtle in your obsession over these women. It's her. Her pictures were sent in to the office. It's *her.*"

Sharon is an intern at some New York literary agency. She's wanted this job for as long as I knew her, but I think she hates it. It's nowhere near as glamorous as it looks on television.

"I thought about telling my bosses, but . . . they're not looking for *her* and if it is her, she needs someone who doesn't want to exploit her." I hear the pause as she flicks a lighter. She quit smoking at least a year ago.

I'm not sure what she's withholding, but I know there's more.

"I'm sorry," I tell her. "Whatever it is, I'm sorry."

I can hear the crackle of burning paper and tobacco through the phone. She's somewhere quiet enough to speak privately—which means she's violating several rules on smoking. New York is on the long list of cities where cigarette bans and restrictions are the norm now.

Finally, she says, "I can't tell you *why* they have a picture of her because of an NDA I signed."

"She's an author?" I try to imagine how the woman I've been thinking of as either dead or hostage to the Carolina Creeper could be living a secret life and writing books. Maybe she wasn't connected to the case at all. Maybe we were wrong about her.

"No." Sharon lets out a sound that's laugh-like, but has no humor in it.

"But you're sure it's her?" I ask again. This doesn't make any sense. Maybe I can ask enough things not to violate her NDA, but if not, I'm still going to find out what Sharon knows.

"Tess. That's this woman's name, Jules." Sharon inhales again. "Fuck. Do you know how hard it is to get into an agency like Wells Literary?"

"I'm sorry," I repeat.

I know what she's about to do before it happens, but I'd bet we both knew what she'd do from the moment she saw the picture. She wouldn't have called if she wasn't going to tell me more than she should.

"Check your phone," Sharon says in an angry voice. "That's her. She's in New Orleans. It's her. I've spent enough time looking at this stuff with you. I know it's her."

"I won't tell anyone that you told me," I promise.

"It'll come out. I can't tell you why. That part, at least, I won't tell you, but it will come out . . . and once Ms. Wells finds out I knew who Tess is and didn't tell anyone, she'll fire me." Sharon's lighter flicks again. After a moment, she continues, "Christ, I hope it's not even her, but Tess . . . *this* Tess at least . . . she's in trouble."

"I love you," I tell her.

"Yeah, you too, Jules." Sharon sounds like she's done exactly what she has, tossed something she wants into a fire to do the right thing, and I wish I could say or do something to make up for that, but the reality of the world is that it's not a meritocracy. Doing the right thing doesn't equate to rewards. In reality, far too often it leads to problems.

Once Sharon hangs up, I open my email. There are a few pictures of a woman who is almost certainly Teresa Morris. She doesn't look like she's the heiress in the photos her mother gave us, but she's the same woman. Dozens of tattoos cover her body —including the flower bud. The tattoo of the victims of the Carolina Creeper marks her wrist.

How did she escape? How is she alive? I debate whether to call Andrew or Henry first. Then it hits me, awkwardly and frighteningly, that Andrew called her *Tess*. It's not what most of the articles call her, or what I call her, but I think back over what Sharon told me and realize that she called Teresa "Tess."

So did Andrew.

He didn't know her. Why would he do that? Was there an article or . . . he didn't know her. He would have told me.

I cannot stop the doubts that fill me. He lied to me. He wants me to stay away from Henry.

He called her Tess.

But just as quickly, I remind myself that Henry investigated Andrew. I remind myself that I trust him. He's been my lover for over a year. He isn't a killer. He wouldn't leave dead bodies for me to find or send that letter.

He isn't the Creeper.

My lover is not the killer.

Why did he call her Tess?

For the first time since I went to bed with Andrew, I doubt my own judgment. I don't call him. I don't call Henry either. What does *Henry* know that he's not told me? I try to think about his attitude to Andrew. Is he colder toward Andrew? Does he know a secret that I ought to know, too? Surely, if they had any reason to think Andrew was a suspect, Henry would tell me.

No, I can't call Henry or Andrew. This is on me. I'd have to tell them how I know to look there.

I have enough money to fly to New Orleans; even if I didn't, I'd find a way. I don't know what I'll say to her when I find her. How do you walk up to someone and say, "Hi, I thought you were dead, but since you aren't, I was wondering if you could tell me if you were or are you the captive of a serial killer?"

As much as I want the answers she probably has, I don't know what to do. I'm used to talking to detectives or employees at various medical examiners' offices. There aren't that many murders, though. I'm only part-time with the PD. Mostly, I deal with mourners, and there's a vast gap between mourning a loss and surviving horrors.

I don't know what to do. I don't know what I *should* do.

Maybe the logical thing to do *is* to tell Henry.

I'm not prepared for this. How do I tell him without sharing my suspicions that Andrew knows more than I realized before now? How do I explain why I found Teresa? Do I tell him that Andrew called her Tess? That Sharon found her?

Before I realize it, an hour has passed. My phone buzzes. Email comes in. Andrew. Both are from him.

I look at flights. It's often expensive to fly last minute, but New Orleans isn't that far from North Carolina by air. There are a few cheap tickets, airlines selling off last minute tickets. It's a short, easy trip. I could do it, go there right now. It's not like she's somewhere in Europe or Canada or even somewhere remote in the U.S. like Montana or Idaho or those other states that seem like they're surely all wilderness I don't know how to handle. She's in a fairly busy city, one filled with tourists.

I flit between the flights and hotels. I look at my schedule and my budget. I can maybe swing going for a week. Uncle Micky can handle the work here, and I doubt that he'd object to me getting away to clear my head.

Dealing with Andrew and with Henry . . . that's a bit more complicated.

I don't know if I can find her, but I don't know if I can afford not to try. I stare at Teresa's face. She doesn't look like the girl in the pictures I have of her. Not really. Admittedly, she's early thirties now.

The only pictures we had were when she was in her early twenties, and she looked like a lot of young women with money. This woman doesn't look like that. She has the appearance of someone who could be homeless or five minutes from it. There's something hard about her.

She's sleeping in one of the pictures Sharon sent. Tattoos spiral down her arms, across her shoulders, along her calves and ankles. It's the one on her wrist that I keep looking at. It's nearly identical to the one I saw on what remained of Ana Menendez. The next picture is different. Teresa is standing in the same park that shows up in most of the tourist brochure pictures of New Orleans. It's shot from farther away. She looks like a wraith, a junkie, starving. It could've been in any number of cities, in any number of years. She's a woman lost.

And she isn't aware that her picture is being taken.

Unlike the vulnerability of the one of her sleeping, this is a different kind of invasive. I have no doubt she was unaware of both photos. And I have no doubt that whatever has happened to Teresa Morris, it wasn't good.

She's alive.

I can't decide if that's good or not.

I save the photos to my phone. Copy and re-save them, edit them slightly—adjust the lighting only—and then email them to myself and re-save again. Then, I call Andrew.

"I have to go out of town," I tell him as I start throwing clothes into my bag. I'm doing this. I'm going to New Orleans. "I'm on my way to the airport, but I'll be back as soon as I can."

He's quiet.

"Andrew?"

"You didn't mention a trip," he says.

I force a laugh. "Yeah? And you didn't mention who gave you a black eye. We had other stuff to talk about, right? We always do."

"Right." His laugh sounds no more genuine than mine probably did. "Where are you headed?"

"Oh. Just New York," I lie. "A friend's getting married. I can call you when I'm back . . . "

"Good. That's good. Alone?"

"Yes," I snap. "Okay . . . I'm going to—"

"I love you, Jules. I know you don't want to hear it, or maybe you don't even want me to feel it, but I do."

I notice that I'm shaking. I can tell myself that it's simply because I want to do this alone, or because I don't want to go away with him, or even that I don't owe him the whole truth. The reality is that whatever he's hiding unsettles me.

"I'll call you when I'm back," I say.

It's the most I can add without further lies.

UNTITLED

A Girl with No Past

Once Edward and I were married, his brothers came by whenever they wanted. Before that, he'd apparently told them to stay away.

"Is he good to you?"

I looked at Edward's younger brother. The oldest one, William, barely spoke to me. The younger brother, Buddy, watched me carefully. He catalogued my bruises, my cuts. He knew that Edward had to send me to the shed twice now.

"Edward loves me." I looked down as I said it.

Earlier that day was the first time Edward hit me repeatedly. I wasn't sure what to do. I would learn over the next few months, but the first time was a surprise. I hadn't been completely sheltered as a child. My family was affluent, and if not for the choice to walk away from them, I suspect my life would be completely unfamiliar to me now. I'd left though, walked away without a backward glance when my mother's latest husband made a pass at me—and my mother blamed me for it.

I was nineteen then.

At the time, it seemed like the worst thing that had ever happened, could ever happen. Then, years later, I learned about real violence.

It was before I'd learned how much he needed to hurt women.

There would be things that hurt worse, but that day

I hadn't even spoken before his fist connected with my face. There was no warning, nothing. Silence and then a fist.

I stumbled backwards. "What—"

He closed the distance between us and hit me a second time. "I thought you were better than the rest of them."

I didn't reply. I might not know why he was angry, but I understood that speaking had led to a second strike. I didn't want a third one.

"What am I to do, Tess? How am I to be okay when I have to worry about you? Do you want to upset me?"

I reached up to touch the blood I could feel on my chin. I touched my teeth with my tongue to see if any were loose. Doing so revealed that my tongue was bleeding.

"Were you with someone else, Tessie?"

"No, Edward! I just went for a walk—"

He had my throat in his hand then, and I knew that there would be fingerprints.

"I thought you were special, that you could be trusted." He shoved me backwards, and I stumbled.

"I can be!"

He stared at me. "Where were you? Were you with someone else?"

Buddy walked into the room, took one look at us, and turned away.

"Do you want to fuck her?" Edward asked him, dragging me across the floor by my throat as he turned.

"She's yours." Buddy didn't even look at me. He kept his gaze firmly fixed on Edward.

"If she's going to be a whore, she might as well do it for you." Edward's hand tightened.

"I don't touch your things, Edward." Buddy shook his head.

"No one should touch my things without my permission." Edward's attention dropped back to me. "Do you understand?"

"Yes, Edward. I was wrong to go out. I won't leave the house again."

"Ever." He stared at me.

I heard footsteps as Buddy turned to walk away.

Then Edward said, "I don't want to have to hurt you, Tess. Prove that you're a good wife."

"I am. I swear it, Edward."

I heard footsteps as Buddy turned to walk away.

"You won't go out again alone," Edward announced. "I don't want to worry like this again."

I nodded. It hadn't seemed like a big deal when I went, but I knew he worried. I didn't want that--or want him to hit me again. I thought I was special. I thought that I could be good enough.

"Sometimes I need to do things, Tess. I thought if you were here, I could stop. I thought you . . . I don't want to hurt you. You know that, right?"

I nodded again.

"Do you love me?"

"I do."

For a moment, he stared at me. I knew he was possessive. I thought it would get better when he was sure of me. It still wasn't enough.

He was silent, and I was afraid.

"I trust you, Edward." I leaned in and kissed him.

He said nothing.

"I belong to you. I love you," I reassured him. "No one else. Never anyone else."

Finally, he spoke. "And you trust me to decide what's best?"

It wasn't really a question, but I answered. "Whatever it takes for you to feel better. I want to be with you, Edward, and I want you not to worry."

He shook his head and pulled me closer. "Don't ever leave me, Tess. Swear it."

"I swear. I love you, Edward."

"I'll kill you if you leave," he told me.

"I'm here. I'm not leaving."

Sometimes, I think that if I knew what he'd intended to do I'd have said something else. The rest of the time, I'm honest enough to admit that I would've agreed to anything to keep from being the one he hurt.

I know that I survived being his wife because Edward hurt other women instead.

I'm alive because he killed other women instead.

During those first months when I realized who he was, what he was, when I had to admit that I slept next to a sociopath every night, I still thought there was an answer. I thought I could be enough—because Edward thought that.

I snorted the cocaine he gave and swallowed the lies he told me. His brothers knew about the women. I knew. When I heard the first one scream, I asked Buddy to help her.

To help me.

Nothing changed.

I stayed in the house. I felt like a pet sometimes when he left and set the alarm. There was no phone. There was no way to go out without an alarm going off—and not one that went to a police station.

I only tried that once.

He killed the next woman in front of me.

TESS

Being in New York is a mistake. I feel out of sorts, out of my
skin, the moment we step off the plane. It's wrong how
quickly you can go from home to a strange land when you fly.
As a girl, I liked it, but it's been years since I was on a plane. I
couldn't afford the sort of holiday trips I was used to growing up,
and Reid simply didn't like to take me with him if he had to
travel. He limited his travel. Sometimes when he took trips, he
used a different name. There was a guy, Robert, who made up
fake IDs. Reid had several. I still have all three of mine. I used to
think Reid would find me if I used any of them, so I have
another name I use if I have to have ID—Teresa Adams.

"Are you okay?" Michael prompts as we climb into the black car
that he's hired to take us to the apartment he rented. I expect
he'll leave me there while he goes to his meetings. That, at least,
is comforting to me. I need time to adjust, to listen to the music
from home that I carried here, to take a few more pills without
having to hide it. I need my tethers.

Few things about this trip make me feel okay. The weather isn't humid enough, and the streets are so silent without the music I use to help keep me focused. There are sounds, horns and voices and the omnipresent rumble of a city, but it's not *my* city.

He leaves with the sort of kiss Reid used to give me when he left for work, a reminder that I matter. It's sweet, reminding of the man Reid could be when he wasn't so focused on the pretty things. People wouldn't understand that if they knew, but Reid was kind when he wasn't awful. He laughed and brushed my hair and brought me breakfast in bed. When he was happy, I was happy. I miss that. I miss mattering to someone.

Maybe that's why I am here with Michael.

The apartment has more personality than my own, but not as much as the one Michael is renting in New Orleans. Both of his rentals are obviously decorated to announce their location. Michael's in New Orleans has photographs of jazz singers, an overflowing bowl of beads, a few parade throws that sit on the mantel, and other assorted announcements that this is a space intended to "feel like" you belong in the city. Those of us who do don't need to prove it.

This apartment functions the same. I wander around the space we are renting. It's sterile. I like that part. Combined with the jazz through the headphones, that is soothing. It reminds me a bit too much of Sterling's house, the casual minimalism, over-done black and white. She had such a stage. I think that was during the era of the husband before the one she had when I left. Gregory. He was new money, kind in a way that heralded his short tenure from before the wedding.

The flowers in the vases are bright and fake. The bedroom furniture is some sort of reclaimed item that was undoubtedly too expensive for its value, but clearly on trend at some point. Sterling would be at ease here. Teresa's friends would be too. I suspect the remnant of Teresa that I can't smother is comfortable too.

For a change, I embrace her. The girl I used to be. The woman who was horrified by life with Reid. She's the person I need to be to face a weekend here.

The mere thought of it makes me feel like running. Teresa remembers too much. Sometimes that's okay. Right now, I don't want to think about the past. I add an extra pill.

Too soon, Michael's back. I don't remember intending to sleep, but maybe I took too many of my Klonapin.

"Tess?"

I nod. That's me. "My mother called me Teresa."

Michael paused before asking, "Do you want me to call you that?"

"No." It's fuzzy in my head, but I know that I'm Tess. The rest helped. The lack of dreams helped even more. The pills are doing what they must. "When I was here before, I was with her. She called me Teresa."

I watch Michael do that thing he does when he's feeling unsure.

"We need to meet Elizabeth in two hours. We could—"

"Walk." I stand and stretch. "We can walk to where we're meeting her."

Again, the pause. Again, the stare. Michael doesn't know what to do, and I can't explain. I'm too quiet. I try not to be, but I am. The lack of New Orleans makes me feel like I'm going to slip.

"Sure, Tess." He smiles, a fake smile, the one I saw when he first arrived in my city, the one in his pictures. He's more real with me usually, but not here. Not now.

Coming here was a mistake—but I already knew that. The only question is how *much* of a mistake it was. I open my luggage and pull out the sort of dress Teresa would wear. It's familiar, like donning the armor that I used to wear so easily, and constricting all at the same time. Tasteful, simple, black. I bought it at a thrift store, but it's still the right sort of dress.

The fact that it doesn't conceal many of my tattoos is a different sort of comfort. I am Tess playing dress up as Teresa. Hopefully, that means I can be the best of both parts of myself.

"You look perfect," Michael says as I slip on tasteful low heels.

The shoes aren't designer, but I'm not seeing Sterling. I'm seeing a woman who ultimately is no one, and I can't let too much of my past out, not unless I want Michael to find out more than is safe. He's already guessed that I have a past with money. He's seen my scars, too. There are only so many details he can be allowed to know.

As we leave the building, Michael watches me. He holds my hand as we walk along the streets of Manhattan. We're meeting his agent. I remind myself of that over and over. It's a business meeting dressed up like a meal.

"Elizabeth is a bit brusque, but she's really looking forward to meeting you."

I nod.

"Are you okay?" Michael stares at me too long again, not missing a step, but fixing me in his gaze long enough to make me squirm.

It strikes me that he's different here too. I'm less tethered. He's more so.

"I don't leave New Orleans," I remind him. "I haven't left her in years."

He laughs. "You do realize the city isn't *really* a woman, Tess."

Again, I nod.

"It's not home. This place isn't home," I offer when he glances at me again. It's the best I can say. I don't tell him that it makes me remember being Teresa. I don't tell him that Teresa couldn't handle what Reid had done. Or what she has done.

I'm not *her*.

I am some part of the same person, but I am not wholly her. I sift through all of the memories I can access, and I remember only the things I have to. Right now, I must remember being Teresa. She would be comfortable in Midtown.

I must remember being Teresa and still not fall apart. I'm not sure I can. Being several versions of me at once is hard.

The city doesn't look like it's changed since I was teenager visiting with my mother. Back then, being in the city was about shopping and lunches at whatever restaurant happened to be declared acceptable to people like her. Vaguely, I wonder if she's somewhere in the city, trying on overpriced shoes that her latest husband will buy.

I know my silence unsettles Michael, but he doesn't press me. Later I can thank him for that gift. Today, I must simply try to let enough of Teresa in that I can handle being in the wrong city.

His agent is already seated when we arrive. We're not late, but she obviously decided to be early. I remember that game. She is of my mother's kind of woman. I dislike every detail of her appearance from the peacockish style of dress and jewelry to her insincere smile.

Reid would have broken her.

I would've let him.

That's the secret I can't tell.

I *let* him.

I was tired. So tired of hurting. So tired of bleeding. He always came back to me because he loved me. It is beautiful to be loved. Every person wants that. Often, though, being loved by Reid hurt. I wasn't good enough to deserve a love without pain. I was never good enough. Not for my mother. Not for Reid.

I'm going to be good enough for Michael.

I straighten my shoulders and let him lead me to my seat. I wait as Teresa would have so he can pull out my seat. My clothes are as well-cut as they ought to be, and I remember long ago manners that are unfamiliar to the woman I am when I fuck Michael.

I ignore both the agent and the writer while they exchange polite greetings. She gives him the same sort of stiff half-hug and faux European kisses that were the norm at parties I grew up attending. She's no more sincere than they were, but neither is Michael. Neither am I. This is how most people live, false in every way. There is no truth in word or act. We hide it all under costumes and masks.

Reid removed those.

My memories surge. Teresa needed masks that Reid wouldn't let us have. She wanted to believe things that made the ugly pieces kinder.

All of the pretty girls dressed in red . . .

So much red.

Sometimes my dreams are red.

I smooth my napkin in my lap. Blue. It's blue. And my dress is black. There is no red here.

I tune them out until I hear Elizabeth order a bottle of red wine.

"White," I insist. "Michael, it *has* to be white."

He exchanges a look with Elizabeth, but he takes the wine list and selects a white wine all the same. "The 2000 Ceretto Blangé Arneis."

The waiter leaves.

Overall, the meal is a stilted affair. Elizabeth opts to direct a few remarks to me, but mostly, I keep my silence. It's exhausting to be in this world. The things I need to do and be in order to avoid embarrassing Michael are things that make me remember more than I can handle here. Sometimes I want that, the remembering. Not today. Not here. I am in the wrong city with the wrong people.

I concentrate on manners and silence. I concentrate on the tattoos that she is surreptitiously studying, the answers etched on my skin that no one here can translate, the very story that has made Michael bring me to this city and this table. I wonder what they'd do if they knew. I know that answer though. I saw it when Reid tore away masks. Under the skin, under a knife, we are not so different. People like to pretend that they are above the horrors they consume in their films and novels, but at the core of it all, all people break. How much they break, how easily they break, those vary. But we all break.

Elizabeth would break.

I broke.

All of the pretty girls broke.

We are the same.

All of us are the same.

The thoughts swirl until I debate excusing myself for another pill. I try to hide them, hide how much chemistry it takes to keep me steady. That is my every day plan with Michael, but right now, it feels daunting. Instead, I open my bag and shake one out.

"Headache," I say.

Michael reaches out for my hand.

Elizabeth's gaze follows. Her already pursed lips tighten.

"That will add to your wrinkles," I explain helpfully.

Michael coughs abruptly. His smile flashes at me almost against his will before he lifts his glass and drinks more than he should in one sip. I'm pleased. This is the man who has been twisting my sheets. His cruelty and his confusion make me calmer. It's more familiar than the stiff expressions that he shares with Elizabeth.

She watches him. She studies me. She pats her lips and then gives up any faux politeness. "What is it you do, Tess?"

"I simply *am*."

Elizabeth stares at me. "I see."

She doesn't, but until you've had a moment when you realize you're likely to die, that the next exhalation should be counted as there are only a few breaths left, it's hard to understand that the sheer act of living is incredible. I don't know that I'm doing anything to make this world better. Most days, though, it's a victory to simply *be*. I survived. There is nothing I wouldn't do to survive. That was the greatest lesson of my life so far.

"Generally, I do whatever I need to do," I offer in an attempt at explanation. The rest of the details are ones I won't tell, not willingly, and certainly not to her.

I glance at the tattoo on my wrist. It tells the story I won't. She just can't translate it to words she can understand.

Elizabeth doesn't seem to know how to respond to the words I do say. "Michael is quite successful," she says after a too-long hesitation.

I laugh. She's not *wrong*, but she's not right either. I think she's being protective of him.

"His first book certainly was. The film helped, though, I'd expect." I glance at Michael, who suddenly looks like he's both fascinated and afraid. I continue, "That second book, though . . ."

Elizabeth lets out a quiet sound that may have been a word. She's a lot like Sterling, a liar to the bone. There are layers here, but I'm not the one who will peel them back. Reid could have, but I don't think there's enough substance under her layers to have held his interest. He wanted me because there was Teresa under Tess, and he knew that there was Tessie in here too. Or maybe Teresa was the deeper layer. It gets confusing sometimes. All I know is that sometimes Reid had to cut me to find the layers inside.

I want another pill.

I want to go home.

I don't want to think about sharp things or being good. I don't want to remember the past when I'm not at home.

I reach out and refill my own glass even though I know it's vulgar to do so.

"My next book will be the best so far," Michael offers mildly, his voice pulling me out of my thoughts and into this strange room in Midtown Manhattan, his words reminding me why we're here.

"I'm excited to read it," Elizabeth says.

"When is the next book due? I'm not sure how that part works. Is it already sold or does he need to write it before . . ." I meet Michael's eyes and smile again.

He looks away.

He's already writing it. I knew he was going to. I knew he was trying to see inside my dark places and steal things, but his sideways glance tells me that he's already started writing.

There are words on a page about me. Already. I knew, but he's told her, too.

There are secrets of mine that he thinks he knows, and he's spilled them like ink on a page instead of onto my skin.

He wants me to see his pressure, as much as he wants me to be wooed by the New York glitter—and like everything, it's an attempt to find out more about my past. The entire trip is his attempt to manipulate me, but the version of myself that I have become after-Reid isn't someone Michael can manipulate without my consent. A niggling feeling pushes at me. The Bad

Things . . . the ones I can't remember . . . the ones I drown in whiskey and pills if I start to remember too clearly . . . they were why I couldn't be with Reid.

But that's why Michael wants me. He wants to know all the bad things. He wants to figure me out, but if he does, he'll know if I'm a monster.

I don't think either of us really should have that answer.

UNTITLED

A Girl with No Past

Life had shrunk a little, reduced to what Edward said, what Edward thought, what Edward wanted. I suspected that it was precisely why people became religious: does my god or church want me to do this? Having that one question enabled every answer to be clear. I did what my husband thought was best.

I didn't decide what I wore, or what I ate, or when I spread my legs for Edward. He had rules for all of that. He kept track of what I ate. He watched me to be sure I did a good job grooming myself. Sometimes, it was hard for both of us. He had a demanding job, far more complicated than I could understand. He explained that to me.

Sometimes he gave me cocaine for days in a row when he needed me to stay awake to take care of him. He always took it away, too, so I didn't become an addict.

Addicts didn't make Edward happy.

Edward's happiness was my job. That was why waitressing and school had to go away. Sometimes, even though I tried my best, I wasn't good enough. It made him angry. Then he had to find someone else to take care of his needs. I tried. I really tried to be good enough so that he wouldn't need them.

I was never good enough.

He brought a new girl home. Courtney.

He offered her coke, but she was crying more than I was. She didn't take it.

"She doesn't want it, Tess. Show her how."

"Yes, Edward." I couldn't move, though.

"Do I need to show her how to be good?"

The pretty things always bleed more when he was angry with me.

"It's your fault," he reminded me. "If you were good . . ."

"I'll try harder," I promised. I did try. I closed my eyes. Sometimes, Edward had stressful days at work. My job was to make him happy. Maybe if he was happy, he wouldn't make Courtney cry. The girls he kept in the bathroom eventually all went away. They stopped crying, and then they . . . left.

I didn't cry. I never cried. Edward liked that I didn't cry. He liked me to say "thank you for taking care of me." If I could let him do more bad things to me, he wouldn't have to have other girls, but I wasn't strong enough for everything he liked—and I wasn't allowed to die—even though I tried.

If I was good enough, strong enough, no one else would get hurt.

After a few days, Courtney didn't fight. She didn't cry much. Usually they stayed longer, but this one was different.

I was in there puking. She watched. I wished I could shower, but she was in the tub I was allowed to use.

"Just do what he says. He won't hurt you as much if you're good." I leaned against the wall, trying to stay upright. I shook all over, and I had fever and chills. I wanted the drugs. I wanted . . .

Sometimes I wanted to be the one who died.

I think Edward knew that. The bathroom door was open. He didn't like it if I closed it. I leaned against it and tried to decide if I had to puke again.

He was afraid I'd find a way to die.

Sometimes I wished they understood that there was an end for them. If they could be good, if they could just be a little patient, it would stop. It never stopped for me.

"He likes good girls," I told her. "If you're good enough, you can leave."

She laughed. It wasn't a good sound. I saw her wrist as she moved. There was a flower on it. Already. The pretty girls he brought home all got flowers. Edward drew them himself.

"Could you leave?" she asked. "If you wanted to leave, to go away from here, could you?"

I didn't know what to say to that either.

I wasn't chained in the tub the way they were. I slept in his bed. I ate at his table. There was an alarm, and no phone, and I only went out with him. Trying to go alone meant time in the shed.

Edward came into the bathroom.

"Could I leave?" I asked.

He went still. His attention fell to Courtney, then it returned back to me. "Do you want to leave me? Like the other girls? Do you want me to take you home?"

Home meant dead. I knew it. He knew it. I wasn't allowed to call it dead, but that's what he meant when he said they were "going home"—to their maker, to the earth.

"I want to be where you are," I said, and it was still mostly true. I didn't want to die just then. He never asked me if I wanted to go home when I was so much pain that I wanted to die.

"No."

"Should I keep her, make her my wife, and take you home, Tess?" He didn't touch me. "Do you want her to stay or you to stay?"

I thought about the others. I thought about their eyes as he carried them away. "I don't want to go home."

"Get out, Tessie." He slapped me. "Close the door."

I did.

I don't know how many days passed. Eventually, he took me in to see her again. She wasn't screaming anymore. I wasn't sure when she'd stopped. They all did eventually though. They learned—

just like I had—that it's for the best to keep him happy. If you keep Edward happy, it's better.

"Do you see how good she is, Tess?" Edward pointed at her.

"Yes, Edward."

I sat on the toilet lid. The girl was silent now. I thought about telling her that she could rest. He was calm now. Soon, she'd get to leave. She could go home now that Edward was calm.

"You need to be good." He motioned at the girl in the tub. "She's good now." He looked at her. "Aren't you?"

Mutely, she stared at him.

"If you were good enough, I wouldn't have needed her," Edward reminded me.

"I want to be good."

"But you weren't, and she had to bleed because of it. You did this, Tessie. You made me need to hurt her." He walked away, leaving us in there.

The girl looked at me. "Help me. Please?"

"You'll get to go home soon," I promised her.

She laughed. It was a strange choking sound. "Help me."

"I can give you a blanket. Or a sandwich. If Edward says . . ."

"Help me," she repeated, louder this time.

And Edward was back.

She watched him, cringing back into the tub.

"We need to let her sleep now, Tess. She's tired." He held out his hand to me. There was blood on it, but there was often blood on Edward when he was in these moods.

I took his hand. "Yes, Edward."

He led me to our bed. "You need to be a good wife, Tessie."

"Yes, Edward."

"Do you want me to have to bring home other girls?" he sat on the bed next to me. When he was like this, when he was gentle, I could almost forget about the other things. I wanted to forget.

I shook my head. "She doesn't want to be here." I swallowed. "I want to be good enough."

"You can sleep." Edward smiled. "I'll take her home tonight."

JULIANA

Getting off the plane in New Orleans feels like a letdown. I'm not sure why I expected anything else, but it feels like any other trip I've taken. An anonymous airport. Another Southern city. In some way, I want this one to *feel* significant. I've spent years with these girls on my table because of him. Sometimes I think I know them better than I know people in my daily life. Knowing that I might find one of them *alive* rather than dead seems impossible.

And yet, the trip is strangely calm.

I want today to feel like the start of the end, the solution to finding the Creeper, the stop of the deaths. It doesn't. It feels like any other day. Worse perhaps. I feel uncertain. Andrew has left me unsettled, and right now, I don't feel like I know Teresa Morris at all. The woman in those photographs shares little with the one that her mother spent hours talking about in interviews.

It doesn't take a second glance to know she's experienced things that haunt her. Confirming that isn't surprising. I've seen the scars on the bodies of the Creeper's victims. I've had nightmares simply from seeing the M.E. reports. If she was with him—and the tattoo she shares with them says she was—then how is she here? Is *he* here? Something about her is different.

I don't know how to find her or what to say when I do.

I grab my bag and head out to the taxi stand outside the airport. The air has a familiar heaviness, a humid weightiness akin to the heart of a Carolina summer. It holds scents captive in the air in a way that makes everything linger: an older woman with too much perfume, a man who has been traveling too long, his clothes tainted with sweat and gin, the exhaust of a car in need of a tune-up. The scents twist and slither together as they tend to do in thick Southern air. I don't know if it's the sensory overload or my rattled nerves that has my stomach in distress. Either way, I feel queasy as I slip into a taxi.

The ride toward the far eastern border of the French Quarter isn't long enough for me to figure out answers I couldn't come up with on my flight here or the hours before that when I paced the RDU airport waiting for the flight. There is no polite way to walk up to a woman and ask if she's been tortured by a killer. There is no kind way to ask if she knows her mother is dead. There are no right words to say to someone who has been victimized.

Maybe I can get Teresa to come with me to talk to the police. That's what we need. The police can stop him.

They have to.

I send a quick text to Uncle Micky: "In New Orleans." And then I send a slightly longer one to Henry: "In New Orleans. Safe. Following a lead."

If I let myself think on it, I will have to ask why I can tell Henry but not Andrew—or why I didn't tell Henry *before* I boarded a plane. I file those thoughts away for another time, one when I'm not in a strange city seeking a woman I'd presumed dead.

Teresa is here. That means she's not his captive. It also means there is another Ana, another Courtney, another Maria out there somewhere. The killer has a woman either as a captive or picked to be his victim. Men like him don't stop until they're dead or caught.

I stare out the window of the taxi as the driver takes me into the French Quarter. I need something in my mind's eye that isn't filled with the faces of his victims, of shallow graves, or letters from a killer.

"How do I find Jackson Square?" I ask the driver.

He grins. I see it in the rear-view mirror. "First time here?"

I nod.

"You can't miss it, darlin." He's gentle, but he has the sort of laughter riding in his tone that tells me that my question was ridiculous. "Right smack in the middle of everything in the French Quarter."

He looks at me again, and I apparently look like a country mouse in the city because he asks, "Are you meeting friends here?"

"I'm here looking for someone," I tell him, feeling foolish at the thought that I ought to explain myself to a random taxi driver, but he has the look of someone's grandfather. I have a flash of the Southern gender rules that I usually find tedious as I add, "I'm not here to drink or party."

He nods.

"There's this woman. She disappeared, and she was here. There's a picture of her here in your city." I find the picture on my phone and lean forward, showing him. "She's lost, and . . . I need to find her."

It sounds impossible saying it aloud. I'm trying to find one woman in the entire city. She might not even live here. She might have been passing through. In some ways I'm no closer to finding Teresa than I was before.

"A lot of people get lost here," he tells me. "Not so many get found."

Without meeting her, I already know that Teresa is the sort of lost that might not be able to stay found, but I need her to surface enough that I can figure out how to stop the Creeper.

The little apartment I'm renting on Esplanade—one of the ubiq-uitous short-term rentals in the city—isn't what I'd call nice or even comfortable. The walls have the sort of stains that say the owners aren't even trying to hide the damage. It's clean in the way of old forgotten houses, dirt layered to the point of creating raised marks on the wooden floor, and water stains on the ceil-ing. Last minute options aren't great. It was either a rental with a kitchen or a room in a soulless hotel. I like having a kitchen.

I drop my bag in the main room, grab my sunglasses, and set out. Unfortunately, med school and funeral director's classes didn't include classes on finding missing people. I suspect it would be easier with help. A part of me wants to ask Henry to come here, but I can't imagine that going well. I'll go to the police department and to the coroner—or let the Durham Police Department handle that.

Right now, I want to see if I can find Teresa. I have four days to walk throughout this city and look for her.

I start by walking into the French Quarter with a vague grid in mind. Street musicians, drunken revelers, and Midwestern couples pace by me. I probably look more than a little wide-eyed. I don't know how many people live in the city or if Teresa lived here when that picture was taken. But whatever Sharon couldn't tell me makes me think that she knew that Teresa was living here and not just temporarily visiting.

Why would a literary agency have pictures of one of the Carolina Creeper's victims? Was someone doing a book on him? I'd like to say that no one would exploit a woman like that, that the people at Sharon's agency would care enough about the women who'd died and one who was lost because of him . . . but nothing Sharon had told me about her co-workers made me think that.

Several hours later, I'm forced to admit that simply walking around looking at strangers wasn't likely to get me anywhere. I stop in a coffee shop on Royal Street and show the barista Teresa's pictures while I wait for my drink.

"I'm looking for this woman."

The man looks at me. "Don't work here."

I try a smile. "Okay . . . but do you know her?"

"No, ma'am. I don't know her, don't know nothing." He hands me my coffee and walks away.

I try a few other shops and stores. Asking around isn't as random as simply staring in the faces of strangers, but the closest I come to any sort of answers is a very tattooed and pierced girl who asks, "Why you want her? Is she in trouble again?"

"Again?" I echo.

She shrugs. "People don't come 'round askin 'bout her 'less she done something."

"So you *do* know her?"

She shrugs again.

"I don't mean her any trouble," I try. "She's been gone, and—"

"Sometimes los' things better off stayin los'." The girl shakes her head, sending a twist of braids and beads rattling. "Let her stay los'. Better for her. Better for you. Better for ever'one."

"I can't. I'm sorry, but I can't. Can you tell me—"

"Don't know her," she interrupts. She folds her arms over her chest. "Musta thought she was someone else at firs', but lots a women look like her come through here. Don't know dem. Don't know her. Don't know *you*."

She starts to walk away.

"Someone hurt her. A man. He killed other women. Tortured them, and I need to find him." I sound desperate. I know it, but I feel even more desperate than I sound. "I need to *stop* him."

Her stern expression doesn't change. "Can't help you."

I follow her.

"I don't want to hurt her. Honestly. I just want to stop him. Maybe I can get her to help or . . ." I'm not going to tell anyone that Teresa's a rich woman, that finding her would mean she got her inheritance. "If you know where she is, can you tell her I'm looking for her? I can leave you my"—I pull out a pen and grab a business card from the store to write on—"numbers and email and . . . *please?*"

For a moment, I think I got through to her. She accepts the card I'm extending to her.

"Thank you," I start.

She says nothing as she drops it in the trash.

MICHAEL

The screams wake me. They're not human. That's my first thought. The next is that they're coming from within the apartment.

"I'm sorry. I'm so sorry. Please." Tess is standing in the middle of the room. Her head is bowed, and her head is turned toward the bathroom. "I know better."

"Tess?"

"I'm sorry. Don't make me leave."

"Is someone here?" I don't see anyone else here; I'm fairly sure that it was Tess who screamed. "What's going on?"

She ignores me, stares toward the bathroom. "I can do it. I *can*. I'm good, Reid."

"What?"

I walk to stand in front of Tess. The touch of my hand on her shoulder is enough to make her start screaming. I've never heard a scream that comes close to this, nothing in a horror film even. It's not a sound that any person should ever make—and it was my touch that did it. I flinch backwards.

She's cringing away from me, crouched on the floor, shrieking. Nothing in my life has prepared me for this. I'm not sure a person *can* prepare for this. When she stops shrieking, I drop to my knees and crawl toward her. I don't know what else to do. I can't touch her if that's how she reacts, and she's not answering me. I'm not sure who she *is* answering, who Reid is.

Right now, to be honest, I'm not sure of much.

"I can do it," she repeats between gasps. "I will."

"Tess!"

"Please! Just don't make me go home."

"Tess, can you hear me?"

She stares, and even though her eyes are open and she's speaking, I'm not sure she's actually awake. I've heard of night terrors, but I thought they were something only children had. Maybe it's a psychological break of some sort? Either way, I try to talk to her as if she were in either a nightmare or a hallucination.

"You're in New York, Tess. Reid's not here. Reid's not here, Tess." I sit on the floor in front of her, filling her entire field of vision.

For a moment, she doesn't react. Then she frowns. "Michael?"

I nod, relieved. I can't call the police, an ambulance, but what do you do when someone loses their grip on reality? I can't write this off as a nightmare. I push away my worries and reassure her: "I'm here."

She stares, shakes her head, and insists, "You need to go. Reid doesn't like it when I talk to people. I can talk to the pretty girls, but . . . he won't want me to talk to you."

My relief disappears as quickly as it had come. Anger flows in, despite my attempts to be kind, and my voice is harsh as I tell her again, "Reid's not here, Tess."

"Where is he?" She looks away, and that's it. She's gone. Her moment of lucidity passes. She's whimpering again.

I'm not prepared for this, not prepared for the parts of Tess everyone warned me about. I don't know who Reid is, but I know this is the secret she's been hiding. Reid is the reason she didn't want to leave New Orleans. He's behind her scars.

A domestic violence case isn't nearly interesting enough for my book. The thought comes unbidden in the moment. I thought she was my sparrow, my start of a story that would prove that I'm more than a one-book-success. Domestic violence, though? That story has been written too often. Despite how heinous it is, domestic violence doesn't even shock readers anymore. I'm not sure it even shocks people when it's real.

"Come back to bed, Tess. Reid's not here. It's just us. In New York. We came here for a holiday." I keep talking as I take her face in my hands and make her look at me. "Reid isn't here."

Again, she stares at me in confusion before replying, and I almost wonder if the whole thing is an act—until I think of those screams. I cannot even begin to fathom what would make a person makes such a horrible noise. I think back to the scars that twist through the tattoos that cover her body. The scars were there before the ink.

"Don't touch me," Tess whispers. "I still have their blood all over me. People will ask questions if you go out with blood on you."

I stare at her.

"Just leave before he gets back, Michael." She still sounds gentle, as if she's the one trying to calm me down. "I'll be okay. He loves me. He only hurts me until I pass out."

I don't know how to reply to her. I don't imagine it will matter. She isn't here, not in the same time and place where I am. Tess' mind is in a memory, one I've entered when she looks my way.

"Where are the others?" I ask. "Do you know them? Are they in danger? Can you help them?"

"No." She looks away again, and in the next moment, she's scurrying backward like a crab. She shrieks again. "I'm sorry. I'll be good. I shouldn't have . . . I won't. I'll be good. Don't make me go."

She grabs a vase, looks down, and slams it on the floor like she's hitting something or someone. She crashes the remaining piece in her hand downward again, shards of pottery slicing her hand.

"I'm sorry," she whispers, staring at the floor.

I don't know if I want to ask what she's beating. I'm starting to fear that in her memory a person was there. I can't look away. Am I watching her kill someone? Is that the thing that she's hiding? Did she kill Reid?

"I don't want to. I don't. I'm sorry." She stands, glances at her hand where the blood is dripping.

A shard of the vase is still clutched in her hand.

Tess looks at me, and I don't think it's me she's seeing. Earlier I intruded into her memories, but right now, she seems like she's only seeing shadows from her past. I just watched her re-enact what I think is a murder, and at the least was a brutal assault—and now she's advancing on me.

I shove her away with enough force that she hits the wall and slides down to the floor.

The shard in her hand drops, and she looks up at me. "Michael?"

TESS

Wen I wake in the New York rental, I find myself in the corner of the room, gasping for air, shaking all over. I hurt. I don't know what happened, what I did, but I can tell I fell.

Five nights. I'd made it five nights. I try to think of the details of the now, try to pull up lists in my memory, try to find a trick to help anchor me.

It isn't working.

Nothing is working.

Michael crouches down in front of me, not touching me but so near to me that he's all I can see. "Tess, are you here? With me?"

I nod. Whatever he saw was bad. I can tell that much. The look on his face is somewhere between horror and fascination. If there were only one memory of mine that would cause that, I'd know more. I lived with Reid for several years though. There are a lot of bad things stored away in my mind. Sometimes, even now, these episodes leave me with new images that I can't fathom forgetting. I will get a tattoo. It's how I process them.

"Where are we?" Michael asks, and I realize that my silence has gone on too long. He's nervous. I don't see any cuts or blood on him though. It couldn't have been too bad if he's intact.

When I have to swallow to speak, I realize my throat is dry. That means I was screaming. I look around: The police aren't here. That's a relief. At home, my neighbors are used to my middle of the night episodes. They don't call the cops. I wasn't sure about people on the road, but I've seen them look away from worse things. Reid held a knife to my throat in a diner. No one called the police then either. Neither New York nor New Orleans is to blame. People are simply too self-serving in a lot of places, small or large.

"New York," I tell Michael. "We're in New York in an apartment you rented for the week."

He stares at me, looking for something in my eyes that I'm hoping he can't find. It's not just my aversion to intimacy that makes me prefer a revolving door on my bedroom. I don't know the whole of the things that happened when I was with Reid, but I remember enough to know that some secrets are best left buried.

Being closer to being *Teresa* made memories come to the top. I know that. The part of me that used to be Teresa feels bad about the things Reid did. The part of me that was raised away from sharp things and dark memories doesn't like what we've done to survive. Sometimes, I think she'd rather we had died in those years when we were with Reid.

The rest of me would do anything to survive. That's the secret of all the secrets. That's what people wouldn't understand. Until that choice is in your hands, there's no way to know how far you'd be willing to sink in order to live. I know that answer. Reid taught me.

I have red on my hands--and on my arms, my belly, my eyes. Death is messy.

It's not only hands that get stained. Death is messy.

"I've never seen anyone have a night terror," Michael says.

I shrug. "It happens."

"Who's Reid?"

I push to my feet, wincing a little as I realize that I've cut myself again. Sometimes the night terrors include attempts to escape my house. In New Orleans, I have a lock on the top of the door where I can't reach it in my nocturnal ramblings. That usually keeps me from waking in the street or on a car hood or sharing a stoop somewhere out in the city like I used to do, but now, in the midst of the terrors I claw at the door. It's easier when I keep my fingernails short. I learned that lesson fairly quickly. Ripping your nails off hurts.

This time, my only concerning injuries are the cuts on my hands. I look down to see the shattered remains of a vase. The memory of flight is common when things come back. Reid hurt me. I learned to let him, but early on, the instinct to resist was hard to overcome. At the end, it was worse. When memories surface too intensely, trying to escape is a constant.

I look at my hand. I obviously grabbed a piece of the broken vase. It gouged my hand deep enough that stitches wouldn't be amiss. I hate stitches though. Going to the hospital leads to questions. It means police. Reid taught me to stitch myself, so I can do that passably well.

I don't think Michael would be okay stitching me back together or seeing me do it.

As I try to step around Michael, he moves back, but he doesn't walk away. "Tess, *who's Reid?*"

"Someone I knew," I offer by way of explanation. It's not anywhere near the whole truth, but no one needs to hear that much truth, especially Michael. He's the first man I thought I could care for. Telling him that Reid is the last man I loved is not an option. Of course, telling him that Reid would kill him for touching me might be wise. If Reid knew that a man held me, if he knew that a man touches the parts of me that were his alone, we would both bleed.

But Reid doesn't know where I am. If he did, I would certainly be his again. I would likely be dead.

"Don't ask so many questions," I tell Michael.

"That . . . that was *not* normal." Michael can't seem to decide if he's horrified or intrigued. "Everyone said . . ."

"That I was a raging mess," I supply. "Dangerous? Only willing to fuck and duck, willing to do unbelievable things, disconnected from *now* here and there? Have I missed anything?"

"Tess . . . I *like* you. You know that, don't you?"

I smile at him. "And I like you. No one has been allowed to sleep next to me in a long time. You just saw why."

"I want to understand."

"It was just a nightmare," I lie. This part I can do. It's easier than the truth. Lies are how the days become manageable. They're like air sometimes, necessary to make me able to keep moving. I ball my hand into a fist to keep the blood contained and add, "Everyone has nightmares sometimes."

He looks at me, shakes his head, and steps back again. He lets the lie stretch and rest there on the floor between us until the moment for calling me out has passed. For that, I'm grateful.

I glance at my hand. "Let me get this cleaned up."

Despite the fist, blood is starting to trickle over the edge of my hand, and I don't want to try to clean it off the hardwood floor. Blood stains too easily on old wood. Carpet is better. Tile can be good. Bleach and a good brush will get it out of most surfaces if you're fast enough, but old wood—or porous tile—can be a real pain.

Bath tubs are best.

I push away the reasons I know those things.

I don't want to think about the pretty women dressed in nothing but red. I don't want to think about the ways Reid hurt them. I don't want to think about the ways he hurt me.

By the time I wash the cut in my hand, making sure there are no tiny pieces of glass in the wound, I realize that I have no proper bandages. I grab a handful of paper towels to absorb the blood for now. Toilet tissue gets messy when it's wet, and the last thing I want is to get anything in the wound where it'll fester. My hand wrapped in paper towels, I walk in to see Michael sitting on the edge of the bed, exactly where I left him.

"I need to go to the Duane Reade and get some gauze."

"That's it?" Michael watches me with an expression I can't interpret and don't know if I want to. "You wake screaming like I've never heard anyone scream, beg some guy called Reid, telling me you have 'their blood' on you, and then you're just going out for gauze?"

I hold up my hand. The paper towels already show bright red. It makes me think of those paper towel commercials on the television where they show which towel picks up the most liquid. Whatever brand these are wouldn't win that contest. "That was a nightmare, and I don't want to get *real* blood everywhere."

Michael shakes his head. He doesn't speak. Reid would've spoken. He wouldn't even have lied.

But Michael and I stay that way, me in the doorway bleeding and him sitting on the edge of the bed staring. He's asking me for more than I can give. He might not be saying it aloud, but he's asking all the same. His silence is because of questions that I can't answer. I can let Michael manipulate me, but not as much as he wants.

He wants to touch my shadows, and that isn't free. Not for either of us.

"I can find my own way back home," I say. "I just need to get this cleaned up first. There's surely a bus or something . . ."

Instead of replying, Michael gets up and gets dressed. Maybe it's easier for him if he's the one to leave. The rental is paid, so I *could* stay here and sleep. I don't want to be in New York; I need to get home where I'm steadier. It's the middle of the night though, and I'm still woozy from the pills and the memories. Once he's gone, I'll tend to my hand and sleep. Tomorrow, I can go home. I might not have money, but I can sell myself for enough for a ticket home or take it if necessary. I don't like hurting people, no matter what Reid said, but I also know that I'm not well enough to be away from home too long. If I need to make someone bleed in order to protect myself, I will. Reid taught me that too.

New Orleans keeps me steady. I need to be back in my home, back where music tethers me. New York doesn't simmer with blues and jazz. New York doesn't have chicory coffee and gris gris and the Mississippi. It isn't my home.

I remain in the doorway of this strange room in this wrong city as Michael pulls on trousers and a shirt. I am motionless as he tugs on socks and shoes. Despite everything, I want to say something to keep him from leaving me, but I can't. He just saw what I'm really like inside. He thought he wanted to know, but my reality is a bit less pretty than the stuff of his fiction.

"Are you coming to the pharmacy with me or waiting here?" He looks over at me. "If you want to stay here, it's okay. I'll get what you need and be right back."

I stare at him.

"If you're coming, though, you need to get dressed," he continues.

"Okay." I walk over to the dresser, careful to avoid the glass still on the floor. I'm not sure what people do in these moments. I've never had one. My nocturnal screams are not something that I've allowed others to witness. No one shares my bed for sleep.

Not since Reid.

Not until Michael.

Trying to figure out how to get dressed without getting blood on my clothes isn't new, but it's harder with the things I packed for this trip. Michael likes me in colors, and the best option I have is a pair of dark blue jeans and a red blouse. There's a black cardigan I can pull over it. I concentrate on the clothes, on the minutia, as I try to figure out what I'm to do.

I no more than pull the jeans out and Michael is there, taking them from me and kneeling at my feet. In that moment, he is so much like Reid that I fear that I'd do anything he asked of me.

"Step in," he says.

Silently, I let him help me, feeling safer now that he's treating me like this. Reid did this, helped me dress after I was hurt. Sometimes he hurt me a little extra while he was helping me, but that was just to make sure I was going to be good again. "Good girls don't cry," Reid always said. "Bad girls *have* to cry." If I was good enough, he didn't make me cry when he dressed me.

Michael isn't hurting me. He buttons my jeans and then picks up my bra from where it had been tossed earlier that night.

"I've never put one of these on a woman. Usually I only take them off." His voice is light, teasing, not pushing me toward the memories.

But even as he

does that, he lets me know I'm not special: plenty of women have touched him. That, too, is about power. It's how he says I'm replaceable.

I'm not. There is no one in the world who can give him what I can. We both know that. I let the illusion stand though. It serves both of us well to pretend I don't matter to him.

"Once upon I time, I was with Reid. He . . . hurt me. There was a tub. And red. And I wasn't sure I'd survive."

Now, Michael looks at me like I'm special now.

He puts my arms through the straps and turns me around. It's oddly non-sexual, as if he's afraid to touch my breasts. He hooks the back, not quite as tight as it should be, but I'm not going to complain. Complaining is bad. That's a rule.

Softly, I say, "Can you . . ."

"What?" he asks.

I turn so I can see him, reach into my bra and pull my breast upward so it's settled in correctly. I don't need to, not really. What I need is for him to see me sexually again. "Can you do like that, but on the other side?"

He complies, trying to be clinical, but I catch his wrist and force his hand to stay where it is. At the same time, I press closer to him so my breast is filling his hand.

"Tess . . ."

I pull his wrist tighter to me, letting him feel how hard my nipple is in his palm. "I had a nightmare, Michael. I'm not any different than I was when you were pounding me into the mattress earlier tonight."

"Point taken."

I release his wrist, and he keeps his hand where it is. He watches my face as he slides his palm to the side so he can pinch my nipple. *This*, this is what I need. I don't want to be the woman in the memory he glimpsed. I don't want to be the person who bled because Reid was angry and the other woman was already dead. I don't want to be the one responsible for her death.

And I really don't want to be the one who had to beg to stay alive.

I want to be a woman so caught in *this* moment, *this* place, that I forget the things that were my past. I want to forget—not forever, but just for a while—that Reid existed. I'm not Teresa. I'm not Tessie. I'm *Tess*. Stronger than Teresa, built from her broken pieces. Stronger than Tessie, whose pieces were stitched together by Reid's will and word.

I walk forward, pushing Michael back toward the bed.

"You don't need—"

"You want me to feel better, right? This will help."

He backs up until he bumps into the mattress. "I don't see how this—"

"Shut up, Michael." I drop to my knees and fumble with his trousers. It's been a while since I've had to do this with my left hand. It isn't as graceful as I like to be when I'm acting the seductress, but Michael is a man. Men are compliant when women go to their knees.

He lets me have control.

I fumble through button and zipper and tug his trousers and boxers out of the way, careful not to let my bloodied hand touch them. A fleeting thought that I'll have to deal with blood on the floor after all crosses my mind, but then Michael objects again, "Tess, you really don't need to do . . ."

I remember the things Reid taught me then:

Good wives don't have to die.

I am a good wife.

I am.

Afterword, I tell Michael about the day I knew that I had to leave Reid—even though I know he'll write it in his book.

Or maybe because he will.

Maybe writing my story in ink on my body isn't enough. Maybe I need Michael write it, maybe that's why I wanted him all along. He's doing it. I know he is. I haven't read it, and I know he lies. It's what men do. It's what writers do. It's what I did to stay alive.

UNTITLED

A Girl with No Past

"Get in." He points at the tub.

When I don't move, he sets the bottle of wine down on the bath-room counter hard enough that I flinch. Red wine. That means it's for guests. Reid likes white. It's cleaner. He likes everything to be clean.

And good.

I try. I really do. Sometimes, the rules shift, and Reid doesn't tell me. Sometimes, he likes to explain my mistakes. He watches for them so he can teach me to be good. Tonight, though, I made a mistake worse than ever before.

"You don't need to use the tub." I look down as I speak; he doesn't like insolence. "I didn't mean to—"

"In the tub, Tessie. Now."

"I was wrong, and—"

"Get off the floor and into the fucking tub." He's not touching me, not moving.

Neither of us are looking at the girl slumped in the corner. She's there on our floor. Dead. I don't know her name. I try to learn their names before they die. It bothers me that I don't know hers before she died. Names are important.

Once I had another name. I had another life. Before Reid.

"Tess!" He pulls me to my feet and drops me in the tub.

I scramble to get out, try to get over the edge and away, even though he's watching. The chains he uses are on the floor. I get one leg out, but then I lose my balance and fall onto the chains. They make a clinking-clattering-angry sound.

"Stop." He grabs my hair with one hand to keep me steady. With the other hand, he knocks my chest and shoves me back into the tub.

I half-fall into the far side of the tub, hitting my arm hard enough that it will bruise. My chest will bruise too. He hits to mark. I start to think about the rest, the list of places that will purple, but there are always marks. My throat will have fingerprints tomorrow too.

Bruises heal.

The things that happen to the girls in the tub don't heal.

Reid turns on the water so it pours down from the shower head. He doesn't bother with the temperature. He doesn't speak. He simply stares at me as the icy water sluices over me.

I look down.

The water running toward the drain is pink.

Blood. He's rinsing the blood off me.

I can't look at him, and I don't want to look at the girl on the floor. She's dead. I'm wet and cold, and she's dead.

"I don't want to stay in the tub." I say, as if what I want matters.

It doesn't, not to Reid.

MICHAEL

O nce Tess was asleep, I slipped out of bed and walk to the living room. I knew there was a story here, but I'd had no idea how much of one until her night terror tonight. The sounds of my pen on the pages seem loud in the tiny apartment, but I want to capture it, every moment, every feeling that she shared.

That chapter seems out of place. *Do I move it?* For now, I write it as she shared it. Mostly.

There's no way this book won't prove the critics wrong. Calling me a has-been? First book a fluke? Once they read about Tess, they'll be *begging* me for interviews.

I write until my eyes are heavy. I will need to go back and make changes. Her Reid is my Edward. He is the modern Rochester, his wife in an attic as he entraps others. He is Angel Clare before his death, a man who created his own demise. He is Victor Frankenstein, destroyed by his monster.

And I am going to be the name on the cover, the one who wrote the tale. I'm creating the story from the pieces I know and the pieces I want to add. Tessa and Edward will be my masterpiece. Her domestic violence tale will be greater, larger, *more* in my hands. What I don't understand is why there were other girls. I wonder if it was one of those many wives things. *That* would make for an interesting twist.

I write for a while longer, playing with revisions on earlier chapters, going back and changing threads.

Do I call him Reid? Or stick with Edward? I make a note to myself. I think Edward has more weight than his real name. I re-read, and then I climb into bed. I don't want her to wake alone. I might not believe in love and all that shit, but I'm not a monster. Tess is a little crazier than I thought, and she obviously needs me.

And I need her story.

As I slip back under the covers, I think about what she did afterwards. That part I don't write down. She was in the throes of a night terror, and instead of comforting her afterwards, I let her suck me off. I feel guilty. Admittedly, being with her usually ends in some sort of guilt, but this was worse. She was begging for her life a few minutes prior. Whoever this Reid was, he hurt her more than I think I'd want to know if not for the book.

There are hints enough sketched on her skin, white lines where her body has healed. The first time I realized how many scars she had, I was grateful I wasn't expected to speak. She's given me an easy way to never mention them, and I've accepted it so far. Now, however, I want to know, to hear the stories that go with each mark. I want to see how they fit into the story I'm writing. But I don't want to hear it when I'm touching her. I like the space that darkness offers. I don't need lights to remember the scars all over her body. *He* did that, tortured her, and she escaped. There were other girls there, and I don't know if any of them escaped too, but Tess is a heroine.

I saw her hit Reid. The memory she was in must have been the night she escaped him. I want to find out who he is, if he was caught. I'm not a true crime writer, but Tess is a heroine. Maybe I ought to consider an "inspired by true events" book.

Even as I think that, I reject it. I should protect her. That's the moral answer. The reality is that I want the fictionalization of her story, making it worse where I need or better if the events are the sort to turn off high street readers. Does it matter why though? If doing it my way keeps her safe, isn't that enough? Media attention would destroy her. She's already fragile.

She moves closer to me in her sleep, and I let my hand fall on her hip. It's not sexual, merely a comforting touch to let her know she's not alone. I can do that when she's asleep. Awake, everything is somehow sexual, a negotiation or a rejection. The entirety of her interaction with people is about power dynamics, and for Tess that's often sexual. It's the coin she best understands.

No, exposing her story too truly would ruin a lot of things. Tess, as beautifully broken as she is, doesn't match the image of a victim that the media would like. She's too brash, too vulgar. Between her tattoos and drugs, her sexual deviance and history of occasional prostitution, the real Tess is not the character I need. She's too much for the readers I want to reach.

Her story, however, is compelling. I'll edit and cut, and soften her edges. I simply need to create a more sympathetic heroine. The fiction of Tess will be heartbreaking in a way that book clubs will embrace, and luckily, she has no desire for fame. I'll take care of her, pay the ridiculously low rent on her home, and she'll stay in her beloved city without the burden of worrying over ending up homeless.

I'll be her savior, and she'll be there as my escape. As often as I need her, I can escape to the city where she thrives. My muse. Maybe if the book's big enough, I'll even write a sequel. All because of Tess, my broken sparrow.

I pull her a little closer. She's turning out to be the answer to a lot of my problems. No one will forget my name after this book releases—because of Tess. *J. Michael Anderson, writer of compelling fictional novels.* I drift to sleep dreaming of accolades.

JULIANA

I'd spent two more days wandering the French Quarter with no more clues than I'd discovered the first night. If I'd been here for any other reason, I'm fairly sure it would be easy to see why people love this city. Music floats from so many corners. Some of the best is on the street, while semi-tuned cover bands blare from more than a few bars. The smells of food, cigarettes, pot, and spilled drinks give way to unmistakably unappealing smells the later it gets. Shops that range from antiques to negligées invite browsing as they blast their AC on full with doors propped open—if the trinkets don't lure you, perhaps the cool will. It's unapologetic in its efforts to sell every visitor *something*. And on a different trip, I could be enchanted, but today, I'm only frustrated.

STREET HUSTLERS LOOK at the pictures of Teresa and shake their heads. Several times, I know they said, "Tess."

When pressed, though, no one admits it. No one will tell me a thing. I've run out of ideas. She's here, or she's been here. I'm sure of it. It's not just because of the picture either. I see the expressions on people's faces that say they recognize her, but they do nothing to help me. They lie. They shrug.

In their reactions, I understand how she's stayed hidden. For whatever reason, no one here is willing to reveal where she is or even put me in touch with her.

I've given my name and number to several dozen people now. No one has called.

I ask every vagrant, musician, and shop worker willing to look at the pictures on my phone. I'm starting to think she is still a captive, and they are afraid of the Creeper. I can't think of too many other reasons to see the flash of fear that comes over their faces more often than I can explain.

On the morning of the third day, my phone chirps. A text from an unknown number says, "Go to NOPD by St Louis 1."

After only a couple of days in the city, I already know where that is. Exploring on foot makes it impossible not to get your bearings. There are several police stations, as in any city, but there is only one cemetery that draws every tourist: St. Louis Cemetery Number One.

That walled cemetary is the supposed resting place of both the voodoo queen, Marie Laveau, and hold the theorized tomb of the serial killer Delphine LaLaurie. I laugh at the fact that even the dead are only *reputed* to be present here. Neither the living woman I'd believed dead nor these infamous dead women are truly locatable in New Orleans. The city, apparently, is designed for hiding women.

I can't be too angry about it, in truth. Teresa Morris deserves to hide if she escaped the Carolina Creeper. With every report I've read, with every photograph of torn flesh, broken bones, and crudely drawn tattoos, I can't imagine surviving after being his victim. Sometimes in the days after my meetings with Andrew I dreamed about the Creeper's victims, but my dreams are often of finding more bodies, of finding him, of being the dead woman staring up and unspeaking. I don't dream of being Teresa or Ana or any of them when they were alive. I don't ever imagine having to live with the things he's done.

The horror of it is more than I can process.

Some days, I could barely face the glimpses of things I can tell he's done to his victims.

I walk to the police station, the one closest to the cemetery, along Rampart Street. The area here is dirtier. Tourists seem to stay closer to either the heart of the French Quarter, or Canal Street where it borders what is called the Central Business District. Other than that, they go further up-river in the Garden District. It makes me think that Teresa must live further away, where she wouldn't be exposed to the constant flood of tourists who could recognize her.

The area around the cemetery seems to be more locals—or people on guided tours.

"What the hell were you *thinking?*" The voice greets me before I see him. Henry Revill, Durham Police Detective, is standing outside the New Orleans Police Department with his arms folded and a glare on his face that could make the sweetest woman confess to any manner of sins just to make him smile again.

I, luckily, am not sweet. I've also been on the receiving end of that glare more times than I can count. "I was thinking that I'm a grown ass woman who can take a trip without permission. Uncle Micky can cover—"

"Don't pretend you don't know why you ought to tell a person when you're leaving town, Jules. There is an investigation. You are . . ." He sighs and looks at me, not like I'm a suspect, but like he just needs to see that I'm okay. That, more than the glare or the words, makes guilt flare to life in me.

"I'm in another city," I say carefully. "He wouldn't know where I—"

"Why? Because it's impossible to find you? Because you're sure he's not watching you?" Henry reaches out like he's ready to snatch me to him, but he doesn't. His hand is outstretched, but not touching me. "Do you have *any* idea how worried I was? I talked to Andrew—"

"Did you tell him where I am?"

"He seems to think you said you'd be in New York. For a wedding . . . but I can tell you right now that he believes it about as much as he believes you're going to take up knitting and cookie baking."

"I can bake."

The look he gives my attempt at levity is not unexpected. He stares at me, visibly takes a second to calm the temper that's come near the surface, and offers me his arm like a proper Southern gentleman. He doesn't say anything further as we begin to walk.

Somewhere between the shock of seeing Henry and the fact that he's rarely been this close to me the last year or so, I am at a loss for words. We are crossing Bourbon Street before I look up at him and say, "I'm sorry I frightened you. I hadn't thought . . . I just had a lead and all I could think about was finding her."

"You do realize that you are not a detective, right?" His slightly kinder tone is the closest he ever gets to saying we're all right again.

It's not much, but I'll take it and be glad. "I know."

We walk quietly, and I realize that instead of waiting until I'm back in Durham, I ought to tell him now. In truth, I should've told him when I found out that Tess is alive. The thought of finding her, of finding a way to save myself and every other woman that the Creeper wanted to hurt, skewed my logic.

"Teresa Morris is alive. I have a photo of her in New Orleans."

Henry stops mid-step, steers me into the doorway of a store, and orders, "Repeat that."

I do.

"And you decided to . . . what?" His tone isn't so light anymore.

We both know I fucked up. I'm not some kid who doesn't know any better. I was wrong. We both know it. Explaining why I did it is another thing entirely. I trust Henry more than almost anyone, but that doesn't make it easier to share my secrets. As I weigh what to tell him, I watch a man walk by in a top hat. He's looking at me, and a few weeks ago, seeing his attention linger on me wouldn't have done more than prickle my skin. That's changed.

"I'm acutely aware that there are awful people in the world, Henry. My job doesn't do much to prove otherwise. I know there are good people, too. Like *you*. You're a good man, but I know you are one of the exceptions."

Henry presses his lips together as if he's keeping words trapped in his mouth.

"You know I have trust issues," I continue. "Hell, I suspect everyone who meets me knows that. Until the letter . . . until he sent that . . . I felt invincible. Now? He took that away. Some sick bastard took away my sense of safety." I hate it, but my voice cracks a little. The calm I am trying to pretend to feel slips a bit. "I don't want to be a victim, Henry."

For a minute, I think he's going to ignore what I'm saying, but he lets out a breath and hugs me.

I'm stiff in his arms. "What are you *doing*?"

He laughs briefly. "That's called a hug, Jules. Maybe you remember it? People hug when someone they care about is alive, and they've been worried. There are others reasons, of course . . . I could remind you of what used to follow it if you want."

When he looks down at me, I squirm to get away. "No kissing!"

He smiles and releases me, before saying gently, "You're not the only one who doesn't want you to be a victim or wants to stop that bastard or who can't stand feeling helpless. It would gut me to lose you, Jules." He stares at me. "Taking off though? That's an asshole move."

"You're not wrong." I squirm under his gaze. "I'm sorry I worried you."

Henry looks like he'd rather not say the next words. "And as much as I dislike Andrew . . . you ought to call him. He seems as worried as I was."

A part of me wishes I could pretend not to care that Andrew was worried or that Henry is a good enough man that he wants me to tell Andrew I'm safe, but the rest of me acknowledges that while I don't owe *anyone* an explanation, it would be the right thing to do. I made sure Uncle Micky wasn't worried. He knew I was safe, going away to clear my head, and I checked my phone faithfully in case he'd called. I hadn't given the same consideration to Andrew.

We weren't exactly the sort of people who talked about everything, but I lied. I had reasons, but . . . I didn't ask. Maybe he has a good explanation. Maybe I'm over-reacting, jumping at shadows.

"Why don't you like him?"

"Aside from the obvious? That he's with you? That without him maybe . . ." Henry's expression is about as friendly as a rabid possum.

I don't reply.

"Something's not right with him. He is hiding something, and I don't like it. The fact that he sets off my alarms *and* sleeps with the woman I . . ." Henry stares at me again, as if he can will me to understand. In truth, he seems more like a cop again in that moment. "Just so you know, Jules, I didn't like him *before* he took up with you."

"Did he do something?"

"He's just not right." Henry shakes his head. "We checked him out. A lot of things aren't there. No real proof that he existed before five years ago, but he has an airtight alibi for several of the murders." He pauses. His lips press together into a disapproving look. "You, Jules. You're the alibi. I'm not sure what he's hiding, but he's not the Creeper."

I text Andrew as Henry watches: "Just checking in. All fine here."

"Do *you* trust him?"

"Maybe," I hedge. I want to say yes. I want to deny the things that have been making me uncomfortable lately. He lied to me. He called Teresa "Tess," and that black eye wasn't something he'd explain. I can't answer Henry. Andrew and I have a thing that works—or, rather, we had one until recently . . . or maybe *I* had a thing that worked for me and he was waiting for it to change. I don't know what to think anymore. I don't know what to think about a lot of things.

All I know is that with Henry at my side, I feel fine to answer when Andrew's name flashes on my screen again a half hour later.

By then, I'm back in the increasingly familiar small section of New Orleans that I've paced for days. Henry is at my side, not talking. He glances my way as I say, "Hi, Andrew."

"Did Revill find you?" Andrew prompts.

"He did." I watch a tour group gathered in a cluster and cross the street to avoid winding through the crowd. It's uncomfortable to thread through crowds. I manage it, but I dislike it all the same.

"Good. He was worried." Andrew pauses as if he's struggling to get the next words out and then says, "I was too."

I glance over at Henry. "I'm sorry. I just needed to get away."

"Where are you?" Andrew lets out a breath in a heaving sigh, and I wonder at his mood. I expected impatience or anger, but he sounds desperate. "You didn't really go to New York for a wedding. I know that. You'd have been home by now. I've met every flight from New York the last two days. You would be on one of them if you were coming back from a weekend there. You're not here. You're not at your house. Micky had no idea why I thought you were in New York, and Revill was looking for you and—"

"Why?"

"Because I love you, and you're in danger." His words are right, and for a moment, all I can think of is that he's been my haven so often that there's no reason for my mistrust right now. He's a good man. Why isn't that enough?

"No, why are you meeting flights?"

Andrew laughs, but in that way that tells me he's frustrated that I don't understand him. "I care about you, Jules. I want to be in your life, to be the one you turn to. You got a letter from a killer. I want to keep you safe from him, protect you the way those other women weren't protected. I don't want him to ever touch you. We might not be what I want, but we are something."

"I'm in New Orleans," I say because I can't answer the rest. I have never been the sort of person who wants to be half of a "we" or believes that there is anything remotely like a fairy tale or fated love. The closest I ever came was with Henry.

But I like my freedom, and he's old school. Henry wants a wife, a family, a home. When I considered it, I was stopped by the thought of Darren, who demanded all of that from sister and it still wasn't enough. I need an exit, space to be on my own.

I like men who don't think that I owe them anything. I need to be with a man I don't need, who doesn't need me. I thought Andrew was like, but right now, Andrew is not acting like the sort of man I want—even though I know he's telling the truth about caring for me.

After a moment that's just shy of too long, I tell him, "Teresa Morris is here somewhere. I'm not sure where, but she is."

"So why did you hide that? Did you stop trusting me, Jules?"

"I don't know. No," I lie. "I just . . . I wanted to find her. It's stupid, but all I could think about were the women I couldn't help, the things he did, and I reacted."

I look at Henry again while I'm talking, but he's pretending not to listen to the awkward call I'm having. We stand on Royal

Street and watch a crowd gathered to listen to a woman singing. She's worth a pause. For a blink of a moment, I wish I was here with Henry, not for work but just to *be*.

"Are you coming home soon?" Andrew's voice is strained.

"I'll let you know when I do. I'm staying here a couple more days."

"And Revill?"

"He's here," I admit, not looking at Henry this time. It's not an answer to the question Andrew asked, but I can't unpack what he really wants to know: why is Henry here not him? I don't know that I'm ready to answer that question for any of us, so I just add, "He found me, and he's here."

"I see."

The thing I should do is tell Andrew there's nothing to worry about, that he ought not doubt me, that I trust him, that Henry is just a friend. Part of that is true. I do still trust Andrew to a degree, but I have doubts about whatever he's hiding. Henry is a friend, but I have a history with him that makes it hard to ignore the feelings that I cannot always hide from myself.

Nothing will come of it right now. I don't cheat. Henry wouldn't ask it of me, either, despite his feelings for me—and dislike for Andrew.

When Andrew doesn't push for answers about Henry or volunteer answers about his secrets, I tell him goodbye and disconnect. I don't want to be cold-hearted, but I can't deal with him right now. What we have has worked for well over a year. We never had the "let's be monogamous" talk or "some day we'll get married" conversations. We simply were what we were, and it worked.

It doesn't feel like it works now.

Henry clears his throat. "Are you okay?"

"Not so much."

"You're a good woman," Henry says awkwardly. "It's only logical that he was worried when you hared off."

It's such a Southern thing to say, a compliment twisted in with an unspoken criticism. I can't fault his logic, but that doesn't mean I feel like engaging it either. I place my hand on his forearm and say, "Walk with me?"

He nods, and we walk from the French Quarter across Canal and into the Central Business District. Henry is more familiar when he's steady and silent instead of hugging me and offering advice. Neither of us comment on the fact that my hand is once again tucked into the fold of his arm. A gentlemanly arm is not the same as infidelity. He might be more affectionate here than he'd be when we are home in North Carolina, but that doesn't change us. It doesn't change all of the reasons I shouldn't cross the line into intimacy with Henry again. Some men aren't ever convenient. They aren't the kind of people who can be in your life casually. Henry is *not* convenient.

And I'm not the sort of woman who wants a partner—even one who flew to another state, using vacation time most likely, and stands at my side like a guardian.

UNTITLED

A Girl with No Past

"Happy Thanksgiving, Tess." Edward's brothers greeted as they came into the house.

"You, too."

Edward looked at his brothers. "Sit. Eat. My Tess made us a traditional dinner."

I had. There was turkey, ham, even green bean casserole.

We said grace. I was still standing, but sometimes Edward when he needed things.

A noise from the back of the house made everyone pause, but no one said a word. Everyone there knew about the girl in the tub. Edward had a difficult week at work. One of his investments had a loss, and he was feeling anxious. I'd tried. I really had. I'd been his for twenty-two months now, and it wasn't getting better.

Last month, I'd spent three days in a row in the shed.

Edward looked at his brothers as I stood there, hoping things weren't going to go poorly, hoping they'd intervene. I couldn't. Not again. I wasn't sure I'd love through the last beating.

"You think the courts wouldn't arrest you too?" he began when he caught Buddy looking at me. "You think they'd ignore it if they found out you knew about the girls and—"

"No one's getting arrested," Buddy said firmly. "So, they found a few bodies. That doesn't mean anything."

"They should never find them unless I want them to."

"It's okay," William said. "It was a mistake. It won't happen again."

I'd never heard them like this, and I had to wonder what had happened. Sure, the pretty things arrived, and then they left. Unlike them, I hadn't been out of the house without Edward or one of his brothers in nearly two years. There was no phone in the house. I had no cell phone. I had no computer. I had no access to anything other than what Edward allowed—and Edward didn't allow much.

No one spoke.

Finally, he looked up at me and said, "You're a good wife, aren't you?"

"I try."

Edward nodded. "Grab drinks."

I went to grab a bottle of wine and opened it. No one spoke as I poured it. Buddy refused to look up from his plate.

"Would you like your own drink?" Edward prompted.

"If it's okay." I was thankful that he let me have a glass, but after I drank a bit, I wasn't sure what to do.

"I'm going out for a smoke," William said.

When no one objected, he pushed his chair back and left. Edward and Buddy weren't speaking yet, and I wasn't sure what to do. Carefully, I reached out for a dinner roll and took a few bites while I waiting.

Buddy shook his head. "I won't ever tell your secrets, Edward. You know that. I never have."

"If I ask you to testify what my brothers did to you, will you?" Edward watched me, and I was glad it wasn't me who had angered him.

Buddy looked away.

"Did William threaten you?"

"Yes, Edward."

"And Buddy? Did he fuck you after you said no and cried?"

"Pretend we're in court, Tessie." Edward's voice had rarely sounded as cold as it did just then. "Could you cry for the judge? Could you tell him how you begged for mercy? Would you tell the judge how my brother hurt you and you had no choice?"

Buddy froze.

"Then do it. I don't want you to have to lie." Edward stood then. "If they come after me because you let them find that girl, you'll be in jail, too." He shoved me toward his brother. "Don't break her too much."

When Edward walked out, Buddy stared at me. "Tess . . . I won't."

For a moment, I wanted to believe that was an option we had. It wasn't. No one disobeyed Edward. I thought of the women. The more they fought, the faster they died.

"I don't want to spend tonight in the shed again," I told Buddy quietly. "I don't want him to hurt me either. You need to do what Edward says."

A few minutes later, Edward returned. "Has he hurt you yet?"

I shook my head.

"Do you want to go to jail, little brother?" Edward stepped closer and put a hand on Buddy's shoulders. He had his after-dinner coffee in the other hand.

Buddy held my gaze. "I can't."

"There's your mistake," Edward said. "I didn't ask what you thought. Tess wants me to be safe. Don't you, baby?"

"Yes, Edward."

He tilted the coffee cup, pouring it down my chest. It wasn't as hot as it could've been. I knew that from experience. I had no need for the hospital.

The coffee burned my chest, my belly, my thighs . . .

Buddy reached out. "Edward—"

"Tell him no," Edward ordered.

I felt his fist. Felt him strip me. And then I was on the floor.

"Please, don't." I felt sick from the burns, and despite best efforts, I tried to get away.

"Fight him, Tess."

So, I did.

Edward stood and watched his brother rape me.

I wouldn't need to lie if we went to court.

TESS

I knew there would be consequences when Michael let me keep my secrets that night. He bandaged my hand with a shirt of his that he cut up with kitchen scissors. I think he was afraid that I wouldn't still be here if he went to the store without me, or maybe he was afraid that I'd run while we were in the store, or maybe he just felt too raw after the night we'd had. I couldn't say any of that was untrue. We didn't go though. We fucked, and I slept.

When I wake, I have the start of a plan.

"You didn't need to debase yourself for me," he whispers as he pulls me close. He likes to sleep with his arm around me, pinning me to him so he wakes every time I slip out of the bed.

Reid held me the same way. It makes me feel safe, being unable to flee. I think sometimes that if any of the men I fucked since Reid had even tried to hold me like this, I might've considered a relationship. They didn't, though. They were content with my fuck-and-roll-away approach to dating. It was easier for everyone.

Michael doesn't want to let me go. It makes me feel needed, wanted, essential. I love that.

After I first left Reid, I only dated married men. I knew they wouldn't try to stay, and even though I knew I was still breaking Reid's rules every time a man touched me without his permission, it felt better if I wasn't the only one breaking my vows. I sometimes found myself excited at the idea of Reid finding out, of him knowing that someone else touched his property, of him seeing that I was happy without him.

After I left, it took two years for me to remove my wedding ring. I wonder if he still wears his. I suspect he does. Reid has flaws, but he understands commitment. He killed women so he could let me live. He kept them in our home so he didn't have to hurt me because I was too weak. I tried to be strong enough though— and I failed. Other women died because I was weak.

Waking up to find Michael still holding me makes everything seem clear. For a moment before I turn and look at him, before he speaks, I pretend that Reid is with me again. I'll be stronger.

This time, I'll have the power.

Lips are on my neck, and a hand slides over my stomach.

"Tess . . ."

"Shhh. Just don't say anything."

He listens, and I part my legs in invitation. Maybe last night was good for us. Michael's not a particularly giving lover. Most of the men I've fucked aren't. Today, though, I feel cherished. His fingers are sure and quick, not like Reid. *He* liked to make me beg, to leave me so close to desperate that I would do anything if only he would continue.

"HARDER," I say.

He stills, but after a moment, he complies. It's closer to the cruelty that I learned to like.

"I won't break."

After a moment, I give him the incentive he needs. I share my plan, still only half-formed. "I'll answer all your questions. Pleasure for words."

His voice is shocked. "I give you pl—"

"*Hurt* me, and I'll tell you my stories, Michael." I press back tighter to him. "Let's play pretend. You can be the monster, and I'll be your victim."

His breath hitches, and his hips surge against me.

"That's what you want, isn't it? You want to understand how to be a monster." I feel him responding even as he struggles to come up with the words to deny it. It's pointless. I wouldn't be here if he didn't have that seed inside him. I nurture it a little more, teasing it out. "Do you want to hear about how I crawled on my hands and knees, naked, bruised?"

He's the one who can help me. Michael is my cure, someone safe who let me take back control.

And Michael wants to hurt me, debase me. I just didn't realize how much until last night. It's not just my secrets he wants. He wants to roll around in my shadows.

"Would you like that? Me kneeling there with your brother watching—"

"My fraternity brothers . . ."

I smile. In that moment, he's mine. Fair, perfectly pure, and good: I own him. He just doesn't know it yet.

"I kneel in front of you, all of your frat brothers see me there, see your teeth marks on my thighs, see my swollen—"

Michael flips me over and does exactly what I tell him. It's not quite like it was with Reid. I never needed to instruct *him*. He knew how to break me, how to hurt me so I wouldn't disobey. Michael is not Reid, but he want to be darker.

"Is that your *best*, Michael? Maybe we need to call in those frat brothers of yours to show you how to do it right."

In the next moment, I let out a shriek of pain, but he doesn't stop.

Afterwards, I think he's going to be the one to run. He keeps staring at the bruises on my thighs. Teeth marks, finger prints, *his* marks.

"Why did you let me do that?"

I shrug.

"Seriously, Tess. You were a mess last night. I heard you begging for your life. Reid . . . That's who did it, right? He was going to kill you. You saw something . . ."

"My . . . *Reid* was a complicated man." I almost slip and say *husband*, almost tell too many truths, but Michael isn't ready for that secret yet. He's still struggling with the violence he just enjoyed. Telling him I'm married to a true monster would be more than he can handle.

"You wanted me to hurt you." It's a question, a plea for reassurance that he's not a bad person.

"You wanted to do it." I sit with my legs wide open so he can see what he's done and because closing my legs will hurt. It's been a while since anyone's been so rough with me. I feel more focused than I have in years. The entire world is crisp, and I think I may actually manage a day without the Adderall. "I need a cold towel, Michael."

He looks like he's going to be sick.

"And my purse," I add.

Michael silently retrieves both. "Are you calling someone?"

"Why would I do that?"

"Because I . . . because you're hurt, Tess. You're bleeding." He gestures to my thigh where one of his bites is, in fact, a little bloodier than I'd like.

"I still got off." I rummage through my pill bottles. I pop a pain pill in my mouth and swallow. "And you learned what your *character* is really like, didn't you? It's not that hard to become the sort of man that nightmares are made of."

Michael just stares at me.

Today, for a rare change, I don't even feel the need for all of my pills. I want to kiss Michael for that, thank him for making me feel more stable than I have in years. I still take the Xanax, though. Skipping everything at once usually goes poorly when I try it.

"We made a deal, Michael. I'll tell you my stories, and you will hurt me," I say quietly. "I think you won't mind as much as you're trying to tell yourself you will. I see it, the edge of that violence, when we're together. You keep it leashed, but it's in you."

He doesn't try to deny it.

"You want to know my story. That's why you wanted me when you met me," I say, pointing out the truth I hadn't made either of us face so clearly until today. "You heard how extremely fucked up I am, and you know there's a reason, a story, and you *want it*. You wanted it more than you want me."

"Not right now," he admits. "I want you."

I smile at the compliment. "But you want to understand the monsters, don't you? To be able to write about them, to be able to get another movie deal. To surpass your last success. To make the failure of your last book the fluke, not prove that the *first* book was the fluke. I knew. I knew the day after we met." I trail my hand over the bruises that are showing dark against my pale skin already. His gaze tracks my fingertips like a predator. "I knew before we fucked. I understand better now though. You want a muse. I can be that. I can show you all the things you need to know to write something horrifying."

"I don't want—"

"Liar." I understand the world so much better now that I've figured out my cure. I can give Michael his story, and he can give me my stability. I was putting the pieces together wrong. I know better now. "Get your pen, Michael. You wanted to know what a monster looks like, feels like, thinks like. I can show you."

He stares at me. This is it: the moment of my salvation if he gives it to me. It's a contract, but not the sort he was offering when he started to date me. He wanted to manipulate me, twist me until I sobbed a little story on his shoulder. He could be strong and kind, and I would give him my pain to turn into a book to pay his bills.

"Everyone thinks that it was a single thing, a memory, the one you saw last night, but that's not true."

Michael wavers.

"You LIKED THAT TASTE, didn't you, Michael? Liked the dark thing that stretched out inside you. You wanted to hit me, but you didn't."

Even now, he stares at me, eyes dropping to my bloodied skin and darting back to my face.

"Reid taught me to survive. He made me who I am now."

"How?" Michael asks. "What he did in your nightmare?"

"Get your pen."

When he doesn't move, I add,

"He killed a few people. Sometimes it was bad."

"He . . ."

I want to laugh. Even now, even having seen me when my shadows were rolling all over me, Michael seems shocked. I don't understand how he thinks to write darkness if he finds murder shocking. It's not the murders that are the story.

"Get your pen," I say for the third time.

JULIANA

I'm not sure how to make sense of the changes with Henry. Last night, he'd escorted me to the rental where I was staying, and this morning, he'd met me there to walk to breakfast with me. The area around my short-term rental isn't bad, not by Durham standards. The part of Esplanade Avenue were I'm staying is a border of sorts, dividing the French Quarter and the Marigny. It's safe enough. Pretty enough.

"Sleep poorly?"

I sip my coffee and ignore the question for a moment. We're in one of the tourist-friendly restaurants in the French Quarter enjoying chicory flavored coffee. There really is nothing quite like it. I'd already bought a bag of it to take home with me. Good coffee, a good conversation, a charming man: it's almost enough to erase the lingering worries from my nightmares.

"My boyfriend is being illegally investigated by my co-worker, and a serial killer sent me a letter." I shake my head. "Right now,

I understand the allure of staying *here*. I don't want to go back to North Carolina."

"So stay here," Henry suggests. "Micky has things under control at home. I can ask the locals to keep an eye on you."

Something about the way he says it tells me that he's leaving out a detail, but I need to be sure. "That's why you didn't ask to sleep on my floor last night. You already asked them to up patrols there."

Henry grins.

"Isn't that abuse of your authority, Detective Revill?"

"I flew on a last-minute flight to track your ass down, Miss Campbell. You are a person of interest, a potential target or witness, in a serial homicide investigation that crosses state lines." Henry has no lightness in his voice now. "Even if I didn't have a romantic interest in you, I'd ask them to watch out for you—just as I asked them to find Teresa Morris and take her into protective custody. You're lucky *you* aren't in protective custody right now."

I sigh and pointedly ignore the romantic interest remark. Instead, I ask, "Protective custody? Really? That's where we are, Henry?"

For the first time since he arrived, Henry obviously decides to ignore all of the very reasonable objections and requests I've put in his way for years. He reaches out and takes both of my hands in his. "Even if you never spoke to me again, I'd make that call if I thought it would keep you safe."

I bow my head. Knowing he means well—hell, knowing he's likely *right*—doesn't change the way it feels to think about being trapped, being in anyone's custody. I don't want to be trapped, not even for my own safety.

"Are you heading home?"

"Eager to get rid of me?"

"No." I'm not sure which of us is more surprised by the admission. "I like being here with you . . . despite everything. No one watching. No one judging. Away from work. It's easier than I remember. I wouldn't have imagined being here with you being so . . . natural."

Henry stares at me as if I'm a puzzle that suddenly became less confusing. Maybe he realizes that this is about as much intimacy as I can rightly handle, though, because he grins suddenly and teases, "You imagined it, then?"

I flip him off.

"Maybe kissing is easier too," he adds. "Should we try that? Just to check?"

"Don't overstep, Henry." I'm smiling, maybe because I know he's half-joking. Henry won't kiss me while I'm still dating someone else. Lightly, I admit, "Kissing wasn't the problem for us."

"True," he agrees. "I don't think I *had* any problems."

I open my mouth to reply, but Henry holds up a hand.

"I know. Forbidden to discuss by order of Juliana Campbell."

"I'm sorry."

"And I'm patient, Jules. I'm still here. I still . . . I'm not giving up on us."

After a moment that's more charged than I know what to do with, we relax and enjoy our meal. It's something I need more than I'd like right now. A few bites of food, even at an average place here, makes it very clear that this is a city for the sensory in every way. The music of at least a dozen artists rises and falls in the streets. The scents and sounds of the city are no less impressive than the sights. And there is nothing quite like the savory dishes that are staple foods at every restaurant.

With Henry, I am seeing the side of New Orleans that escaped me when I was pacing the streets begging for clues about Tess. He is not the same man I see at home. It's not as if we've never been alone together. I've known him in some way or another most of my life. He's only a couple of years older than me, but as kids, a few years is the same as decades sometimes. We'd met when I'd been in North Carolina to visit Uncle Micky, but even as a kid, Henry was serious and silent. Our first encounter was when he saw me punch a boy. My "mind yourself or I'll deck you too" wasn't the response he'd expected to his chastisement that "girls don't need to do that." Thirteen-year-old me was confused that he thought I needed protection. Thirty-two year me is still a little baffled.

"Why are doing this?" I ask after the drinks and food are ordered.

"Eating?"

"No. Dredging up the past."

"Don't overthink it, Jules," he says lightly. "I liked you when you were a kid, and I like you now. It's not that complicated. You're smart, funny, and not hard to look at . . . even with those purple crime scene gloves."

I flip him off again.

"I learned to cook because you were lousy at it, you know." He glances at me briefly, and I know he's not joking.

"I make coffee. I know how to order take-out. What else do you need?"

"Next time we have breakfast, I'll show you." Henry, the police officer I know and respect, is briefly replaced with the man I cannot help but want. There is something inherently sexy about men who respects your strength but still want to take care of you. However, there is still reality to face, and the reality is that I am not looking to be a wife. A woman who dates Henry Revill has to accept that there is either a time limit or a trap in the end.

"Don't make it weirder than it has to be, Henry," I say in the same tone he used.

"It wouldn't have to be weird."

"Are we really going to talk about this?" I wrap my hand around the glass of water the server dropped off. No liquor for me. Not when I'm alone with Henry. Not when I'm capable of supremely bad choices.

He leans back, legs extended so that they are to the side of the small round table instead of under it. Everything in his body language says he's calm and in control of this moment. He is every bit the interrogating detective suddenly. "Yes" is all he says.

"Why now?"

"Maybe thinking I might have lost you made me a little less patient." He doesn't look away. "The Creeper—"

"No. Not today. I can deal with a lot, but just for a few hours, I don't want to think about him."

"Fair enough."

"You *know* me Revill"—I hold his gaze, half daring him to call me out on trying to make everything less familiar, but he simply smiles as I continue—"and I'm never going to be the sort of woman you need."

"Oh? Did I have a list I forgot about?"

"You want kids." I say it more like an accusation than I mean to. It's not; kids are a deal breaker. "I'll never be a mother."

He nods. He knows why. For all of my independence, I've broken down over my memories of holding my nephew in my arms, of watching him, of wishing I could get custody of him. Henry held my hand over drinks now and again.

"What if I didn't w—"

"Don't," I cut him off. "I like the way we are now. Can we just . . . not do this?"

"Ignoring it won't change it. Sooner or later, you're going to have to deal with the number of times you've kissed me—and the fact that you want to do it again." He stares at me, challenging me to deny it. When I don't say anything, he adds, "I like it, too, you know."

"Ignoring it has worked for me the last two years."

Henry sighs. He's not pushed this hard since we were barely legal. I wonder how much different things would be in my life if he had.

Fortunately, he lets it drop, but when he speaks again, I almost wish we'd stayed on the last argument: "I ran Andrew's fingerprints. You ought to know that."

"You *what?*"

"Not because of wanting to date you and see what comes of this." He motions between us. "Because you vanished. I don't trust him. Never have. I took his prints and DNA. Not legally. Not in any way that will stand in court."

I close my eyes.

"I'm not going to lie to you, Jules." Henry reaches out and touches my wrist. It's just the tip of his fingers, a barely there brush of skin, but it makes me jump. "If he'd have hurt you . . ."

"He didn't."

"You vanished. Gone. No word other than a terse text message. How was I to know that you weren't in danger?"

I shake my head. "Ask Uncle Micky? Call me?"

"I did."

"I don't know, but . . . really? His DNA? His prints?" I pause as the server brings our food.

"He's not in the system, but there's something not right about him. He's hiding something."

I can't argue. Sometimes I think that whatever Andrew is hiding is something I'd rather not know. He's been good to me, and I don't think he's a bad person. He loves me. Maybe we're not forever, but he loves me. That counts for something—at least it did until this past week.

"I wish you wouldn't have done that," I tell Henry.

HENRY SIPS the chicory flavored coffee, savoring it before saying, "Things don't add up with Andrew. You know it, too."

We slip into silence after that, not the comfortable kind I'm used to with Andrew either. It's a silence as heavy as the ones that fill the funeral home where I work. There's a weight to it that I can't quite shake off. Small talk fails. We eat without words because the alternative is admitting that Henry has never once been wrong in my experience when it comes to matters of law.

After our meal, he takes me back to the apartment I've been renting and goes to the N.O.P.D. without me. I'd object, but they'll talk to Henry more openly without me there.

I'm not very good at waiting, so I go out again, walking through the French Quarter into the Central Business District toward the Garden District. The city has myriad ways to get around—

the streetcar, horse drawn carriages, pedicabs, Uber, taxi, or Lyft. None of those let me set my own pace or pop into stores to ask if anyone's seen Teresa. Henry can go through the proper channels; I'll ask the people who are still annoyingly resistant to sharing answers.

MICHAEL

Tess closes her eyes often as she tells me things that are either truth or lies shaded by the drugs she takes constantly. There are moments when she opens her eyes and stares at me, as if the anchor of seeing where and when she is tethers her.

If I were writing a different story, I'd include that detail. I'd include the *now* version of the woman who stretches out naked in this rented bed, sharing things that would be too graphic for the film I'm hoping to have made of this novel. I see it sometimes as I write, the cameras trying to capture the elusive fluctuations of reality and memory that comprise the woman whose voice lilts like a lullaby as she says, "The smell of blood never gets better, or maybe it's the things that follow when a body stops. With no muscles, they let go. Blood, and shit, and piss. Death smells bad."

She stares at me as she pauses, and I nod.

I wanted this, her story. It's the first time I write the details of her life as she watches me. I've been revising *A Girl with No Past* as I learn more—her mother's name is Sterling, for example. In my novel, Tessa's mother has the same name. I'm not changing Edward to Reid, though. There is so much more weight to an *Edward*—Rochester of *Jane Eyre or Ferrars from Sense and Sensibility*, or Edward Scissorhands and Edward Cullen from the eponymous film or the pop sensation *Twilight*. Reid doesn't have the allusions that Edward offers.

My pages, so far, are but a draft, a mix of my imagination and the slivers of reality I gleaned from her. Tessa, the character, is much more . . . appealing than the real Tess in front of me. Her fictional doppelganger is appropriately broken, meek, submissive—whereas the Tess in my bed is something else. The more I know Tess, the more I realize that she's smarter than anyone might notice at first when they meet her.

She's in control when she can be, vicious as needed, and I am both afraid and entrapped by her.

She controls me. I didn't realize how much until this trip.

There is a fierce practicality in how she exercises that tendency. I had hints of it, but after the night terror, after realizing that she felt the need to be hurt, after hearing her screams, I believe that Tess is alive because of a combination of ruthlessness, luck, and intellect. Whatever she fled when she left Edward/Reid may have been more than I can express in a novel. All along I've been excluding things in my pages, softnesses and delusions, but *those* aren't the things that readers won't be able to accept. Like Hardy's Tess, my Tess isn't so easily situated in the role of sympathetic victim. There is a darkness in her that would make the masses hate her—and I want their emotions to be more sympathy or pity.

People prefer monsters to be wholly monstrous. We like our heroines to be battered but morally intact. Tess manages to be both simultaneously. I don't know if she could be one without the other.

I cannot write her as she truly is.

Right now, she's humming. She been doing that more since we left New Orleans, as if the lack of music that rises up in every shadowed alcove of that city could be corrected by her attempts at song. Or perhaps she hears that music in her mind and the humming is a consequence of it. It's hard to say with Tess. What I do know is that I'd doubted her when she said she couldn't leave the city, but having been here with her, having woken to her terror-laden shrieking, I think she was speaking a truth that I couldn't have understood before this trip.

"Did you kill that bum?"

Tess frowns at my question, and after a moment, I realize that it's not over the accusation of murder but over the act of remembering. She'd not sure if she did or not.

"When?"

"In the Marigny. Luke or Lee or . . . I don't know. The drunk." I watch her as I repeat the question, "Did you kill him?

"Lucus!" She smiles, proudly, as she recalls the man she may have murdered.

"I went to look for him. I couldn't find him. No one saw him after that night." I confess my amateur sleuthing.

"I gave him money so he could leave." Her tone is matter-of-fact, as if it excuses what I expect her to say next, what I know she is about to admit. "Sometimes when people know things . . . it's not safe."

"Did you kill him?"

"Maybe?" She sits up, stretches, and stands. "Is he dead? If he's dead, maybe I did. I think I might have. I can't always be sure, but I might have done." She nods, her humming and nodding flow into the off-kilter cadence of her words. "Sometimes when people know things . . . it's not safe. Lucas knew things."

She smiles at me as she admits that she will kill, that she *has* killed. I hear it, the warning in her words.

Careful to sound casual, I ask, "So if people know . . . too much, you kill them?"

She laughs. "Not always. I haven't killed you, Michael." She laughs.

"Lucas knew secrets. He drank too much, and he might have talked when he was drunk. That happens. It's dangerous though." She pauses, tilting her head in thought like a small child might do. "I probably killed him. It's very important that no one tell tales. Reid taught me that. All the pretty things . . . none could talk when they went home. They couldn't leave if they would tell stories. Telling tales is bad. That was a rule. Even the pretty things have to follow the rules."

"The pretty things?"

Tess kisses me and says, "I need to shower. That helps keep infections out of cuts. We'll need some antibiotic cream too. You can put it on me later."

It's weirdly seductive when she says it, as if treating the injuries that I've left on her body is intended to be sexual. She watches me to be sure I understand, and when she's satisfied, she strips and walks out of the room.

Nothing could have prepared me for the way I feel now. I'd cling to my own illusions: I thought of her as the broken sparrow, a fragile thing, but coming to New York makes me realize that there's something more akin to a bird of prey in Tess. She's still been victimized, still broken, but she's swallowed a bit of darkness along the way. People aren't always one way or the other, not really. The interesting ones are several things at once, often contradictory things at that.

Logic kicks in and tells me I ought to be afraid: I'm sleeping with a killer. That should upset me, but it evokes a very different reaction. I can't look at too closely, that part of me, that shadow is one I don't dwell on very often. There is something glorious in power. It's why I want to succeed in my career.

If I'm completely honest, it's why I "date" the sort of women I do.

Sometimes, however, the temptation to squeeze a little tighter, shove a lover down a little harder, push them to do things I can tell they don't want to do . . . it's there. Tess saw it.

Whatever Reid did to her is why she wants me. It's not my money. It's not my body. It's something in me that most women pretend not to notice. A rush of shame fills me at the thoughts that rise up in me. Tess is the sort of broken that means she has very few limits; she's already showing me that.

How far could I go? Would she let me act out the kind of fantasies that I would never have admitted aloud before her?

Unbidden, a darker thought comes to me—or maybe it's just a different shade of dark: Tess has taken lives. She's willing to talk about it. How much more would she be willing to do? I want to be able to understand what it means to take a life, but there's never been anyone who was willing to let me into the world that Tess knows. I've tried. When *The Ruins of a Carriage House* failed, I was the man at the back of the kinds of bars where the dim light hid what I was pretty certain were bloodstains. I didn't necessarily want to *draw* blood, but I want to witness it. I want to see it done. I want to let my senses fill with it. How else am I to write it properly? I want to be a master of words, of realistic darkness. That takes research.

Tess somehow sees that needs. For all of her madness, I feel like she understands me in ways no one else ever has. I wonder if it's why she came out to dinner with me the first night. She said it so casually, told me about Reid's history as if it was mundane. *He killed a few people.* How do you reach that place where death is casual? She's taken lives, too. I realized it before she admitted it.

I spoke to a man she killed.

There was a man I spoke to, and now he's dead.

Tess did that. She ended his life.

When she gets out of the shower, she stares at me with such an odd smile. Then she says, "You want to know about dying."

"I'm a writer," I start, quickly pushing away the things I'd been thinking.

Tess doesn't allow me even that much distance, that scant comfort. She crosses her arms as she stares at me, and I realize that there is an odd sanity that darkness seems to allow her. I wonder if the way she is, that floating disconnectedness, the almost desperate hurtling toward violence in the dark, is something she's always carried or if the years with Reid created it.

"I'm not lying."

"Really, Michael?"

It's a bargain. There are terms to everything with her, and I'm beginning to understand it more and more. I exhale. "I want to know everything."

"Well, let's go then."

"Go?"

"Hunting."

A part of me wants to ask what she means, but the rest of me is afraid of the answer, I can't decide if I'm afraid that it'll be what I expect or if I'm afraid it won't. I play out alibis in my mind.

My agent, Elizabeth, would vouch for me. That's the benefit of being a former cash cow, willing to offer her the golden teat again: her morals are as lax as mine. Sometimes I think that Tess, mad and unpredictable Tess, is the most moral person I know. Her ethics certainly don't adhere to the tenets of any faith, but she lives her truth, and she's obviously bled for it.

We leave the building and walk for several minutes in silence. I'm not sure what to say, and she's not offering. We walk. Tess hums. An hour later, I've almost forgotten what she's said. Hunting? Who hunts in the city? We walk through the streets of New York, and I relax.

It's like she can sense it.

"The first key," she whispers from my side, "is learning to assess them. Not every lamb is created alike."

"Lamb?"

She pauses mid-step, and consequently, midway through an intersection. "That's what you want isn't it? To find the lost lambs?"

I stare at her. There are layers twisted into Tess' words.

"You can't cull the herd if you don't know which are lambs and which are other things." Tess is seemingly oblivious to the cars now honking at us. "There are lambs and there are hunters."

I take her hand and tug her toward the sidewalk. "What are you?"

"It depends on the day. I used to be a lamb, but I bled so very much." Something darker than I want to face slides into her posture and voice. "I won't be a lamb again, Michael. Not ever."

Almost as if the words are forced from my tongue, I ask, "What am I?"

She waves at a man who yells obscenities at us. "A lamb who wants teeth."

"I'm not a killer," I tell her or maybe I tell myself. I'm not sure which of us needs to hear it more. A part of me thinks that it's me.

"*Everyone* is a potential killer unless they want to be a potential victim." Tess shrugs. "I want to live. So, I will never ever be a lamb again."

I want to ask how many bodies litter her memories. I want to know everything. In time, I will.

SHE SPEAKS as of her way of reducing the world to those who kill and those who die is a casual truth. For her, I think it is. Tess had to decide to be a killer in order to survive. That's the key, the secret, the thing she's willing to share now—because I hurt her when she asked me to do so.

As I stare at her, Tess walks away, leaving me standing at the edge of the street. Logic says I ought to contact the police. Logic says I ought to fear her. There is no statute of limitations on murder. I should act.

But the people she killed are long dead.

Except Lucas.

Do I can about a drunk vagrant? In public, I would say yes. In the privacy of my mind, I think that Tess did what Tess does: she protected herself. It makes me realize that he died for the very thing I could: he knew her secrets.

Is my life in danger?

DESPITE THAT NIGGLING FEAR, I want to know more. I *need* to. I'm never going to meet anyone else like Tess.

I follow her. She's waiting, leaning against a building, smoking.

"You left because he killed people. Reid."

Tess shakes her head. "No. I left because if I stayed he'd kill me. For a long time, I thought that if I was good enough, did everything right, he'd stop killing them and I'd be safe. *Everyone* would be safe."

"Did he kill . . . many people?"

Tess looks away, staring at a group of young men laughing and talking as they prowled the street. They were the same sort of men you can see in every city, every town, young and full of confidence. These were dressed well enough to mark them as affluent, but that was the only true difference I could see.

"I was raised with more money than you might think. I know you realize that I come from money, but"—Tess lowers her voice —"you'd recognize my family name, Michael. We've likely been at the same galas, the same tedious events where everyone believes they are so much better than whichever unfortunate will benefit from their latest charity donations. I left them. I left that world . . . and Reid found me."

This is the story I thought I wanted, but it's not. I'm not sure what or why, but there is more to Tess' past than she's revealing, even now. "And so, you knew he was a killer after you were with him?"

"I always knew that he wasn't a lamb." She twines her fingers with mine and pulls me closer. "This is what you want, isn't it? To understand?"

We walk for a while, and Tess makes no further comment. She doesn't comment on the people we pass or ask me any further questions. She hums to herself for a while, that strange little song that seems to lack any similarity to music or actual song. I don't know quite what to call it other than music, but it's a discordant tumble of sounds more than anything else.

We're standing in Times Square when she speaks again: "Sometimes it's the way people watch you, the way their eyes follow you like they want their feet to do. That's part of collecting a lamb. You need to see them clearly." She lets her attention drift visibly to a young woman who is watching us. "That one has promise, but she's the sort of girl you can't manage quickly. "

"Manage?"

Tess smiles, a secretive little grin that frightens me a bit. "She's looked at her phone several times while we were standing here. Either she is texting or on social media. She's not a proper lamb. People know where she is, possibly even know that she's headed somewhere else. Livestock like her aren't impossible, but they're not as easy to cull."

"I thought you said Reid was the killer." The question is clear even if I don't phrase it as such.

Tess shrugs. "There are things I learned. He watched them, all the time. The pretty things who would be dressed in red . . . Little lambs who lost their way . . ." She steps away from me then. "I tried to stop him. I tried to be good. I really did, but . . . I *was never enough*."

"What do you mean?"

She shrugs. "I *survived*, Michael. What I did was survive. Until he finds me, I'm alive."

I'm not sure why, but until that moment, I'd thought Reid was dead. I stared at her. She'd lived with a killer and left him.

"You're hiding," I say stupidly. "He's still out there, and you're hiding. Why would he look for you? It's been years, hasn't it?" I think back over everything I know, the bits of her past, the stories I know and the things she's admitted today.

"I'm his wife."

"You're . . ." My mind boggles at this revelation.

"And Michael? Teresa Morris was my name then."

I have no words. The woman in my bed is the wife of a known serial killer.

Tess is still talking. "The missing heiress? Escaped or most likely killed by the Carolina Creeper?" Tess smiles at me as she confesses her true name.

The last piece is too much. Teresa Morris, Tess, Tessa in my book . . . This woman *was* a victim of the Carolina Creeper. The only known survivor. There was no way I could keep all of this to myself. There was no way I could avoid talking to the police.

UNTITLED

A Girl with No Past

Being with a man like Edward changed me. He saw me, the potential and the weaknesses both. I didn't know how unmolded I was until he started to shape me.

"Why, Tess?"

"So I understand." I swallowed the blood in my mouth. He was always gentle with my face. It made him sad when he had to hit my face, so he always did it carefully. His palm open, more slap than punch. Rarely did he punch me now.

In our earliest months together, I was disobedient more often. Now, I am much, much better.

"You know it hurts me that you make me do these things." He kissed me, roughly enough that he could taste my blood.

I didn't resist.

When he pulled away, I promised, "I can do better."

"And you will."

"I will." I reached out to touch him, to make up for my slip-up tonight.

He looked past me to the source of my mistake. The girl in our bathtub wasn't awake, but that didn't mean that I should've bothered him.

"What do you want me to do?" I bowed my head like he preferred. "To make you happy?"

"Be good," he reminded me.

"I try, Edward. I do. I want to be good."

He kicked me. "Please don't interrupt me, Tessie."

The thud of my body hitting the wall didn't wake her. The girl in the tub kept her eyes closed, and I was grateful for that small mercy.

I leaned forward and put my hands on the floor to push to my feet. Simply trying to stand up hurt. I'd learned to brace myself when he'd hit my stomach or ribs.

"Stay down."

"Yes, Edward." I stayed on all fours where I was. I didn't even look up at him.

I wanted to ask for instructions, but I was afraid that this was test. Was I to know? Was I to try things? Sometimes he changed the rules but forgot to tell me.

Slowly, I counted to fifty. He still hadn't spoken or touched me by then, so I reached up with one hand. He slapped it away.

"Look at her."

I did. The girl in our bathtub was a little older than me, brown hair, short-shorts and a tank top.

He grabbed my hips and jerked me to my feet.

My back was to him, and he shoved me forward again, not quite punching me between my shoulders but hard enough that I'd have a new bruise there.

"Look at her!"

"Yes, Edward." My face was close enough to the tub that I'd had to put my hands out to stop from tumbling in on top of her. I gripped the edge of the tub and stared at the woman he'd left in the tub.

"Is that what you want to be? Is it?"

Tears were on her face. I wasn't sure if she was crying for me or for herself.

Edward stood beside me then. A knife was in his hand. He was so angry lately. Nothing I did calmed him. Nothing appeased him. He'd taken several weeks of his vacation time from the company. We were on day ten, and I wasn't convinced I was going to survive the last four days.

"Do you love me, Tess?"

I nodded.

"Enough?" He ran the tip of the knife over my side, drawing a line of blood that stung. He was good at shallow cuts, ones that barely scarred. I had scars, of course, but a lot of pain doesn't scar.

"I try."

"Would you do whatever I needed, Tess?"

I froze. I wanted to give him the right words, but sometimes, even after three years in his house, I didn't know them. It took several tries, but I managed it finally: "I would."

"Deal with this." He walked out then.

"Run," she said when it was just us.

I was crying. There were things I never wanted. I tried to be good enough that he didn't steal women, didn't torture of kill them. I was never strong enough. Eventually, I was too injured, and he brought someone home.

"I want to rescue you," I whispered. "I try. I try all the time."

"Kill me." She grabbed my arm. "I want it to end. Please?"

The girl in the tub went home that night. I set her free. I cried the whole time.

Edward carried her to the car and took her away then.

When they left, I cleaned. The tub. The floor. The walls. I threw out the shower curtain, towels, rags. I bought them in bulk. These

—as usual—would be burned. Edward didn't like to see proof that any of the pretty things had been here after they were gone.

Tomorrow, he'd light candles and draw me a bath. He liked to see me soaking in the tub after one of the pretty things left. He always made love to me once they were gone, treated me with softness that only came after they had taken the edges off his moods and I'd removed evidence that one of them was here.

The blood bothered him when they were gone.

The smell bothered him once they left.

I cleaned, and I lit candles.

I dressed in one of the night dresses he liked—and I waited.

Later, the light came into the room as he opened the door.

"Tess?"

"I try to be good," I whispered.

"I know you do." Edward stood in the doorway. "I don't want to lose you. I can't lose you. If you . . . maybe if you help me with them more . . ."

When he sounded like this, lost and small, I was afraid. Edward wasn't often afraid, but sometimes the thing that most scared him was what lived inside his skin. We both knew there was a darkness in him that he couldn't always contain.

"You killed her," he whispered. "No one has ever done that for me, with me. Only you, Tessie."

"She needed to go home."

I thought maybe that would be what saved me, saved all of the pretty things. Maybe she would be the last one. Maybe I was finally good enough to save them—and myself.

TESS

I leave a note with an excuse for Michael, and I slip away in the night while he sleeps. I'll see him in New Orleans unless I die in the next few hours. I can share the rest of my story with him, but I can't take him where I'm going.

The flight to Raleigh Durham International Airport isn't long. In less than two hours, I'm on the ground in North Carolina, the one state where I really don't want to be. Simon's state. Simon's hunting ground. I am here where he is, where Buddy is, where Eddie is . . . where the pretty things died and were buried.

Before the next morning, I'll be back in New Orleans. I just need to get through this. One day. I can do one day.

I fumble for pills. It's hard with gloves, but I put the gloves on in New York, and I'm not taking them off until I'm on the next flight. It's not that I'm afraid, that's far too simple. I am *terrified*. If he sees me, he will kill me. That's been the truth I've held onto for years. He wouldn't kill me immediately. I suspect it would be slow.

A part of me thinks he has moved on—or maybe that's just hope.

I feel arrogant for thinking I still matter, except that I know I do. There were victims before me, and there were victims after me. I know that now. I might not have a computer in my house, but I've used the library ones. I've read about my husband. I didn't mean to, not at first. I knew Simon killed people, but not that he'd been so public about where he left the bodies these days.

The flower buds were the clue. I looked up "dead women with flower bud tattoos," and there it all was.

It's not that I didn't realize he was a serial killer during our marriage. I just didn't realize he'd been one *before* me, and I didn't realize he'd been so sloppy that he left enough bodies that they'd given him a name. People keep saying things about him wanting to be caught. He doesn't. I know that.

Simon isn't trying to get caught. He just doesn't think anyone is clever enough to catch him. He's been doing this for years. A decade at least. Longer, I'd bet.

Some people kill. It's just who they are. It's who Simon is.

Not everyone with his past becomes evil. Bad things happen to kids. They happen to adults. Some people become fiends; some don't. It doesn't matter why he became a devil, only that he is one.

Simon wants to survive, and he's taught me how much I want the same. We'd both do anything to survive. I didn't think that way until he rebuilt me, but it's who I am now. I'd do anything to survive.

Kill others. Leave him. Turn on him. Kill him.

My husband taught me that no one, no matter how much they think they're special, can resist being remade if they want to survive. When it was death or murder, I chose not to die. When it was die or live knowing you will be abused, Simon chose not to die. I think the pretty things would've chosen to murder me if it saved them.

Or maybe they're better than me, and that's why he kills them in the end. I am like him, broken and bloodied. I chose murder. I am more like Simon than like they are.

I am alive.

The year after I left, I added to my flower tattoo. Much like the changes I've made since then, the new pieces don't entirely blot out the past. If someone knows where to look, they can still see the proof that I belonged to Simon.

Once I thought dying was the only way out—until I ran. Since then, I've been waiting. Hiding. Expecting him to come and kill me. Telling Michael was the first time I realized that I was ready to be done hiding.

I thought I'd made my peace with the inevitability of death, that if he came for me it was simply the way things had always been meant to end.

Now? I am done waiting. Something snapped or clicked or I don't even know. I want a life. That means he needs to be in jail or dead. It's *his* turn to hide.

In Durham, I pick up a car. Technically, I steal it. I don't want to leave proof that I was here. The plane ticket was unavoidable. The ID I used isn't my real name. I think of the list of crimes that I will have to deny. I'll lie on the stand—or maybe it's a different kind of truth if I say it right. Did I kill people? Technically, yes, but I killed them because it was an act of survival. Simon was in charge—has *stayed* in charge—but no more.

There wasn't a cost I would refuse to survive. Simon forced me to learn that lesson, too. There still isn't a price too high.

I think about it as I stop at a neighborhood I haven't visited in years. The young men on the streets aren't the same ones, but they might as well be. If the police wanted to clean up the streets, they would. They don't. Far better to contain them to neighborhoods, and then if the police or some candidate needs a PR boost, they can do a "round up." Easy day. Easy targets. It's bullshit.

It's also convenient today.

I cruise past the men selling crack until I find one who catches my attention. I roll up and tell him what I need. My foot is ready to slip off the brake, and the car is in gear. There's not anywhere to box me in. There's no way for anyone to get in my passenger door without me seeing, not with the rear and side windows tilted right. Is it safe? More so than my next steps.

Aside from a too-long look at the gloves on my hands, the transaction goes smoothly. The seller calls a guy who brings a presumably clean gun. They wipe it down for prints and hand it over wrapped in a dirty shirt when they give it to me. There's no doubt that the gun will be used in a crime. I hope it has a ballistic history, too. Tying it to someone else's crimes isn't a bad thing.

Gun in a bag on the seat next to me, I drive to Simon's house. Technically, it is our house. I am his legal wife. *Still*. His house, his things, I would own half of them if I filed for divorce—and thanks to our marriage, he'd get all of my inheritance if I died. He threatened that.

I never threatened to divorce him. It's the other reason why I stayed hidden. He does not deserve my money—not via divorce or my death.

There are no cars in the drive. There are no lights. I debate thinking that means no one is home. It might mean that. It might not. I still park in the road.

I check the 9millimeter that I just bought, slide the clip in, and make sure the safety is off. I'm not sure I can kill Simon, but it's either that or let the police handle it. I can't decide which is crueler.

I get out of the car, leaving it unlocked, and walk toward the house. I swore I'd never come back here. I swore I'd run until I ran out of places to hide. I guess I lied about that, too.

I don't ring the bell.

I walk around the side of the house and smash a window. Fuck it. He'll know someone was here. I'm not trying to hide it.

For a moment, I brace myself for him to come running at the sound of falling glass. The gun is out of the bag and in my hand. In that instant, I think I could really kill him.

But Simon doesn't come.

I climb inside, gun still held tightly, and walk to my bedroom. Our bed. The smell of it, of Simon, overwhelms me. Old memories wash over me.

He'd kill me if he saw me.

I'd kill him if I had to.

Inside the bureau is a box, and in the box are mementos of every pretty thing. His tattoo machine is there, too. So is our marriage certificate. I take all of it, shove it in my bag, and leave the room. I don't touch the bed. I don't take any of his shirts to sleep in like I did when I first left.

I walk through the house until I reach the bathroom. I'll grab the chains, too. I know about DNA. The chains will have DNA.

But inside the tub is a woman. She stares up at me, and too many memories crash over me at once.

"Help me. Please?" The words are more whisper than speech.

If there's a woman, he'll be back soon.

"I will. Just . . ." I turn to leave the room, praying to anyone actually out there that he won't come home and find me here with her.

I'll call the cops once I'm away from the house. I'll— . . . there is a phone. I stare at it with a sort of remembered desperation. How many times had I prayed for that? How often had I wished there was a way to call for help? When I lived here, there was no landline.

I pick it up, hands shaking.

The phone works. I grab it, dial 911 as I walk back to the bathroom, and say, "Ambulance. Now."

I shove the phone into her hands, and I run. They're coming, or Simon will come first. Either way, I'm not ready. Death or prison. Neither sounds great.

I shove open the door, bag of evidence in my arms, gun in my hands, and I run to my stolen car. The gun I didn't get to use is a liability now. I toss in the first body of water I see—a farmer's pond by the looks of it. Maybe the police will arrest Simon, and that will be that. If not, I still have what I came for.

If I need to defend myself, I have it.

If he comes looking for me, I have proof—and our marriage certificate. It's probably not valid. The name on it isn't my real name, but it's proof that I was *there*. I don't want that in the police's hands. I don't want to go to jail. The evidence of my presence there is gone, and now they are coming to his house.

I drive toward the airport, carefully, and I ditch the car. I might not even need to do anything else. Once again, the presence of another woman has saved my life.

I'll watch the news, and once I know they have arrested him, I'll decide if I need to give them some of the things I stashed in my suitcase.

For now, I go back to New York. From there, I'll fly home. To Michael. To a new life. To freedom.

Finally.

JULIANA

After I left Henry at the police department and headed back to the little apartment I'd rented, I tried not to think about the fact that he leaned in to kiss my cheek before we separated. That's not who we are. It's not who we can be. I force the thoughts away, check my email, and stare at the window.

When I step out of the taxi, I find Andrew there waiting. It's weird enough that Henry had found me, but to see Andrew here is more than I can handle. I want to know how.

And I don't want him here.

"Jules . . ." He looks as if he hasn't had a decent night's sleep since I left.

The driver, who doesn't look bulky enough to withstand a strong wind let alone a fight, looks from me to Andrew and scowls. "You okay, miss?"

I hesitate before nodding. "Thank you."

Andrew has made me uncomfortable, but I'm not afraid he'll hurt me. He hasn't ever acted in a threatening way. The simple fact that he's here, that's he's traveled, alarms me.

"You're *sure* you're okay?" The driver asks as I hand him some cash.

I look away from the taxi driver and study Andrew where he waits on the street. I don't trust easily, but I still trust him. I should. He's been in my life long enough that he's earned my trust—or maybe I trust him because I know Henry checked him out again.

"I'm sure."

The driver shakes his head. "Do you want me to wait for you to get inside?"

"I'm good." I take my receipt and get out.

The car drives away.

Andrew and I are standing on the sidewalk, as awkward as if we're strangers. This is a man who's touched every inch of my body, a man who has shared my meals, a man whose bed I've slept in regularly. We shouldn't feel like this.

Still, Andrew says nothing. I want him to speak, to give me an answer that would explain why he's here. He shifts on his feet.

"How did you find me?"

"Micky."

I nod. It hadn't occurred to me not to send my uncle my address. Henry already knew where I was, and Andrew knew I was in

New Orleans. I guess I'd assumed Uncle Micky wouldn't share the specifics. It seemed out of character. "He told you?"

"I looked on his phone."

I close my eyes and push my temper away. "Why?"

"You need to understand. If I thought you'd actually find Tess, I'd have obstructed you more. Let this go, Juliana. Let her go. She's safer this way." He stares at me as he speaks, and fear starts to fill me. Fear of Andrew. "Right now, she's alive, but if you lead him to her—"

"You know her. Teresa. You know the woman who could help me catch the Creeper."

Andrew nods.

"And the Creeper watches me, you know that more than because of the letter, don't you?"

Andrew holds my gaze. "I tried to stop it."

"Are you—"

"No!" He steps toward me.

I back up. I can't help it. The secret Andrew has been keeping, apparently, is that he could find not just the killer but the woman we need to locate to catch the killer. He knows more than he's admitted about the monster who's killing women and leaving their bodies for me to tend.

"I wouldn't do those things, Jules. You know me. You may not love me, but you *know* me."

"I thought I did." I fold my arms over my chest. "You know Teresa."

"Tess," he corrects. "It always feels weird to call her Teresa. She hates that name. She went by Tess when we met."

He smiles in a way that's more revealing even than his words. Whatever she was to him, it wasn't simple friendship. There's love in his eyes. It's painfully obvious that Teresa matters to him enough that he's known where she was and hidden it, hidden her, even as other women died. He did so even when he knew the killer was watching me. For now, that's all my mind can process. The bigger thing—the fact that he knows more about the killer—is too much.

"You don't understand, Jules," Andrew starts. "If I told you, if we went to Tess, he'd find her. He's watching you—"

"Because of you." I step backward again, moving closer to the building.

I scan the street, looking for the killer. I don't know what he looks like. I'm not sure I'd even be able to tell if he were here, watching me. I clutch the keys in one hand and reach into my jacket pocket to grip my phone with the other. "He found me because he was watching *you*."

Andrew sighs, but his gaze doesn't falter. He doesn't look away. "Yes."

I don't know whether to run or lock myself in the rental or call Henry. I don't know what to think or do. I trust Andrew, or rather, I *used* to trust Andrew. Right now, I'm somewhere between furious and terrified.

"He thought I knew where Tess was," Andrew adds, as if that explains anything.

I exhale, watching cars as they drive past us on Esplanade. Even if the Creeper isn't on the street, he could be in any one of those cars. I'm assailed by memories of graves, of bodies, of cataloguing the injuries that were obviously pre-mortem.

I look away from traffic to fix Andrew in my gaze. "You knew where she was and did nothing."

"I know," Andrew says gently. "You have to understand, though. Tess can't be found. She shouldn't be. She's lived here for years, and the best thing I could do was to hide her. I don't go anywhere because I didn't want him to think *that* was where she was. I haven't visited her, but I know she's not well."

I can't help but ask, "Physically?"

He shrugs. "She's an addict, but she's not *sick* in other ways. No cancer. Nothing like that." He steps toward me and lowers his already quiet voice. "She survived some horrible things, Jules. She's would not do well testifying or anything. She's . . . just not *well*. I had to protect her."

I push away the very real fact that he chose to protect Teresa at the risk of my safety. I don't discount the things she undoubtedly suffered. I've seen the bodies of the women who didn't escape. I don't want Teresa to suffer more, but the police could've protected her. There are victim support programs. Hell, there's Witness Protection. He had information to stop a killer, to save lives, to protect *me* too, and he chose to withhold it.

"Tell me why you know her. Tell me you're not . . . tell me you're not a killer, Andrew."

"Jules . . ." He shakes his head. "Do you honestly think I could do those things? I've seen the pictures, too. Do you think I'm capable of that?"

"Yesterday? No. Today? I'm not sure." I scan the street again. If the Creeper was watching him, watching me, he knows we're here. I pull out my cell phone. "I need to call Henry."

Andrew lurches at me and grabs my phone. "I'm sorry, but you can't do that."

I fight for it, grab his wrist and twist it away from him. The phone drops, and I dive toward it. Andrew shoves me aside with one hand and stomps on my phone, shattering the screen.

"I can take you to her, Jules. If that's what you want, I'll take you to see Tess." Andrew stares down at me. "You can come with me, or you can walk away."

"And you?"

"I'm going to her. I helped her disappear once, and I can do it again. If you want to talk to her before she goes, you can, but that's it." He holds a hand out to me.

"What about . . ." I can't make myself finish that sentence though.

"Us?" Andrew laughs in a way that I'd rather have not heard. "You're not the first woman who didn't think I was good enough. Tess never loved me. She just needed me to think she did so she could use me." He squats down in front of me. "I forgave her, and I forgive you. It's okay, Jules. I enjoyed what we had, even though I knew I was never really the man you wanted. I *do* love you. I love her still, too."

I can't move as Andrew reaches out and cups my face in his hands. He leans in and kisses me, and for a moment, I don't pull away. That passes quickly, and I crabwalk backward.

Andrew stands and holds out a hand again. "Come with me to meet her. You can ask your questions before I take her away."

I stand, without his hand, and brush myself off. "Henry could help you both into witness protection. You don't have to—"

"Tess isn't an innocent, Jules. They wouldn't let her go free, not if she spoke to the police, and I'd rather she and I both die than see her become a prisoner again." He smiles. "I know you. You follow the rules. You won't be talking about *helping* her once you realize the things she's done."

He starts walking.

"Wait."

Andrew looks back. "Come or stay. It's your choice."

I picture Henry's face. He'd likely be furious if he knew what I'm about to do, but I don't want to ignore the best clue we have. The woman who has the answers to help us find and stop the Carolina Creeper is in reach, and she's about to disappear.

And Andrew? He knows far more than he's admitted so far. He has information that he's withheld. I'll get it. Meet her. Suggest Witness Protection to her. It's that or wait on Henry. My mind fills with the images of the dead women—and a small voice I don't like to admit whispers that if I'd have been braver when I saw the signs that Darren was a threat to Sophie and Tommy, if *anyone* had been braver, my sister and nephew might be alive.

Knowing Andrew knows Teresa isn't enough of a lead. I think about the people I couldn't save, and I think about the women the Creeper hasn't yet killed, and

I follow Andrew.

TESS

Returning to New Orleans after my excitement in North Carolina has left me high on my own courage. I expected to feel relief, but I didn't expect how proud I am. I feel like I freed myself. It means I can try to be with Michael. I can live a life. I could even claim my inheritance.

I texted Michael as I left the airport to head home, but instead of going there, we met at my favorite breakfast place: The Ruby Slipper. They opened after Katrina, and they serve some of the best breakfasts in the city. I came into their locations over on Canal the first morning I was in New Orleans, and since then, it's become part of my stabilizing routine. When I am at my worst, I go to one of their locations to eat. Today, we're at the Mid-City location.

I'm home, at a beloved restaurant, and all is well. I was able to be Teresa for a lot of minutes. I haven't been able to be *her* for more than a hot minute since I left Reid. Neither Teresa nor Tessie handles life after Reid very well. We struggle. We remember, and the remembering isn't good. Teresa wants to die because of the things we did, and Tessie wants to go home because it's easier if Reid tells us what to do. Neither of those are okay, though, not if we want to survive.

"You need to file a report, Tess." Michael brings it up again on our first morning back in the Crescent City. In some way, I see him trying to create the lie that he is appalled. It's what he should feel, and so he's trying to do that. He forgets that he liked hunting the lost lambs.

I don't forget: he liked the feeling of power. I saw it.

"Why would I go to *them*?" I don't admit that I already have. That's between me and my guilt.

"Seriously?" Michael's voice is horrified. "You know the identity"—he looks around—"of a killer."

"Who would kill me if he knew where I was. Do you think he wouldn't come here?"

Even now, Michael cannot understand. He thinks he does, thinks that writing down the stories I share will make the darkness make sense. People don't understand, though, not unless you peel back their masks. Pain clarifies. Bleeding illuminates. I understood before I ran.

Michael's hands are too clean to understand. Even the best writer can't say anything real until he has the right ink. That's what he wants from me.

"No police, Michael." I smile at him, and it's Tessie's smile curving my lips. "Unless you want me to tell them things your agent wouldn't like."

He stares at me until I take his hand in mine. My fingernails cut into the underside of his wrist, not enough to do anything other than twinge as I lead his hand to my thigh. Silently, I direct his grip to the edge of where I am still red and tender. "I am not a lamb, but I know exactly how to sound just like one of them. I can be very convincing when I have to be."

He gapes at me.

"There is nothing I wouldn't do to survive. You need to understand that. Do you?"

And I see that he's still thinking like we are researching, like this is an exercise in storytelling. He nods, but if he understood, he'd be more fearful than he is. He'd look like Lucas did when he realized that I am always a little bit Tessie even though I try very hard to be Tess.

"It's not your fault, but I get not wanting to tell *that*. It's self-defense, obviously, but if you didn't tell *that* part . . . You could tell the rest. Let them know that you escaped." He lowers his voice. "Tell them who he is."

The server, a new girl with tattoos that speak stories if you study them long enough, stops by the table. I stare at her. I don't like new. Not here. Not when I'm trying to be okay again.

One of my regular waiters comes bustling over before the new server reaches her second sentence. He stands beside her, angling so he can push her away from me if he needs to protect her.

"Sorry, Tess." He gestures at the tattooed girl. "She didn't know you were particular and—"

"I'm good today," I interrupt. "Focused."

He nods. I think his name is River or maybe Storm. Hell, it could be Puddle for all I truly know. My memory is filled with gaps, and even those gaps have a few holes.

"No pills even," I tell River/Puddle.

He beams. "Good on you, *cher*."

Michael watches in silence. He's never seen me without any of my walls in place. I thought that if he did he'd run. I see the truth now. This is what he wants, and if he's going to play this game with me, it's what I need to share.

I look at the tattooed girl. "You can be my waitress, but we need a minute. Grab us coffee while we look at the menu. Black."

She leaves, and River/Puddle follows her. We both know he's going to give her warnings about me, tell her not to touch me, strongly suggest approaching only when I can see her walking toward me. That's part of what I like here. They are okay with customers who are particular.

"It wasn't Reid I hit," I tell Michael when they're gone. "Lucas was not the first person I made unable to talk. You know that, Michael. You may not be asking me the questions, but you know it."

The tattooed waitress returns with our coffee. It's chicory coffee, which means I am in New Orleans. Like music in the street, the river at the edge of the city, this is a sign that I am in my city. I cradle my cup in my hands and sip it.

"Three Little Pigs omelet, right?" the server asks.

"Usually, but I'm trying new things this week. Let's do the Bananas Foster Pain Perdu."

Michael orders something, but I don't know what. I'm staring at the top tendril of something on her neck. It looks she has a tentacle, maybe octopus but possibly a squid, tattooed on her chest. I debate asking, but tattoos are personal and I'm not sure the price of asking for her story.

Once she's gone, Michael leans partway over the table. "Are you saying I saw you . . . that I understand what you *did*, but that it wasn't Reid on the floor?"

"Yes."

He stares at me. "Jesus, Tess."

I drink my coffee in silence as he lets this new part of the truth settle into his ever-shifting vision of me. He's been pulling threads of stories out of me like he's a weaver trying to steal all my pieces for his new tapestry. I let him. As much as I want to be a good wife, keep Reid's secrets so he has no new reason to come after me, I also want the things Michael dangles in front of me like cream for an alley cat who has been living on vinegar.

As I study him, I see the worry, the questions he's having, the doubts. I straighten my shoulders and meet his gaze as I never would've done with Reid. "Stories for action, Michael. You want stories; you can buy them . . . but there will be no police."

I stand and walk out, knowing he can't follow me because they haven't even brought the bill. I walk to the door and keep going.

Michael calls out, but if we're going to play this way, I have to walk out. Even now, I'm not willing to betray Reid by speaking to the police. There are a lot of things I'd be willing to do, things that Michael considers wrong or "debasing," but I've done them.

I walk along Magazine Street, headed toward Canal and back to the ever-open bars of the Quarter. It's early enough not to be bothered by the tourists. Sometimes, I like them, foolish men acting as if New Orleans is still the city that she was in the 1800s. We have the strange honor of having the nation's first legal—or pseudo-legal—Red Light District. In a city that was populated by prisoners and adventurers, it's no surprise that being a whore became big business here. Bourbon Street, a stretch of gaudy blocks of neon and nonsense, is the modern location of that past. No longer Gallatin Street, or Basin Street, but the girls still wiggle their asses and free the tourists from their money. I've done a turn or two on Bourbon, both in the legal and less legal ways of it.

This morning, however, I simply want cheap drinks and silence for a moment.

Being in my bed is an invitation to look into the darker parts of what Michael could be. He's tiptoeing toward darkness, but whether he slides or runs, he's still headed that way. Instead of being grateful to Reid for making this trip possible, Michael wants me to *betray* him. He's asking me to invite police into my life. Nothing else would so clearly lead to my death—and once I sought that. I wanted death because it was the only freedom there was. Now, I have other things. I have a life in this city. If Michael pays attention, I'll have a future with him.

I'm in a bar with my second gin in hand already when Michael finds me.

"You left me there," he says as he comes to stand beside me.

"There are rules, Michael. I don't know how else to explain that. There are rules I can't break, not for you, not for anyone."

"Because you're afraid," he supplies in barely a whisper. "He's not here. You're *safe*."

I laugh. Maybe it's wrong of me, but I can't help myself. I'm never going to be safe. One day Reid will find me. If I go to the police . . . he'll find me faster. I'm not sure how, but he will.

"I won't go to the police," I say in a level but loud voice.

The bartender looks my way, not obviously, but I've spent a lot of nights in bars. The best bartenders notice everything, hear everything, and know when to pretend not to recall most of it.

"You shouldn't have followed me," I add, sounded increasingly more lamblike than Michael notices.

"Seriously? I know where you live, Tess. We're going to sort this out."

The bartender comes over, hearing things in Michael's words that aren't there.

Michael barely acknowledges the bartender. "Vodka, rocks."

I meet the man's eyes and smile. "I'm good. Thanks."

There's a part of me that finds it sweet that Michael can't even hear the subtext, doesn't see that his words sound alarming. He's so used to being fawned over these days that he forgets that people everywhere are listening. I never forget. Even when I'm falling down drunk, there are things I won't say. Reid's secrets are buried in a place that no amount of liquor or pills can reach.

He'd be proud of me if he knew.

Well, after he hurt me enough to make sure I wasn't lying. Pain is the only way to know for sure if you could trust people. If you hurt them enough, if you made them think that they might die, if you let yourself be willing to kill them, they told you the whole truth. If Reid found me, he'd have to ask if I kept his secrets.

I didn't want to have that conversation.

"Did you kill someone there? Is that why you're afraid? Just don't *tell* them that part." Michael keeps his voice low after the bartender walks away.

"You're missing the point." I swirl the ice in my glass.

I KEEP my silence until after the bartender brings Michael's drink. I nod at the man as he asks again if I'm okay. It's cute that he worries—or maybe he sees that same spark in Michael that excites me.

"She stopped hurting because of me," I explain.

"She was a *person*."

"So am I." I poke my finger into my drink, stir it around, and then suck the gin off my skin.

Michael watches, as he should.

"I hated her," I say conversationally. "Not her specifically, but all of them."

Silently, Michael drinks, listening, watching, trying to understand. He can't. He cannot image what it's like to hurt so much to want to die. I envied them. I hated them because they got to be free after only a few days.

I toss the rest of my drink back. "Does it matter? They're dead. They all died."

When Michael finally speaks, he says only, "Why not you?"

That's the question I used to ask myself. It took me years to answer it. There's no way for me to explain it easily right now, not yet. Michael is still trying to understand why he wants these answers.

"I killed, not all of them, but sometimes I killed them. They stopped crying, and it . . . I can't explain it. I just wanted them to be done, to leave. I wanted it to stop."

Michael stares at me.

"I didn't think he'd kill me, not really. For two years, I thought I'd find a way to make him happy. That he'd get better, that I'd be enough. He said if I was good he'd stop hurting them. I survived so much, so he wouldn't catch another lamb. It never worked. He got worse. He hurt me more and more. Did things. Made me do things. I wanted to die—and he wouldn't let me. He was going to kill me sooner or later. Maybe an accident. But first . . . first he would keep hurting me." I shake my head. It's hard to understand; I know that. "He hurt them worse than he hurt me, and when I wasn't good enough he made me watch all the ways he hurt them. If I cried or looked away or looked at the wrong thing, if I wasn't good enough, he hurt them more. I hated them. They all got to stop hurting. I didn't. I healed. Then he did it all again."

Michael keeps staring at me. He doesn't take out his pen. He doesn't ask questions. He listens, and I know he's horrified.

Teresa was too.

I look at Michael, catch his gaze, and will him to understand. "There is nothing I won't do to survive, Michael. Nothing. The memory you saw? I killed a girl because it was that or we both died. Reid watched, and I killed her."

Michael looks at me, opens his mouth, and closes it without saying a word.

"You watched me kill. That's what you saw me remember. I killed her in front of him." I toss back my drink, take his hand in mine, and say, "Let's go."

He stands.

"They all died. When Reid picked them, they would die. I'm alive, Michael. You're alive." I try to sound like it doesn't haunt me. It does, though. I wake screaming. I tried to save them—first by being strong enough and then by ending their suffering. I was trapped in ways no one will ever understand. Sometimes I feel guilty for surviving, for wanting to survive, for wanting a life. Maybe that, at the end of it all, is why I want Michael. I know that when he writes his book, Reid will know I talked. He'll come at me then, and one of us will die. Maybe we'll both die. Me and Reid: Dead because of our sins.

I'm ready to leave and Michael is unmoving. I prompt again, "Michael?"

Michael still doesn't move. All he says is, "How many?"

I shrug. There's no way I can answer that. I used to try to remember them all. I can't. They fade and roll into a single image. Their faces blend into people after I left Reid, faces of men and women I spoke to when I shouldn't, strangers and the lovers. I have a lot of blood on my hands.

"I'm *alive*, Michael," I say again. "Come with me."

Finally, he lets me lead him out of the bar, and we drown ourselves in drink. The more of my secrets he knows, the more he suffers. If Reid were here, Michael wouldn't be strong enough to endure. He's lucky my husband didn't target men. If our lives had been reversed, Michael would've died years before I reached the point of fleeing.

UNTITLED

Girl with No Past

When I decided to leave Edward, I was terrified. There was no way around it, but every fear I'd had was writhing under my skin. I considered taking a knife to my arms to let my fears bleed out.

Everything had changed. Nothing I could do appeased Edward since I'd started helping him. I flinched too much. I didn't smile right. My tears fell too often.

I wanted to die. They were luckier. They were free . . . and I was never going to be free. Several years had passed. I was still his. I started out a girlfriend, a wife, and I'd been his victim for years. I had so many scars that I couldn't remember all of the reasons. I couldn't remember all of the things I'd survived or seen or done.

The others he brought here were only here a few days or maybe weeks. I'd endured his fists and knives and . . . other pains . . . for years. Not even the drugs he gave me to make me sleep or hurt less were enough.

I couldn't continue to live like this, and he refused to let me die. The others got to die. They got to be free. I set them free sometimes. And I envied the dead.

After the only time I tried to kill myself, he was in the sort of rage I didn't think would end. Several women died. One every few days. My punishment. Well, the first of my punishments.

I needed to go. I. needed to try to escape—even if he caught me and finally killed me. That, at least, I was freedom.

"Do you like me?" I asked Buddy as he drove me home from the store one night.

He drove me places more and more since Thanksgiving the year before. I think Edward trusted him now because he didn't act different raping me. I trusted him more too, but for the opposite reason. I saw what Edward missed: Buddy liked me. He liked me more than anyone had for a very long time—and that was how I could get out of Edward's house.

Buddy glanced over at me. "Sure, Tess."

"But really, do you like me?"

"What do you mean?" He refused to look away from the wheel this time. That alone told me to keep going.

"If I were a good woman for you, a really good woman, would you help me?"

Without a word, Buddy pulled his truck to the side of the road, cut off the engine, and turned to stare at me. "What's going on?"

"I'm afraid of him."

Buddy sighed. "Now? Now, you're afraid? Not when he tortured you? Not when he made me rape you?"

"Yes. Now."

"Christ." Buddy looked away again, staring out the front window. "Do I even want to know what he did to scare you?"

The truck stayed silent. The only sounds were the passing of other cars. I've been in silent spaces often enough that waiting isn't hard for me. But quiet wasn't enough--I had to make him want to help me, so I reached out and put my hand on his thigh.

"Tess . . ." His voice was filled with fear.

I ignored it and slid my hand up his thigh until my fingertips brushed his sudden erection. "You've thought about it, haven't you?"

"He might kill me if I touched you without permission. You're his, Tess." He watched my hand as I stroked him through his jeans.

"What if I told you that I loved you?"

He jerked his gaze from my hand to my face. "You . . . no."

But I heard the hope. Edward taught me better than I'd realized. In Buddy's voice, I heard exactly what I needed to make him help me. "I do. Sometimes at night, I close my eyes and imagine that you're the one touching me."

He swallowed visibly. His hands clenched on the steering wheel. I tried not to think about Edward would do when he found out. He'd kill his brother. He'd kill me.

"*Do you think about it?*"

He nodded. He looked so guilty that I'd feel bad if I had the time for that sort of thing. I don't. Edward would kill me if I didn't get away. I didn't like Buddy. In some ways, he was as much of a monster as Edward. Buddy had hidden the bodies. He'd known I was there, that they were there, and he did nothing.

And he raped me.

"*Tell me what you think.*"

He stared straight ahead. "I think about being the one who's naked and trapped and you . . . you do it. I can't stop you. It's not my fault. It's not my fault, so he won't kill me for it."

"*Do I kiss you?*"

"*Never. That would be wrong.*"

"*Edward's away working tonight.*"

Buddy glanced at me.

"*You could record it," I suggested.*

If I was going to convince him to risk death, I needed to deliver the fantasy. "That way you'd have it to watch whenever you want. You'd have all the power. Anything you wanted me to do I'd have to do because you'd have the proof. Not like he does with the other women. You're better than him. He scares them, makes them do things with pain. You wouldn't need that. I'd be afraid, just because you had the recording."

For a moment, Buddy was silent, and I could see the debate in his eyes.

"Edward wouldn't let anyone hurt me when I was little. He kept me safe. Marie too, and after Marie . . . after we lost her, Edward's parents had to die. They weren't to touch Marie or me. They weren't to let anyone touch us or make us touch the men that came to the house. Edward and William did the bad things, but they were the parents' kids. Me and Marie . . . we were Edward's kids. He did the things they made him do, and his mom had us. He did all the things as long as we were safe."

Buddy looked at me. He didn't tell the rest, the details. I didn't need to know. What I did know then was that Edward wasn't Buddy's brother. Edward was Buddy's father—and his half-brother, too.

I couldn't react. I couldn't say anything.

"They were bad people," I told Buddy. "Edward's parents. They were bad."

He nodded. "Edward warned them. They let someone hurt Marie, and she was his . . . daughter. He loved her. He loves me, too. They let someone hurt Marie, and then they died." Buddy held my gaze. "Edward raised me. Him and William. We were all together after Edward killed his parents. He kept me safe. I know what he does is wrong, but he's my whole family, Tess."

The possibility of guilt returned, but the fear of dying was stronger.

"He loves you," I said. "I know that. Maybe you could call him and ask if you can. He might even say yes. He let you have sex with me before. He wants you to be happy, right?"

Buddy shivered. "I don't know."

"Okay . . . if you don't want to ask, we can keep it our secret. You'll have the proof if you ever want to tell him though." I paused before adding in an even softer voice, "You're special to him. He wouldn't be angry if you explained. You know that, don't you? I've seen it. You're his son. No wonder he wanted you to have me on Thanksgiving."

The things I'm saying are the sort of lies that make sense to Buddy. He raped me once. At his father-brother's order. He liked it. What a fucked up mess they were!

Instead of answering, Buddy started the truck and drove to a motel. Inside, he locked the door.

He stripped and watched me, so I followed his lead and did the same. Once we were both naked, he walked past me and into the motel bathroom. "Come on."

I wanted to be surprised that Buddy was peculiar about bathing, too. I wasn't. We're all tainted by the lives we've lived.

Buddy washed me, not gently but thoroughly. He stared at me as he did so, and I saw the same hope that Edward has always had when he did bad things to me.

"Pain?" I asked as he dried me afterwards. "I am used to it, and last time—"

"No." He held my gaze and took my hand. "No. I just want . . . not being in control. I trust you. I shouldn't. He's going to kill me when he finds out."

"Then I'd better be worth it."

He handed me his phone. It was already recording.

I looked into it. "I love you, Edward. Buddy does too, but I asked him for this. I need him to do this. I want you to understand that. I want you to forgive him."

I felt bolder than I'd felt in years. I propped the phone up so it was aimed at the bed.

Then I led my husband's son-brother to a cheap motel bed.

Afterwards, I turned off the recording.

"He'll kill me if I stay," I told Buddy as I rolled over to look at him. I admitted the truth aloud as I'd never dared, even to myself. "I need cash so I can get out. No trail. Then I need a ride to the bus station."

"How much?"

"A few grand so I can get settled."

He said nothing for several moments, and I was glad that the recording was over. This was something far scarier than infidelity.

"It'll take a few weeks."

I cried. I couldn't decide if it was relief or sorrow or fear. Maybe it was everything at once.

After a few moments of Buddy holding me, he said, "I could come with you."

I needed his help, but he was a means to an end, a way out. A future with a man who raped me and was loyal to my husband was a horrible plan. He wasn't anything but a pawn—to Edward, to me--but I needed him to believe he mattered to me.

"Let me go first," I said. "Then I'll send you a message, and if you still want to come, you can. If we go together, Edward will look for us."

"He'll look for you anyhow."

I nodded. "He'll find me eventually, too."

There was never any doubt that I would get caught. There was no chance of freedom. For a few years, I could try to live. I could avoid bleeding. That was more than I would have if I stayed. Edward loved me. I never doubted that, but being loved by Edward was going to kill me. The only other choice was his death, and I didn't think I could do that. Not even to save myself. Not even to save the pretty things.

I was too weak to kill my husband, even though I dreamed of it the way a younger me had dreamed of freedom from my mother.

JULIANA

W e walk up to a little house not unlike the rest of those that line various streets of the city. It's a double shot-gun, painted a shade of pink that is oddly common here. The porch creaks a little, not in a dangerous way but in the way of houses with history. It makes Andrew smile.

"What?"

"Smart. She would hear anyone out here walking," he says. There's a pride in his voice that I don't quite know what to do with right now. He's still the man I've gone to for my own needs over the last year, but there's an entire aspect to his personality that I didn't know existed until today.

"Just knock."

"I'm sorry, Jules. This was never a thing that I wanted to come between us." He reaches out for my hand. "I wish I handled it better."

He raps on the door with his other hand.

I'm not sure how I feel about going into a strange house, but despite the fact that Andrew has lied to me, I still trust him enough to go with him—or maybe I just don't feel like I have a lot of choices. He takes my hand in his, and the familiarity of it comforts my nerves.

"Tess?" Andrew calls. "Are you in there?"

He knocks again. No one answers, and Andrew suddenly seems tense.

"

I'LL CALL YOU LATER. You can meet her, but I think you need to go."

HE OPENS the door and walks into the house.

I hesitate. I don't believe he'll really call. I'm not sure if it's better or worse to go in with him, but I don't have a better idea. I can't call Henry. I can't stand here pointlessly either. After several moments of indecision, I open the door and go inside after Andrew. I'll wait with him.

Inside, the house is barren. There is no indication of personality, of permanence. The furniture is nondescript. The floors are hardwood. The walls are unadorned. The most striking thing in the room is a vase of fresh flowers. They seem out of place, more of a gift bouquet than one a person buys for herself.

A small two-person table in the kitchen stands in for a dining room. In the shadows, Andrew is staring at something. I wonder if Teresa is there, injured, dead. Have we come all this way for nothing?

And then

Andrew looks at me, and whatever I thought before I walked in the house, I was wrong. "Go, Jules. Get—"

"Enough, little brother."

Andrew steps in front of me, and I know. Without hearing another word, I *know* who's in the room. And as the words spoken hit me, I know more than I ever wanted to know.

"I'm sorry," Andrew whispers.

"She was your sister-in-law. Teresa was your sister-in-law."

My words are as much question as statement. I pray that I'm wrong. If I'm not, if the horrible truth settling in on me is true, I've been sleeping with the brother of the man who's been mutilating women.

The man standing in the living room, a slightly older version of Andrew, is handsome. It isn't shocking. A lot of serial killers are attractive. They lure in victims. Either looks or charisma is a part of their arsenal. The 9mm gun atop the back cushions of the ugly floral sofa beside him is more shocking than the look of the man.

"I wasn't expecting *you*." The happiness in the Carolina Creeper's voice makes my skin crawl.

"Then I can leave." I take two steps backwards.

He laughs and lifts the gun from the back of the sofa. "You know me, Juliana. No lies. Not with us. My little brother is the liar here. Not you. Not me."

"Let her go, Reid," Andrew pleads. "I'm here. I'll stay and—"

"Shut up." The Creeper, *Reid*, is no longer sounding the least bit happy. "Did you think I wouldn't find out? That I wouldn't *notice*? That I wouldn't figure out that you stole her?"

"I saved her."

"She's. My. Wife." Reid punches Andrew.

The force of it makes Andrew stumble, but he rights himself quickly. "Tess would be dead by now if I hadn't helped her back then," Andrew insists. "She wasn't going to survive being your wife. You were killing her . . . like the others, just slower."

Reid smiles, and I know that we're not going to get away. Every nightmare I've had about the Creeper pales in comparison to the fear flooding my system.

"You'd be surprised what people can survive, little brother." Reid looks past him to meet my eyes. "*You* know, though, don't you? You ran those hands over my pretty things. You felt what I did to them. Did you think of me? In that room? In your room? I thought of you, Juliana."

Andrew steps backwards, closer to me, as if he can block his brother from touching me.

"You think you're her knight?" Reid doesn't look away from me. His words may be directed to Andrew, but they're for me. "If you loved her, you'd do anything to keep her safe. You'd keep her where no one can touch her, where no one can hurt her, where she isn't able to be found."

He smiles again.

"I kept my Tessie safe. She never left the house alone. She never had to deal with people touching her without my permission. I trusted my brothers . . . Did you tell her?" He looks at Andrew only for a moment. "Did you tell Juliana that you fucked my wife? Did you tell her how you raped her?"

I feel like I might vomit.

"Did you tell her that you saw my pretty things?" He watches me the whole time. "He did, you know. He always knew, and he knew I'd need even more of them because he stole *my wife*. He never told you, though, did he? Those women I sent to you, Juliana. He saw them when they were alive and begging. He knew where they were."

I can't speak. The best I can do is shake my head. Images of Ana, of Christine, of Courtney . . . I can see them in my mind, their bodies, their blood.

"Did you know he went with me sometimes, Juliana? He walked through bars and diners and truck stops." Reid advances on us as he speaks. "He was there when I picked up Ana. He liked her. That's why I picked her. He said she looked a lot like the woman he loved . . . but I was never sure if he meant *my* wife or *you*."

He's inches from Andrew, who has backed up so that he is pressed against my body like a shield.

"If you'd kept her happy, if you'd kept her safe, she wouldn't be here," Reid tells us both. "You took my wife, little brother. I'll take yours."

I want to be strong. I want to think of a way to escape or at the least not whimper, but the man in front of me is a monster. I've seen the proof myself.

Reid reaches past Andrew and strokes my face.

"I'm so sorry, Jules." Andrew's voice breaks, and I don't even know which thing he's apologizing for right now. I can't think about the things Reid has just told me, things Andrew didn't refute.

I'm just like my sister. Darren took his violence out on Sophie, and Andrew raped a woman. Andrew saw the victims when they were alive. I feel my stomach tighten like I'm about to vomit.

"Do you think he'll want to watch when I take you into the bathroom or just listen like he usually does?" Reid presses the barrel of the gun to Andrew's head. "Or should I just kill you, little brother?"

"Let her go," Andrew begs again. "Please. . . you can . . . do whatever you want to me. Just let her go, Reid. She's never done anything wrong."

Reid lowers the gun.

"I betrayed you," Andrew says. "*I'm* the one you're angry at."

"Step away from her."

I clutch at Andrew's shirt. It's a reflex more than a choice. I still have no words. I'm not sure there are words that could help.

"I'll let you choose, little brother. Juliana or Tessie. Who do I take into the bathroom?"

Andrew says nothing for a moment. It's a sob-gasp noise he makes, but then he manages to say, "Me. You can hurt *me*."

With a calmness that I cannot interpret, Reid gestures to me with the gun. "Move aside, Juliana. No cowering behind him. You're better than that."

Mutely, I force my hands to release Andrew's shirt and move sideways.

"Sit." He points at the sofa.

Once I do, he tells Andrew, "Go to the kitchen. Get the biggest knives you can find in her drawers. Not my knives. Those are for later."

A cry escapes me again, but neither man looks at me.

"If you try to hurt me, I'll shoot her." Reid doesn't take him gaze away from me.

Once Andrew's out of the room, Reid shakes his head. "If you're a good girl, you'll survive. Tessie survived. She was a good wife." He looks at Andrew as he returns with a bread knife, a ten-inch chef's knife, and a paring knife. "There were two more, Buddy. Do you want Juliana to pay for your lies?"

"No."

Reid sighs and tells me, "I don't like the thought of hurting him, you know? I let him fuck Tessie. I offered him the pretty things, too. There was no need for him to take my wife away from me."

I swallow. Arguing seems dangerous, but I can't agree with him. I can hardly think.

Andrew returns with the first set of knives as well as a second chef knife, a six inch one this time, and a tomato knife. He hands all of them to Reid.

"Sit."

Andrew obeys.

"We have choices," Reid says. "*You* have choices. Juliana or Tessie?"

"No." Andrew stares at his brother.

"You or me?" Reid lifts the paring knife and extends it toward my chest. The tip of it traces along my collar bone, not breaking the skin. "Do you love her enough to tell me that you'd rather hurt my wife than her? Are you too weak to hurt her? Do you love *me* enough to give her to me?"

Andrew is sobbing now.

"Andrew! He'll do it. He'll . . . hurt me." I try not to think of the things I know he's done to other women. I don't want to bleed, but even more than that, I don't want Reid to be the one holding knives to my skin. "Andrew can do it. Not you."

Reid laughs. He trails the knife up the side of my throat until it's under my jaw. This time, he presses hard enough to cut me. Not a deep cut, but I cry out in pain.

"I have an even better plan, pretty Juliana," he says. "Why don't you show my little brother what Ana felt?"

TESS

M ichael wants to understand. That's the difficult part. He wants to, but he can't. Not with words.

"Do you trust me?" I ask. We're in his apartment now. I feel able to be here after New York, so I've stayed with him.

He closes his laptop and looks at me. "Of course, I do."

"No matter what?"

Michael smiles at me, and I see the edges falter a little. "I do," he says.

"Then we're going to play a game." I walk away, leaving him there, and go to fix my coffee. He needs this, needs to feel why I stayed with Reid. I've been trying to come up with another answer, but there isn't one that will explain it so clearly.

I have to show him.

By the time I've poured my coffee and taken the first sip, Michael has followed me into his kitchen.

"Good boy," I murmur.

His eyes widen, but he doesn't comment.

"That's what you want, isn't it, Michael? To understand your *protagonist*? I know what you're doing, how you're taking my words, my life, and making it a book."

Michael says nothing.

"You want to understand her . . . *me*." I drink my coffee and let him stand there in confusion. "You want to understand how I allowed someone to use me. Why I let him. Why I let you. You're acting like you're *him*, but you're not writing about him, are you? You need to understand *me*."

I drink the rest of my coffee as he stands there waiting for me to explain. He's good at this too, at being told what to do. If I were a different sort of woman, I think I'd be enjoying this.

"Today, you'll do whatever I ask of you," I explain to Michael. "If you don't, I'll destroy you. I have proof, you know, of you hitting me. I like to keep videos."

Michael tenses. "Videos?"

"The other night, when you fucked me until I was sobbing and begging you not to hurt me." I wash my cup carefully. Tidiness matters. "I kept it."

"You told me to do that. You said that you'd ask me to stop, but I wasn't to listen. You told me—"

"International bestseller and rapist," I say. "It sounds so much different when you add the last word, don't you think?"

"How . . . why would you . . ." He stalks toward me.

"The video is just for me," I assure him. "If you're a good boy, no one has to ever know. If not . . ."

MICHAEL ISN'T REID. He takes several breaths and asks, "What do you want me to do?"

I'm disappointed, but I'll help him write a better book. He's coming to understand Reid, but he still doesn't know what it feels like to be me. I'm going to show him.

"Knees."

He stares at me, and I open the kitchen drawer. There are a few knives there. Nothing terribly exotic, but a couple decent sized knives. I pull one out and place it on the counter with a quiet clatter.

"Knees," I repeat.

When he obeys, I remove my clothes and lift one leg so my foot is on the edge of the counter. I don't say anything other than, "Gently, as if I matter to you."

"You do."

I lift the knife and use it to direct him.

Once he's there, doing as he has never done so very thoroughly, I lower the knife so the edge is resting against his neck. It's not somewhere that would truly hurt him even if I slipped, but it's still enough to make him falter.

"Do you trust me?" I ask again.

He starts to pull back to answer, and I push the knife down until it cuts his skin. He can pull away in order to answer me, but moving means bleeding.

"I didn't say you could stop, Michael. I should be enjoying this. If you were *good enough*, I would be."

There's a right answer. There's always a right answer. Reid taught me that all tests must have the possibility of right answers. It's no use if you set someone up to fail. They can't learn, can't improve.

Michael's attentions increase until I buck into his face.

The knife cuts him again as my hand presses down, and he whimpers.

"Shhh, you're a good boy, Michael," I reassure him.

His hands slide up, fingers entering me. He knows my body, knows I like it when he's rough with my soft places.

"No. Mouth only." I hate that I have to stop him, but he'll fail the test if I don't.

Blood trickles slowly from the cuts on his neck, and I trace them with my finger tips. Once the blood coats them, I slide them down, tracing my own skin.

He looks up, cutting himself further. He's a good student.

. . .

FINALLY, he passes the test. He holds me tightly so I can't move, can't cut him further as I shake and thrash.

When the pleasure passes, I pull the knife away. "Do you still trust me?"

"Maybe?"

"Even though I just had a knife to your throat?"

He nods, and then he starts to stand. "That was insane, Tess. That's the lesson? To get cut? I don't—"

"I can email the video or we can do this." I shake my head.

He stares at me, still missing the point despite his body's reaction.

"You like it, Michael." I stare pointedly at the proof. "You like it because *you trust me*. You know that I won't do anything so awful that you can't deal with it because you *trust me*."

"Tess . . ."

"It's your choice. No one is making you do these things." I dig my fingers into the cut on his shoulder, drawing fresh blood. "Every minute of today is one you are choosing to participate in."

He glares at me. "Not entirely. You are blackmailing me."

"You're letting me." I fold my arms over my chest. "Either give me your notebooks, and I'll leave now . . . or come to my house. I need to pick some things up before we go out."

Michael stands. For a moment, I think he's going to hit me or maybe even say he'll let the story go. Instead, he says, "I have limits to what I'll do."

I laugh. Everyone thinks they have limits until they cross them. I had limits. I had a lot of limits, and Reid took them all away.

Me? I was born with every opportunity, every advantage, and I chose to become Reid's wife.

In the end, I was as much of a monster as my husband.

Michael's blood is on my hands this morning because I am Reid's wife. I always will be. The pills and the drink and the sex all help me hide. They help keep the monster asleep, but I remember enough to know that I am not innocent.

No one is if you cut them enough.

No one is if you give them the choice between pain and survival.

Reid re-made me in his image.

Those are the memories that haunt me. That is the lesson I can't outrun.

JULIANA

I can't do it. Even when I know it means that there's a growing chance that it will mean that Reid will torture me, I can't.

"Pretend he's dead," Reid suggests. "Pretend it's your trocar."

He puts his hand over mine and forced me to press the tip of the knife into Andrew's belly. Not far. The sound of pain makes me look at Andrew's face.

"It's okay, Jules." Andrew holds my gaze. "I love you. It's okay."

Reid lets out a sound of frustration and releases my hand. He steps back and stomps around the little living room. He wants me to be someone I can't even pretend to be.

I'm sitting beside Andrew on the ugly sofa. The knife is still in my hand. Without Reid holding it, my arm is limp. The knife rests on Andrew's legs.

"You need to do what he says," Andrew tells me quietly. "If you don't, he'll hurt you. Just go along with him. It's the only chance."

"I can't kill you."

"But you can *hurt* me, Jules." He stares at me. "You're here because of me. He's not lying about me. I knew about the women. I knew what he did and—"

"Don't."

"Think about that, and it will help you do what he says. Whatever you do. I forgive you." He leans toward me like he's going to kiss me, but I can't.

I lean away.

Reid laughs.

I hadn't heard him come back, but he's there watching us and laughing.

"Tell her about Tessie. Have you told her? Does she know?" Reid strokes my hair. "Do you, Juliana?"

Andrew stares at me intently, and I know he wants me to play along. I'm not sure he's right, but this fiend is his brother. He obviously knows him better than I do.

"That he slept with Teresa?"

"*Tessie*," Reid says.

I nod.

"Do you think he pretended you were her when he fucked you?" Reid asks.

I look at Andrew, who is still staring at me as if willing words into my mind. I force myself to say, "Maybe."

I'm still staring at Andrew when Reid adds, "I pretended some of my pretty things were you, too, Juliana."

Against my will, my attention snaps to him.

"Either you cut him or we can go see how much of my pretend was right." Reid leans in and kisses the top of my head. "Shall I pretend you're my wife? Shall I pretend to be Andrew the day he raped my wife? She fought him."

Whatever mess is in his head, Reid has twisted me and Teresa and the rest of his victims into a jumble. Serial killers often enact scenarios; they have rituals. I do not want to be any part of his scenario.

My voice wavers as I ask, "How . . . how do you want me to cut him?"

My hand shakes, but I lift it.

And then I do exactly what he says. Over and over.

I don't know whether it's an hour or ten hours. It feels like time it ticking by so slowly that this will never end. I'm sitting on Andrew's lap, cutting his skin in strips.

"You can end it at any time," Reid murmurs. "His throat? His balls? What do you want to slice?"

"Nothing." I'm shaking.

"It's no different than an autopsy, Juliana," Reid chides. "Steady cuts."

"No."

"It's okay." Andrew sounds like he's choking on the sounds he's trying not to make. "Do what he says, Jules. I love you. I forgive you."

I'm sobbing. "I can't. I *can't*."

Suddenly, Reid sighs. He leans forward, slices across Andrew's throat, and says, "There."

The blood splashes me. *Andrew's* blood. I feel him die, smell it, see it. The man who has been my lover, who comforted me time and again, is dead.

I can't move.

But Reid pulls me up and leads me toward the bathroom. He points at the tub. "In."

"Please . . ."

"In the tub, Juliana."

"I did what you said."

He lifts me. I'm scrambling to get out of his arms as soon as he touches me, so when he drops me in the tub, I flail. My head thunks against it. I'm in a clawfoot tub, covered in Andrew's blood.

I'm going to die.

Like they dead. Like my nightmares.

I try to get out. Push to my feet and throw myself forward. I'm not even clear of the tub before he has me back in it.

The water comes on, freezing cold and pouring from the shower head attachment. I shriek.

"Be a good girl." Reid hits me along the shoulder with the shower attachment.

When I cry out, he aims the water at my face while he holds my head steady with a handful of my hair. I can't make a sound because of gagging.

"Be a good girl, Juliana, and I won't have to hurt you. Do you understand?" He loosens his hold just enough that I can nod.

"Hold out your leg. Over the edge of the tub."

"Please, I don't—"

The water hits my face again. I obey. I think of the things I know his victims endured, and I don't think I can survive as long as some of them obviously did.

Reid turns off the water.

I'm soaked, shivering, still bloody from Andrew's murder, bleeding from where Reid hit me, and terrified.

Reid lifts a restraint attached to a chain and fastens it to one leg. Then he stands and looks down at me. "Be a good girl, and I will take care of you. My brother took my wife, so once I deal with her, you can be my new wife."

"I won't ever—" My words die as Reid's hand covers my mouth.

"I don't want to hurt you, Juliana. I've been lonely. None of them understood me. Tess did. *You* do." His hand stays over my mouth. "I've read everything you've said about me. You have questions, and I can answer them. I'll teach you to be a good wife. Better than Tess."

His other hand caresses my breast, my stomach. His fingers slide down and open the button of my jeans.

I'm trying to squirm away. There is nowhere to go inside a tub. There is no way to get away from him.

"I won't hurt you if you're good," he tells me.

I pull my knee up to try to kick him. I can't move the other leg because of the restraint, but I can move one. Maybe it's stupid. I don't know. All I can say for sure is that in that moment, I can't just lie there and let him touch me.

Reid doesn't react beyond smiling.

"I don't mind hurting you if you like it," he says lightly. "Some girls do. Tess did eventually."

Then he stands. He gets a shirt and tears it. "I don't have any coke. Usually that helps." He ties the shirt over my mouth so tightly that I can't speak. "For now, this will have to be over your mouth."

I stare at him.

"Later, after I handle Tess, I'll go find some coke. It'll help. Once you get high, you'll enjoy our time together more. Once I take it away, you'll do anything to get a taste of it. I know how to train you to be good. I learned when I was a kid. That's what my mother did for me. She taught me to be a good boy."

He wraps a hand around my throat. The other hand trails over my cheek, my chest, my stomach, and stops between my legs. He stares down at me.

"The pretty things were distractions." He sighs. "I had a wife out there somewhere. I couldn't marry again until she dies, but after today, I'll be a widower."

I choke on my sob and close my eyes.

"You'll learn to be a good wife, and I won't make the mistakes I did with Tessie." His voice catches. "I can't. My son is dead. I need a child, Juliana. And a wife to give me that chid."

I open my eyes at that.

"Andrew," he confirms. Then he leaves me there, chained and gagged in a tub, and closes the door behind him.

TESS

Andrew is on my sofa. He's dead. That's the first thing I notice when I walk into the house. Michael is behind me. A part of me thinks that I should tell him to go, but the rest of me knows that it'll go worse for me if he does. Michael is about to discover how far I will go to survive.

I step to the side and reach back to lock the door behind us. "Reid's here."

"Reid? Your—"

"Husband," Reid cuts in as he comes out of my bathroom. He stares at me, and for a moment, it's not rage I see. He looks at me like he's been too long without sight, like I'm something he's coveted and been denied.

I can't speak. I'd like to pretend it's only fear stopping my words, and underneath there *is* a sea of terror churning. It's more than that, though. He trained me to never disappoint him, to please him, to feel guilt at my flaws. He taught me to love him more than I loved anything, anyone.

He trained me to belong to him.

But the fear rises up through the rest. I don't think I could look upon him and not feel fear. Reid taught me the depths of that word in a way I couldn't comprehend before I became his. I still wake screaming because of him. I turn on lights because of him. He is the thing that haunts me. I was essential to him, the air he needed, and I see it now in the way he studies me.

Maybe I'm broken in the ways people think. Maybe I'm weak after all.

"I missed you."

He looks weary in a way he didn't used to be. Tiny lines stretch from the corners of his eyes. Strands of grey hair twine into the darker pieces. Reid has aged since I left. He's still fit. I can tell that even though he's covered with a wet, bloodied shirt. A hunting knife is in his hand. It's not one I remember, but it's similar to knives I remember.

"Do you want me to wash that before the blood sets in?"

"Tess!" Michael reaches out to grab me, to pull me away or stop me from going to my husband. I'm not sure.

I look back at him. "I'm a good wife."

Reid laughs. "You're a whore. If you were a *wife* you wouldn't have been hiding in this cesspool."

"New Orleans is not a cesspool."

"But you're still a whore," Reid adds, pointing the tip of the knife at me in emphasis.

I shrug. I've never claimed to be an angel, even before I started at the Red Light, I had a list of sins attached to my soul. Now, there were a few more. I wasn't about to waste my energy arguing over it. There are only a few ways things could go from here. My husband has found me; worse still, he's found me with another man. My best hope is that he decides I'm too useless to drag home. The only other future that can exist is one in which he kills me.

Once, before the night of the Bad Thing, I thought I was special; I thought that, despite Reid's flaws, he loved me in a way that kept me safe from dying. I know better now. I left him to stay alive, not because of the things he did to other people, not even because of the things he made me do. I left because I realized that if I stayed one of us had to die. That hasn't changed.

"Who's he?" Reid gestures with the knife.

"A writer." I shrug. I care about Michael, but he'll die faster if Reid doesn't realize that.

"Are you fucking him?"

I nod.

Reid's punch isn't unexpected.

I had braced for it. That doesn't mean the taste of blood is pleasant. "I don't like you hitting my face."

He scoffs, but then he narrows his gaze and peers at me like he can see inside me. "Did you know that someone was in our house? That my things were searched, that the woman I left there was taken away."

"I know."

"Was it you?"

I nod. I see no need to lie. "I stopped off there to kill you."

Michael, behind me, makes a horrible noise. I don't think he could ever imagine the story he's a part of now. The book he could write if he survived would be incredible. He won't survive, though. For a heartbeat, the sorrow of his death washes over me. I glance behind me and tell him, "I am sorry, Michael."

He stares at me.

"You tell *him* you're sorry?" Reid's hand is on my forearm now, bruising me. The familiarity of it is enough to weaken my knees. "Who the fuck is he that you tell him you're sorry?"

"He's a novelist. I've been telling him about us."

Reid stares at Michael, assessing him the way he weighs and measures everyone.

"I would write your story however you wanted." Michael isn't begging, but there is an edge of weakness in it that Reid undoubtedly hears.

I certainly hear it.

"Sit." Again, Reid motions with the knife like its an extension of his hand.

"What?" Michael frowns.

"If you're going to act like a bitch, you might as well take orders like one." Reid points again to the sofa where Buddy's body lists to the side. "Sit."

Michael obeys.

A noise from the bathroom, a familiar clanging of chain on metal, rings out. Reid looks at me and smiles.

"SHE LOOKS LIKE YOU, TESSIE." He points to Andrew. "His girlfriend."

"Oh? I'm surprised it took this long for you to kill him."

"Do you think my brother thought about you when he fucked her?" ""Do you think my brother thought about you when he fucked her? I think of you. I stab them and pretend it's you. I imagine that each of those pretty things is my wife. My *loyal* wife. Fucking my brother. Abandoning me. Should I do that to pretty little Juliana?"

Michael gapes at us. He looks at the dead man beside him. In truth, he's coping far better than I expected.

"No." I reach out finally. The palm of my hand flattens on his chest. My husband. I'm touching my husband again after seven years. Memories of the pain that follows such moments make my hands shake. I whisper, "You don't need her. I'm here. We can leave, just you and me."

Reid kisses me so tenderly that tears fill my eyes. "I gave you my vow, Tessie. I took you as my wife. In sickness and health. In richer or poorer."

"I know." I want to point out that he imagined that those women were me before I left, that if I hadn't left I'd have died by now. I don't. Angering him isn't going to help.

"You gave me *your* vow, didn't you?" Reid prompts.

"I did. I *do*."

"And yet, you told *Michael* about me. About us. You let him fuck you." The rage I've been expecting starts to seep into Reid's voice, but his caresses are still gentle. "My wife. My body. This is mine. . . and someone else fucked it."

I don't move.

"He wasn't the first. That was Andrew."

Reid steps back from me. "How many?"

"I don't know. They didn't matter. Sometimes I was lonely, and sometimes I just needed money, and . . . they didn't matter."

"*Michael* does." He walks over and shoves the knife into Michael's thigh, sinks it hilt-deep as Michael screams.

"I'm sorry. I was wrong." I don't know why, but it hurts to see Buddy there dead. It upsets me knowing there's another woman in my house—in my safe little house in the city that saved me. I flinch at seeing Michael bleed, at knowing that he's about to die.

Reid jerks the knife out.

"I'll be a good wife." I put my hand on his biceps. "You don't need to do this. I'm *yours*."

"Liar, liar." He shoves me aside. "I'm not sure you could ever be good again, Tessie."

I stumble, but I don't fall.

Reid looks at me. "I gave my brother a choice: her or you? I gave Juliana a choice, too. Buddy or herself. He's dead."

"WHAT DID SHE PICK?"

Reid smiles at his brother. "Juliana wouldn't kill him. She didn't listen to me or to him."

I understand before he puts the question to me. I think I understood before he spoke at all. I nod.

"Do you love me, Tessie?" Reid asks softly.

"I do."

He holds out the knife. "You can save him or her. The man you're fucking or the woman Buddy loved enough that he couldn't decide whether *you* got to live or *she* did."

"Tess?" Michael looks at me. He starts to try to stand.

"Stay." Reid picks up a gun from beside his brother's corpse and points it at Michael.

Michael shakes his head at me.

I feel sorry for him, but the girl in the tub loved Andrew, who saved me. She tried to save him, and that means I'm alive because of her. Later, Reid will ask me to choose her or me. I know this game all too well.

Right now, though, it's her or Michael.

If the girl in the tub dies, the only one left for Reid to hurt and fuck is me.

"I'm sorry, Michael."

"No!" He tries again to get up.

Reid shoves him down. He stands to his side and hits Michael with the gun. All the while, he stares at me. They both stare at me as I stab Michael over and over.

It's not the first time I've killed a person at Reid's side. I couldn't admit how often I've done so, not even to Michael. He knows now. As Michael dies, he understands the story he was asking me to share.

Afterwards, I hand the knife back to Reid. "Let Juliana go."

"We'll see."

We stand there. Blood-covered. Silent. I'm not sure what happens now. I used to know what to do at times like these, but it's been a lot of years.

"Go to bed, Tessie. I need to think." Reid gestures to my bedroom.

Mutely, I go. It feels wrong to crawl into my clean sheets when I'm covered with filth, but I know better than to go into the bathroom where Juliana is being kept. So, I lie down in my bed and wait.

I don't know if my husband will come to bed or not. The fear of it makes it impossible to relax.

I'm not sure how long I'm there in my darkened room. I don't take my pills, but I sleep eventually. When I wake, he's holding me so tightly that I couldn't move an inch away if I tried.

TESS

The thought of murder isn't new. The memory of it, of Reid killing people, had been a part of my life for years. After I left him, I'd tried to forget. I'd pushed the details so far down that for a while they only came out when I was asleep. Then they'd come screaming to the surface, and I would have night terrors that made it impossible to let anyone into my bed.

I remember more and more now. I remember a lot of things I wish I hadn't. I open Michael's bag and look at his notes. If Reid saw them, he would know how much I told Michael. Maybe he will. Maybe Juliana will. If one of us is alive tomorrow, the answers are waiting in Michael's notebooks. Maybe someone else will finish the story—maybe they'll even make it true. Michael's version of me is wrong. I have a flicker of a wish that I could ask him if he saw me that way.

He'll never speak to me again.

If I survive, though, I'll send his chapters to his agent.

. . .

I THINK ABOUT HIS DEATH. That, too, is my fault. Michael's is different, but in truth, he shares a fate with all of the women. I wasn't good enough to save any of them.

I don't forgive Reid, but I can't forgive myself either. We are both guilty. I won't let Juliana stay in my tub. Not another one. Not a woman who could not kill Andrew.

I wake my husband with a kiss. I know what I have to do. I've been ready for today for several years. I tried another ending. My sojourn to North Carolina.

Today, though, I must be Tessie. I must be the version of me that barely survived. I must be the woman who loved a monster, or I'll die here.

Gently, I say, "Reid?"

He stares at me, and for a moment, I see the man I loved. The monster sleeps. I loved the monster, too. I had to in order to survive. I think sometimes that the bones are his, and the meat belongs to the man.

Or maybe it works the other way.

"Happy anniversary," I say, leaning down to kiss him. No matter what blood or lies we've let come between us, I taste a sweetness, a promise we'll never reach.

"You weren't home for any of our anniversaries." Reid cups my face in his hands. "I fucked strangers that looked like you though."

I think about them, pretty things all dressed in red. They died and bled in my place. He did that. He killed women who looked like me.

Juliana looks like me, too.

"You can do whatever you need so you can forgive me," I offer.

I walk over to my closet and pull out the suitcase of things I've gathered in his absence. It was a strange compulsion to buy things that he'd like, things I hate, but I knew this day would come. It was inevitable.

I bought other things, too.

Reid picks up a spiked baton and runs his fingers over it. "You bought this?"

I nod. I'd ordered it from a guy I'd met at a club. They were used by the Chinese police. "There's one with electricity too."

He glances into the box. When he looks at me, he stares at me as if I'm his goddess, like only I can understand him. It's the sort of trust that held us together for so long, and I've brought it back in this offering. I want nothing more than to make this moment the end, to freeze our lives here--before the bleeding and pain.

He picks up a strip of leather with metal bits knotted into it.

"Will it make you forgive me? Will you let Juliana alive and untouched if I let you hurt me instead of her?"

"Yes."

I strip.

~

BY THE TIME Reid is sated, I'm shaking and sobbing. Being willing to be tortured isn't the same as it not hurting. My mattress is ruined, and I know I'll need stitches on my back.

"No one's ever trusted me like that, not without wearing chains so they couldn't escape." His fingers trail through the blood on my belly. I'm fairly sure most of it is from the deep cut on my breast, but there are other shallow cuts on my stomach too.

I don't speak. I'm not sure if I can.

"Sometimes, I just can't stop. I dream about hurting you. I used to pretend they were you when I killed them. It's not that I don't love you, Tessie. It's because you love me."

"It's okay." I'm glad to finally have it spoken between us, to have the truth on the bloodied sheets. He wants my death. "It's okay."

"You'll need to heal before we travel." Reid has propped up on one arm, staring down at the bruises that are already purpling on my skin. The look of awe is still on his face.

I pull him close, so I can kiss him. I whimper a little, but he likes that, the proof that I hurt and still want him. When he pulls away, I ask, "May I me get a bottle of wine?"

He nods, and I go to the kitchen. One bottle. One corkscrew. One glass.

"Let's toast to new starts," I suggest as I hand it all to him.

Reid looks more at peace than he ever has before as he opens the bottle and pours the wine into the glass. It's that ridiculous pink wine he always bought for me. I keep a bottle of it for this day.

After he fills the goblet, he holds it up. "To us."

"To us," I echo.

He drinks, swallowing most of the measure he's poured. Reid never was one for doing things by halves. I'd worried about that, but Reid is unchanged.

When he holds it out, I touch my lips to it, but none of the drugged liquid even touches my tongue. There was no reason for him to suspect a thing. I'd injected the drugs through the cork.

If I had to, I'd drink it, too. I'd choose death rather than a return to being his prisoner. I want to live, but I am willing to die. Anything to survive, that's the lesson of my life. And with Reid, death is closer to survival than a life as his wife.

He's not paying attention, though. His eyes are on the rivulets of blood that trickle over my body, and I can see that the sight of my blood still excites him. Maybe it's knowing that he drew it, or maybe he's just a little darker than most men. Either way, his gaze is on the results of the punishment he delivered.

I move, reaching out for the bottle of tainted wine again, wincing from the motion, and fill it up. I don't know how much it will take.

"If you were gentle, we could make love again," I whisper as I extend the cup to him. The mere thought of it makes me cringe, but there are two dead men in my house and a woman trapped in my bathroom, and I cannot let him live. "Would you mind being gentle?"

"I can do that." He empties the glass, and then he lays me on my bed so carefully that I imagine myself as hand-blown glass, too fragile, too rare. I think of us, of the way we found this peace at last, as we make love. For a moment, I remember the way it was at the beginning. I remember how he offered me safety and care. I remember how lucky I felt—before I realized that my beloved was a serial killer.

When Reid rolls me over so I'm on the top, my blood drips onto him, and his look of awe expands until I think we've reached something magical.

"I love you," I remind him. A part of me always will. Tessie will love him. That was the only way to survive. I loved him.

I see the drugs taking hold, the hitch in his breathing, the blinking as his vision blurs. I wasn't sure of the dosage, so I mixed Rohypnol, Ketamine, and some Ambien too. Probably any of those would do the job, and mixed with wine they'd knock him out quickly. If necessary, I think drinking enough of it would kill us both, but I couldn't be sure. I need to be sure at least one of us dies here.

I'd rather it's Reid.

"Tessie?"

"Shhhh. This is for the best,"

. . .

I TELL HIM, even though he's unconscious now.

Gingerly, I climb out of bed and walk across the room, trailing blood as I go. That can't be helped. There are many worse things all through my house. Dying is messy, and this house wasn't meant for death.

I go to the kitchen.

There's never been a trace of me before when there were bodies to find. Today, there is no choice. My fingerprints are all over the house, and there will be three dead bodies here by the time the police come. I'll be in their system. There's no avoiding it. Not now. I don't know if I'll be able to disappear again. I want to, but first I have to end my marriage.

I take the knife that he tossed onto my counter. Blood is crusted on it. Andrew's blood. Reid and his brother will share this too. It has to be a knife. Guns are noisy. People will come too soon if I shoot my husband.

Knife in hand, I return to bed. There's something strange about how still Reid is when I go back into my room. I knew he was unconscious, but it seems wrong to see him that way.

I'm careful as I crawl onto the bed. I lower the knife tip to his belly and put my weight into pushing it through the flesh and into his body. What we think of as "stomach" from the outside of our skin is really intestine, but I'm not looking to kill him yet. I want him to bleed, to start to die. I want him to die as he has killed, with cuts and wounds, with slowness and care.

Reid jerks as the blade slides into his belly.

Carefully, I stab him again. This time, I aim higher, hoping to catch the liver. That's a better spot to stab someone.

Killing my husband doesn't take as long as it feels.

As I stab him, he thrashes, but the drugs do their job perfectly. They'll wear off, but unless someone asks for an autopsy too soon, I'm not expecting anyone to ever know about the drugs. On TV or movies, people always get autopsied, but the cause of Reid's death will be readily apparent—and no one will ask a lot of questions about his death. If they do know, it doesn't really matter.

I'll be gone. Freedom has cost me my city, but I am alive. I have survived.

There are a lot of things I don't remember, but so many of the ones I do are awful. If the police find me, here or somewhere else, I will not be able to give them all of the answers. Even if I could remember all of the lies, some things are not ones we can forgive.

If I died here, too, no one would be left to mourn me.

Not Michael.

Not Andrew.

Not Reid.

I'm no different than the girls in the tub. Reid chose women with no families, no lovers, no one to look for them. I had money, and a mother I barely spoke to. Now, I don't have those things either. I'm just like they were.

I LOOK at the bodies in my living room as I walk toward the bathroom. Juliana is the last girl who will be in the tub. She's the last detail to sort out before I leave New Orleans.

JULIANA

When the door opens, I'm not sure what to expect. I know that Reid's attention is all on Tess, but sooner or later, that will change. I brace myself. I've seen the bodies. I don't think I'll survive long.

It's not Reid.

Tess stands in the doorway. She's naked and bleeding in so many places I can't figure out where to look. I hope that at least some of that blood isn't hers.

"He's dead. Reid, I mean. My husband." Tess pauses. "Michael, too. Andrew. They're all dead. My lovers. All three. Dead. You are not, though."

I nod. There are no words that can find their way to my mind or my mouth. I don't think the Teresa I sought is the same as the woman in front of me now.

There's a knife in her hand still. I'm not sure what to think. She's far from stable; on that at least, Andrew told the truth. I wince at the thought of Andrew. He's dead. Michael, who arrived with Tess, is too.

Reid is. The Carolina Creeper is dead. That, at least, is a victory.

But if that's all her blood, I'm not entirely sure if Tess will live.

Although, I'm also not sure if she's here to kill me.

"Can I help you, Tess?" I ask as carefully as I can when she stands silently bleeding. "If you have bandages . . ."

She nods.

I tug on the chains on my arms. "If you unlock me, I can help you."

She nods again.

That's all she does. She doesn't move or react. I'm not sure how she's standing. There are bruises, dried blood, and torn skin.

"He's dead," she repeats. "They're all dead. But not you."

Tess stares at me, and I wonder if there's any chance of survival for either or us. If Reid were in the room, there wouldn't be. She saved me from him. I just don't know if she means to kill me or free me.

"You can't leave here like that." I talk to her as I've spoken to so many mourners in my life. "You need to cover up. People would stop you if you left like that. You may be going into shock."

Again, she nods.

Obviously, this isn't working, so I try a new tactic: "Unchain me, Tess."

She meets my gaze. "If I do, you can't leave yet. I don't want to hurt you, but I can't go to prison." She holds out the hand with the bloodied knife. "My husband did bad things, but it was wrong to kill him. *They'll* think so. It was all I could do. He wanted to hurt you."

"You saved me." It's the truth, but I know it's not enough. His death was likely self-defense, but what about the rest? If Andrew was to be believed, Tess would be hospitalized for her crimes.

I could lie to her, tell her that won't happen, but I can't be sure what she'd do if I tried to stop her. I have a theory; it's not good.

"You need to get out of the tub so I can wash," she says. Then, after a too long moment, she adds, "I don't want you to have to die. Do you understand that?"

Carefully, I say, "You want me to be safe, but you'll stop me if I try to leave before you say it's okay. Is that right?"

She nods.

"I promise, Tess." I mean it, too.

Maybe that's the wrong answer, but it's the one that feels right. There are three dead men in the house. The only person in danger is me. Waiting an hour won't change anything.

Moving so slowly that I want to weep for her, she comes closer and unhooks the handcuff that has held me captive. The chains clatter to the floor beside the beautiful claw-foot tub.

"Stay in the room."

I see her staring at the tub as if the thought of climbing into it is akin to scaling a mountain. Softly, I ask, "Can I help you?"

Tess nods again, and I help her into the tub. Over the next two hours, I help her. Eventually, the water isn't red, and her wounds are bandaged. I apply antibiotic ointment to the worst of her wounds. Some are days old, so I know Reid wasn't the one who inflicted them.

"Did Michael do that?"

"He wanted to understand Reid." Tess looks at me like she's asking a question. "J. Michael Anderson . . . he was a writer. I was his muse."

I am no longer so sure that the other man's murder is a crime.

"Tess?"

She meets my eyes in the mirror as I stitch her back. I try not to think about how different it is to stitch the living. My experiences with stitching flesh are on the dead. Tess stays as still as a corpse, despite the lack of pain relief.

"No man should hurt you," I tell her. "What Michael did, what Reid did . . . you deserve better. You deserve kindness."

She laughs. It's not a pretty sound. "I don't. They weren't the only monsters in this house. When I'm gone . . . Michael wrote things. Memories. You should take them. Send them to his agent or throw them away."

I don't know what they say, but I am sure that I don't want to know either.

"They're only partway truth." Tess watches me in the mirror. "But they have one big truth: I'm not a good person."

There's nothing to say to that. I can't argue because I don't know what she's done. I don't know what Andrew's done either. I probably never will know the whole of it. After today, there is no chance of answers other than the pages Michael has apparently written.

"Did Andrew rape you? Did he rape the other women?" I blurt the questions before I can think better of it.

She shakes her head. "He did the first time, but Reid made him. The next time, I seduced him. He wanted to save me. He wanted to run away with me. If not for him . . . I'd have died."

"Reid said—"

"He wasn't strong enough to say no., but he helped me escape. If not for him, I'd have died there. He was better than Michael. Better than Reid. You were right not to kill him."

I follow her, stopping in the living room. The stink of death and sight of Andrew and the writer, both dead, are too much. I don't want to be here, but I don't know that I want to have Tess go to jail either.

"Come with me? I need to go in there . . ." Tess looks away. "I'm scared. He's dead, but . . ."

She stares at the door of her bedroom. I don't know that I can face that. Tess, apparently, isn't sure she can either.

Together, we step into the room. The smell is worse. I look at him, the killer who haunted me all these years. He's mutilated, bloody, and staring sightlessly at me from her bed.

She dresses as I stare at the Creeper. I can't summon any remorse. I'm not sure anything that happened to him could be too awful. My mind starts a litany of names of his dead: Courtney, Ana, Andrew, Michael. I picture him alive and threatening me. I picture the bodies, the graves, and then I look again at Tess —his living victim.

"Will you help me?"

Her voice startles me, and I realize that there is no way I can do anything but help her. She saved my life—and countless others today.

I nod, and as quickly as I can, I help Tess pack clothes and sundries.

"Please," I say awkwardly, "don't let anyone hurt you—and don't hurt them."

Teresa Morris, Tess, nods. She smiles at me, and I'm still not sure she sees me. The variety of pills she packs is shocking, and the stack of cash she removes from under a board in the floor is equally unexpected. In that instant, I know that she has spent years prepared to run again.

"At least twenty minutes." She hands me a cell phone, and I'm not sure whose it is. "I need that. I killed him"—she points at the corpse—"so he didn't kill you. I need time."

I take the phone.

"There are videos on here. Of Michael. Use them if you need them." She grabs a few notebooks and gives me those as well.

"Tell me you will not let anyone hurt you." I stare at her. "That you will not hurt anyone. I need to know that, Tess. I need to know that, so I can be okay with this."

"Yes," she says.

It's not a real answer, but I hope it means she agrees. I'm strong enough, especially as she is so injured, but emotionally, I can't try to force her to stay, but I am well aware that I am letting a killer walk out of the house.

Then Tess is gone, and I am left in a three-room house with three dead bodies.

I return to the bathroom. It's the only room without a body. I could leave, walk until my twenty minutes are up, but I don't think I can walk by the corpses again. It's a strange thing for a mortician to feel, but these are not simply corpses—they are my lover and the murder who tormented me, who sent dead bodies to me, who was my lover's only living family member.

Whether in curiosity or as a way to distract myself so I can wait as I promised,

I start to watch videos, to look at the things stored on J. Michael Anderson's phone. It's awful. He wasn't as vile as Reid was, but he was still a monster in his way. He exploited Tess.

His emails to his agent about Tess horrify me.

His notes to himself disgust me.

I look at the notebooks. Skim. His manuscript leaves me unable to understand how anyone could justify the things he has done.

I don't finish the pieces of his book that I have in my hands, but I read enough to know that Tess is better off without him.

It's just under an hour when I stop reading *A Girl with No Past*. Longer than Tess asked for, but long enough to give her a fair start at flight.

I call Henry. Call N.O.P.D.

It's not twenty minutes more before Henry is coming in the house calling my name. It's only two minutes more before he is holding me, and I am crying.

"Where is she?"

"Gone. Tess is gone."

An officer stands in the doorway. He has the look of a man who has seen bad things, but nothing like this. I want to comfort him, to pull out the tricks that got me through harsh crime scenes. I can't. I am not working here.

I am a victim.

"Andrew is—"

"I know," I cut Henry off.

He's still studying me, looking at me as if he can't decide if he ought to send me to the paramedics or clutch me to him. I don't know either. I am alive. I am not bleeding badly; I have not been raped. The rest . . . the rest is all details.

"Henry?"

He looks at me.

"That's him, the Creeper. That's him. Teresa Morris killed him. She saved me." I give my statement. "I am alive because she killed him."

"And Andrew was—"

"His brother. I had no idea until I met Reid." I want to be strong, to not let strangers see me shaking as I now am. There are blankets around me. I wrap them tighter. "Andrew was why—"

"Later," Henry says gently. "We can deal with it later."

And in that moment, I see the man who lives behind the job. He was afraid. He doesn't need to say the words to tell me he remembers the bodies we've seen. He doesn't need to admit he imagined that I would be the next one.

"I could have died," I say, testing the words. "The things he would have done . . ."

"Where is she, Jules?"

I shake my head. I don't know. I didn't ask where she was going, and she didn't tell me. I finally found Teresa Morris, but I didn't save her. She saved me. Without her kindness or madness, because I'm not sure which it was that made her choose to kill Reid this time, I would've died.

I won't talk about her, not yet. I can't. Later, I'll tell Henry everything.

"Tess is gone." I give him the phone and the book. "She saved me, and she left these. That's all I know."

It wasn't. I knew a lot more. I'd seen the video. I'd spoken to Tess. I'd met the Creeper. I'd read some of the contents of the phone. The biggest thing I knew, the thing that I couldn't say just then, was that I was glad that the three men were all dead.

And I was glad that Tess was alive.

EPILOGUE

I open the mailbox. There's another postcard this week. A few times a year, I get one. They never say anything new, but what they say is enough.

No one has hurt me.

I have hurt no one.

You are okay.

She's out there, and I'm never sure where. They come from all over the country. I could track her. I'm sure there is a file still open where someone is doing just that. I know Henry still looks for her. Sometimes, I think about telling him.

Without him, I'm not sure how I would've been able to recover. Some nights, his arms are the only thing that bring me enough comfort to allow me to sleep. Other nights, I know he checks the locks on our house more than once in order to find peace of his own.

So, I do what I've always done with Tess' postcards: I shred them. I don't know if she's found peace, or if she could. I know that I have. With Henry, I have found peace and a healthy relationship with a man I love, and I'm not willing to risk losing it. If he knew, Henry would forgive me for keeping my secret. He loves me and accepts me, but I don't know if I could forgive myself for exposing Tess.

Some secrets, some people, are better off hidden.

ACKNOWLEDGMENTS

Thank you to the following:

Merrilee, you never gave up on this one. My book of my heart. Weird, twisted, and written from my own darkest places, and you stood at my side for it the whole time.

Kelley Armstrong and Kim Derting, every time I faltered, you were there. Thank you for faith and for standing at my side at Cyn's memorial. You're family in my heart.

Jeanette Battista, Tom Pollock, Laura Kalnajs and Jeaniene Frost, your edits and insights were essential.

Bayou & Cave Creek Retreaters, you're my people. From swamp tours, feral pigs, Pilates classes, murder plotting, and delicious meals, you are a haven.

Grey Sweeney Perkins, you are a treasure.

Frank, who doesn't adore a man who can help with body dumps?

Todd Harra, I still fondly call you "*my* mortician." I'm ever grateful that my regard for your profession doesn't bother you and that you still answer my weird questions.

Diana Williams, I am far less worried about forensics thanks to your expert eyes to this one.

(Please note that errors on forensics, mortuary, or New Orleans aspects are my fault.)

Dedication: To all of you who are fighting for the silenced or violated, you are superheroes.

ABOUT THE AUTHOR

Melissa Marr is a former university literature instructor who writes fiction for adults, teens, and children. Her books have been translated into twenty-eight languages and have been best-sellers internationally (Germany, France, Sweden, Australia, et. al.) as well as domestically. She is best known for the Wicked Lovely series for teens, *Graveminder* for adults, and her debut picture book *Bunny Roo, I Love You*.

In her free time, she practices medieval swordfighting, kayaks, hikes, and raises kids in the Arizona desert.

facebook.com/MelissaMarrBooks

twitter.com/melissa_marr

goodreads.com/melissa_marr

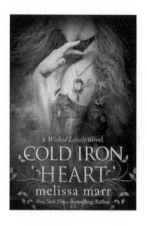

Available Now!

How far would you go to escape fate?

In this prequel to the international bestselling WICKED LOVELY series, the Faery Courts collide a century before the mortals in *Wicked Lovely* are born.

Thelma Foy, a jeweler with the Second Sight in iron-bedecked 1890s New Orleans, wasn't expecting to be caught in a faery conflict. Tam can see through the glamours faeries wear to hide themselves from mortals, but if her secret were revealed, the fey would steal her eyes, her life, or her freedom. So, Tam doesn't respond when they trail thorn-crusted fingertips through her hair at the French Market or when the Dark King sings along with her in the bayou.

But when the Dark King, Irial, rescues her, Tam must confront everything she thought she knew about faeries, men, and love.

Too soon, New Orleans is filling with faeries who are looking for her, and Irial is the only one who can keep her safe.

Unbeknownst to Tam, she is the prize in a centuries-old fight between Summer Court and Winter Court. To protect her, Irial must risk a war he can't win--or surrender the first mortal woman he's loved.

The Wicked & The Dead is AVAILABLE NOW!

"I loved *The Wicked and The Dead*! A sassy, ass-kicking heroine, a deliciously mysterious fae hero, and a wonderful mix of action and romance. Add that to Melissa's usual great world-building, and I'm already looking forward to book 2!"
— Jeaniene Frost, *NYT* Bestselling Author

Geneviève Crowe makes her living beheading the dead. But now, her magic has gone sideways, and the only person strong enough to help her is the one man who could tempt her to think about picket fences: Eli Stonecroft, a faery bar-owner in New Orleans.

When human businessmen start turning up as *draugar*, the queen of the again-walkers and the wealthy son of one of the victims, both hire Geneviève to figure it out. She works to keep her magic in check, the dead from crawling out of their graves, and enough money for a future that might be a lot longer than she'd like. Neither her heart nor her life are safe now that she's juggling a faery, murder, and magic.

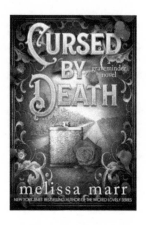

A vailable now: *Cursed by Death*!

The dead don't always stay dead in Claysville . . . and in the afterlife, Death himself can't be trusted.

Amity Blue has begun to remember strange impossible events, her ex trying to bite her and people vanishing like mist. Everyone in town swears a mountain lion is responsible for the recent deaths, but Amity is sure that there's more to the story.

After a stalker—a dead stalker—appears at the bar where she works, Amity discovers that the dead don't always stay dead in Claysville. Along with the current Graveminder, Rebekkah Barrow, Amity seeks out the enigmatic Mr D, who seems to be Death himself, only to discover that the centuries-old contract to protect Claysville has been broken.

Caught between life in a cursed town and Death himself, Amity and Rebekkah must find a way to put the dead where they belong—because if the Hungry Dead keep rising, everyone in town will be lost.

Return to the world of Graveminder, Goodreads Choice Winner for Best Horror Novel in this stand-alone Graveminder novel (also includes two Grave-minder short stories.).

PRAISE FOR MELISSA MARR'S BOOKS:

PRAISE FOR THE WICKED LOVELY SERIES:

"Marr offers readers a fully imagined faery world that runs alongside an everyday world, which even non-fantasy (or faerie) lovers will want to delve into" *--Publisher's Weekly* (starred review)

"This is a magical novel... the first book in a trilogy that will guarantee to have you itching for the next installment." *Bliss*

"Fans of the fey world will devour this sequel to Wicked Lovely. Marr has created a world both harsh and lush, at once urban and natural." *--School Library Journal*

"Complex and involving." *-New York Times Book Review*

PRAISE FOR GRAVEMINDER:

"If anyone can put the goth in Southern Gothic, it's Melissa Marr. . . . She's also careful to ensure that the book's wider themes —how and if we accept the roles life assigns us, and what happens to us when we refuse them—matter to us as much as the multiple cases of heebie-jeebies she doles out..." —NPR.org

"Spooky enough to please but not too disturbing to read in bed." —*Washington Post*

"Dark and dreamy. . . . Rod Serling would have loved *Graveminder*. . . . Marr is not tapping into the latest horde of zombie novels, she's created a new kind of undead creature. . . . A creatively creepy gothic tale for grown-ups."—*USA Today*

"Plan ahead to read this one, because you won't be able to put it down! Haunting, captivating, brilliant!" —*Library Journal* (starred review)

"Marr serves up a quirky dark fantasy fashioned around themes of fate, free will—and zombies. . . . Well-drawn characters and their dramatic interactions keep the tale loose and lively." — *Publishers Weekly*

"The emotional dance between Rebekkah and Byron will captivate female readers. . . . Fantasy-horror fans will demand more." —*Kirkus Reviews*

"No one builds worlds like Melissa Marr." —Charlaine Harris, *New York Times* bestselling author of the Sookie Stackhouse series

"Welcome to the return of the great American gothic." —Del Howison, Bram Stoker Award-winning editor of *Dark Delicacies*